Praise for the Bitter Wind Mysteries

"A slow-burning cold case with copious clues, conscientious detection, a high body count, periodic interruptions from the killer's viewpoint, and all the pages and pages of unraveling you'd expect from such a generously plotted mystery."—*Kirkus Reviews*

"Wendelboe is a skilled writer who ratchets up the suspense."—Margaret Coel, *New York Times* bestselling author of *Winter's Child*

Also by C. M. Wendelboe

– for Midnight Ink –
Hunting the Five Point Killer (2017)

– for Five Star –
Backed to the Wall (2017)

– for Berkley Prime Crime –
Death Along the Spirit Road (2011)
Death Where the Bad Rocks Live (2012)
Death on the Greasy Grass (2013)

C. M. WENDELBOE

HUNTING
THE
SATURDAY
NIGHT
STRANGLER

A BITTER WIND MYSTERY

MIDNIGHT INK
WOODBURY, MINNESOTA

FIRST EDITION
First Printing, 2018

Book format by Bob Gaul
Cover design by Kevin R. Brown
Cover illustration by Dominick Finelle / The July Group

Midnight Ink, an imprint of Llewellyn Worldwide Ltd.

Library of Congress Cataloging-in-Publication Data
Names: Wendelboe, C. M., author.
Title: Hunting the Saturday Night Strangler: a bitter wind mystery / C.M. Wendelboe.
Description: First Edition. | Woodbury, Minnesota: Midnight Ink, [2018] | Series: A bitter wind mystery; #2.
Identifiers: LCCN 2018017602 (print) | LCCN 2018022734 (ebook) | ISBN 9780738755243 (ebook) | ISBN 9780738753621 (alk. paper)
Subjects: | GSAFD: Mystery fiction.
Classification: LCC PS3623.E53 (ebook) | LCC PS3623.E53 H89 2018 (print) | DDC 813/.6—dc23
LC record available at https://lccn.loc.gov/2018017602

Midnight Ink
Llewellyn Worldwide Ltd.
2143 Wooddale Drive
Woodbury, MN 55125-2989
www.midnightinkbooks.com

Printed in the United States of America

I dedicate this novel to my wife, Heather,
who is my constant sounding board and a mentor.

"Only those are fit to live who are not afraid to die."

— General Douglas MacArthur —

One

A FULL MOON—A RUSTLER'S moon—peeks from low-hanging clouds and casts eerie shadows across the grassy pasture. The Midnight Sheepherder, as the Wyoming Wool Growers Association refers to the rustler that's plagued ranchers hereabouts for a year, douses the pickup lights while still on the county road. Easing up to the fence, the thief climbs out, drops the barbed wire gate, and lays it aside. The sheepherder has had close calls with the Association's range detective before, and the last thing needed tonight would be having to stop and open the gate before fleeing. If caught.

The dog in the seat trembles with anticipation as the rustler eases the truck and trailer into the pasture, the moon the only illumination necessary. How many times has moonlight aided in the thieving? And how many times has the rustler gotten away undetected? The original plan last year had been to steal a trailer full of sheep: twenty-five to thirty head a night for a couple nights. Use the money for necessities and quit while ahead. But it was all too easy, with the odds against the lone stock detective the Association put their faith in. The detective, after all, was renowned for solving homicides. Not catching rustlers.

The sheepherder idles toward a deep depression in the pasture, where sheep mill about like frightened children, and climbs out. The dog jumps down from the seat and sits while the trailer ramp is dropped. The hollow cries of bleating sheep sound like the cries of babies, echoing off the walls of the natural depression of land. A wave of the hand, a silent signal to the willing accomplice, and the dog happily bounds after a group of sheep at the near end of the pasture. The dog doesn't know she's an accessory—she's just doing what she knows and loves: rounding sheep up to be sold out of state.

The dog herds four sheep up the ramp into the trailer when … the sound of a pickup approaches in the field above the rustler. Light floods the hillside. Instinctively, the sheepherder crouches even though the approaching vehicle is well above the depression in the pasture, the truck and trailer hidden. Another wave of the hand and the dog returns to sit beside the ramp. Her muscles twitch with the thought of herding more sheep, and she pants with anticipation. But for now, she sits, her tongue lolling out her mouth like she's testing the hot, dry night air. Dog and thief have weathered near misses before. Last month at a ranch on the Snowy Range, the Association's stock detective nearly caught them. But hunkering down, letting the danger pass, had saved them. And would do so tonight.

The rancher—for it has to be the landowner prowling around this time of night—stops the truck. A door slams. Muffled voices rise and fall with the stiff breeze.

As the rustler reaches inside the trailer for a granola bar, a scream pierces the night. Dog and thief scramble up the hillside and peek over the bank. A man in baggy jeans and shirt too big for him drags a woman screaming by her hair out of a truck. She kicks and claws at the man, but to no avail. He slams her against the hood, and head-lights momentarily illuminate them. The woman tries biting his hand, but he backhands her across the face. She slumps and he hauls her erect, shaking her awake, prolonging her anguish.

The rustler keeps quiet. A family fight is no business of—

The man rips off the woman's blouse. He clamps a hand over her mouth, but she bites hard. He punches her in the gut, and she lets go. With one hand on her throat, the man grabs something from his back pocket—a leather thong perhaps—and swiftly wraps it around the woman's neck. Her screams cease. Her eyes bulge out. Her feet kick the air as the man hoists her off the ground with the strangling, when...

The dog barks.

Just a faint nip, but the sound carries well on this hot night. And it carries to the couple fighting in front of the pickup.

The man looks up, his eyes reflecting his headlights, a grimace of hate on his face visible even at this distance. He spots the dog, and the rustler beside her.

The man drops the woman and runs toward the bank.

Toward rustler and dog.

The rustler stumbles to the truck. Trips over a rock. Tumbles down to the bottom of the hill. Recovers and whistles to the dog. She leaps onto the seat of the truck as the thief stomps on the foot feed. Dirt and rocks from the spinning truck tires ping the side of the trailer in a race to get as far and as fast away from the pasture as possible. Sheep tumble down the ramp dragging on the ground.

The Midnight Sheepherder makes it to the pasture gate, caroms off the gateposts. The ramp slides, a gravel storm kicked up by the tires. The rustler will put the ramp up later. For now, the only thing that matters is escape.

And survival.

Two

HE DRAGS JILLIE FROM the truck by her hair. She kicks and claws and fights like most ranch girls would. He admires her spunk.

He throws her hard onto the hood, the head-to-metal sound echoing in the hot night air. She bounces off the hood and tries biting him. He backhands her. She slumps, and he violently shakes her awake. It's not her time yet.

He rips her blouse—not because he has a desire to have sex with this woman, but because her humiliation will add to the pleasure of what he's about to do. As it always does.

She screams. Loud enough that someone might hear her, and he clamps a hand over her mouth. She sinks her teeth hard into his hand. Sticky blood runs down his forearm. He punches her in the pit of the stomach, and she lets go with a whoosh of a drunk's putrid air.

The fingers of one hand wrap around her throat. She sucks in a breath as she tries breaking his grasp. Fingers claw at his bloody hand, the fingernails of her other hand gouging furrows on his neck, but he only increases pressure.

He takes a leather bootlace from his back pocket and wraps it around her neck. He twists the lace, and it digs into the flesh of her neck as he lifts her off the ground. She gasps, coughs, a deep rasping comes from her collapsed windpipe, legs flailing in the empty air beneath her. At death's doorstep, he lets up. She sucks in great gulps, seeming to recover, when he tightens the bootlace again. Her eyes bulge, her legs slowly kick the empty air, when ...

A dog barks.

The attacker's head jerks around to where the noise came from. A cowboy hat just peeks up over the hill. A panting dog sits beside the hat.

He drops the woman. She falls lifeless on the ground as he sprints toward the hill, to the sound of a truck kicking up dirt speeding away. He makes it to the edge of the bank and looks down: the truck and trailer are like most others in Wyoming. Except this one has sheep tumbling out the back of the trailer as it races for an open gate.

Even if he raced after the truck, he wouldn't catch it. Besides, he has a body to dispose of.

He walks back to the corpse and bends over her when headlights illuminate the truck. The rancher is approaching from the gate where he entered, coming on fast.

He abandons the body in the tall grass and jumps in his truck. He slaps the lever into four-wheel drive and bounds over the hill, making a run toward the gate where the witness fled moments before.

As he starts through the gate, his headlights reflect off something red on the ground beside the fence: a broken taillight from the witness's pickup.

He stops long enough to pick up the broken piece before speeding away. He looks back toward the hill, but the rancher has turned around, driving the way he came from, leaving the woman's body unfound. For now.

Later this morning—when the excitement of the kill has worn off and he can once again think straight—he'll go hunting the witness. And dispose of the body.

He shakes anew at the thought of finding the driver of that truck. He just hopes the witness has as much spunk as this last one did.

Three

ARN ANDERSON NEVER PLANNED to take a job as a range detective when he retired from Metro Denver Homicide. All he could think about was that he'd be associated with the last famous range detective: Tom Horn. Unlike Horn, Arn had no intention of getting himself hung for bushwhacking. But his pension didn't come close to paying the bills, especially now that he'd undertaken the restoration of his boyhood home in Cheyenne, which he referred to as the MP—the Money Pit. And his pension didn't allow him the luxury of buying another vehicle, like a pickup that would be better suited to driving the pastures and back country roads than his Oldsmobile 4-4-2.

He opened the gate and let himself into the field. "Wooly" Hank Doss, rancher and victim of considerable sheep thefts recently, had called this morning. Wooly Hank belonged to the Wyoming Wool Growers Association and, within the last year, had joined the group of ranchers who'd pooled their resources to hire Arn as a stock detective.

"It's damned sure the Midnight Sheepherder," Wooly Hank had sputtered over the phone.

Arn had quickly washed up just enough to go out in public. "How many sheep are you missing?" he asked as he knocked his whiskers down with a disposable Bic.

"I don't know."

"Do you at least have a general idea of how many got stole?"

"No, I do not," Wooly Hank answered. "I haven't been out to my pasture this morning."

"Then how do you know you have sheep missing?"

"Last night," Wooly Hank said, as if that were the only explanation needed, and Arn waited for the punch line. "Trucks woke me and the missus up last night."

"Did you call the sheriff's office?"

"I thought about it. We've had trouble with kids sneaking into the east pasture and drinking beer. Partying. Damned near burned some grassland this spring with a bonfire you could've seen from the space shuttle. But by the time I pulled my britches on and drove to the pasture last night, the last outfit had roared off. I didn't think I'd get an accurate head count of missing livestock until daybreak, so I went back to sleep. Figured I'd count up the stolen ones this morning and call the law then."

Arn groaned. Getting any information from Wooly Hank was like pulling hen's teeth. "So, did you count them this morning?"

"I figured I might as well wait for the range detective—that be you—to do the counting."

"I'll be there as soon as I can."

Arn took his time dressing. Danny—his formerly homeless houseguest and cook par excellence—had left some cinnamon rolls under a cake plate, and Arn snatched one on the fly. He'd stop by Starbucks on the way—Wooly Hank could just wait a few moments for Arn to wake up.

By the time he pulled off the county road into Wooly Hank's pasture, overhead lights of a sheriff's Expedition reflected from water trickling into a stock tank in the pasture. Wooly Hank stood by his truck staring at the sheriff's unit. When he spotted Arn, he waved him over. Arn climbed out of his car and stretched, catching Wooly Hank grinning at his Olds.

"What you gonna do in that pretty car when it snows?" the rancher called.

"Chain it up," Arn answered and chin-pointed to the sheriff's vehicle. "You must have found some sheep missing."

"They're not here for that." Wooly Hank beckoned with a bony finger, and Arn followed him across the pasture. Yellow evidence tape flapping in the wind—anchored by stakes sealing off a crime scene—caught Arn's attention. "The deputy said not to come any closer."

Arn moved laterally along the perimeter of the evidence tape before he spotted a body on the ground forty yards inside the barrier tape. A uniformed deputy and another man squatted by the corpse taking pictures. "Did you shoot the Midnight Sheepherder?"

"I would have if I'd have caught him," Wooly Hank answered, then shook as he recalled the body he'd found that morning at daybreak. "After I phoned you I came out here to start the count when I spotted … a body. I'm no trained lawman, but I knowed right off she was dead." He rubbed his temple. "I never noticed a body when I drove out here last night. It—she—was just laying there hidden by those clumps of sagebrush and buffalo grass. Naked from the waist up, she were."

"Know her?"

Wooly Hank stuffed Copenhagen into his lower lip. He offered Arn a dip, but he waved it off. "She's Jillie Reilly. Little Jim Reilly's daughter." Little Jim was, as Arn recalled, half-again as large as his teammates when he'd played line for University of Wyoming decades ago. Arn had the misfortune of delivering the death notification when Little Jim's wife had died in a car accident when Arn worked for Cheyenne PD years ago. He was grateful someone else would notify Little Jim about his daughter.

"Deputy Slade there said he's got to secure the pasture until the crime scene technicians arrive."

"Mike Slade, I'm guessing."

Wooly Hank nodded.

When Arn worked the Butch Spangler homicide last winter, Ned Oblanski, the Cheyenne police chief, had warned him to stay clear of Mike Slade. "He hates big city cops," Oblanski had said. "Especially big city detectives. Slade's one of the SO's investigators and fancies himself a sharp officer. Even drives up to the academy in Douglas to give rookie classes every session. He has delusions of adequacy." Yet here Arn was, standing in a pasture with Sergeant Mike Slade approaching, that delusional swagger coming out. He could have been a poster boy for DQ, with his long, lean legs, his bleached blond hair slicked back and pasted down with ... Vaseline?

The deputy stepped over the evidence tape and stopped in front of Arn, looking down. He had Arn by two inches, and he stood a little taller on his toes to accentuate his size difference. He puffed his chest out like it meant something. "Look who showed up—the old retired Denver investigator. Playing range detective, I hear."

"When I can."

"And I hear you haven't actually caught this Midnight Sheepherder after damned near half a year looking?"

"You heard right," Arn said.

"Well, that's just what I want to be when I retire—a stock detective. That's only slightly above sneaking around to get the goods on a cheating spouse."

Arn breathed deeply to calm himself. Even though Jillie Reilly was no concern of his, his cop DNA wanted to know more about it. And right now, Slade was the only soul who could tell him. "Homicide?"

"You *are* sharp," Slade said. "You figure that out just by looking at the body from forty yards away?"

"No. I figured you and your partner wouldn't be squatting next to a corpse if she just died naturally," Arn said. "We call that critical thinking in the big city."

"Well, stay out of my hair—"

"What was the cause of death?"

Slade turned back and faced Arn. He put his hands on his hips and smiled. "Cause of death will prove to be cerebral hypoxia."

"Just say the victim was strangled?"

Slade's smirk faded.

It was Arn's turn to smile. "At least that's what you would tell your rookie officers in class."

Slade's face turned red and his jaw muscles tightened.

"And while you're at it, what was the mechanism of her death?"

"You damned civilians don't need to know anything about this investigation."

"Look," Arn said. "I worked your side of the street for thirty years. Call it professional curiosity."

Slade kicked at a clump of sheep shit with his shiny cowboy boot. "I suppose your bud Ned Oblanski will tell you anyway." He jerked his thumb toward where the other deputy had just collapsed his camera tripod. "Victim was strangled and left where you see her."

"Any theories?"

Slade stroked his handlebar mustache. "Way I figure it, Jillie was with the Midnight Sheepherder last night. Like she always was, as I figure it. The two had an argument, maybe over the split from the night's theft. Maybe something else, like she got a case of conscience and threatened to expose their operation. Either way, her partner killed her and dumped her there."

"Hank says he came into his field and chased a truck down the hill." Arn nodded to the bank leading to a steep drop-off.

Slade glared at Wooly Hank. "He should have called right off."

"You guys never caught any kids partying before," Wooly Hank said. "How do you think you'd catch this guy?"

"He's got a point," Arn said. "All you got to do is find the truck that Hank put the run on and you might have your man. You might catch a break and find a tire print on down the hill you can cast for comparison when you find a suspect."

Slade waved his hand around the tall grass prairie. "Sure. All we got to do is find a distinctive tire pattern in grass. Now if there's dirt or gravel where the killer drove through—"

"There is." Arn motioned for Slade to squat beside him. He looked back into the sun and pointed out where the grass had bent down in the direction the truck fled. Just like Wooly Hank said. "Over that hill it's mostly dirt where the sheep have cropped the grass close. If it were me—and you understand this is just a range detective talking—I'd send my crime scene tech down there and look for tire impressions."

Slade's face turned red once again. "Maybe I already told my tech to do just that." He turned on his heel and stomped across the field toward a mobile crime scene lab entering the pasture. "Just stay out of my way, Anderson."

Wooly Hank watched Slade swagger toward the approaching van. "Might be a while before that damned fool is finished. Let's drive up to the house and have some coffee and jaw for a spell until they're done."

After two pots of coffee that thoroughly woke Arn up, and an apple fritter that Wooly Hank's missus baked, Slade and his evidence van left the pasture. Arn climbed back into Hank's old Dodge dually truck and they bounced across the field toward where Hank's sheep grazed. "And you're certain you didn't lose any sheep last night?"

"I just looked them over quick like." Wooly Hank downshifted, and the gears on his old truck gnashed in protest. "I'll do a detailed head count later now the law has left, but I'd bet they're all here."

"Then let's go back to where you found Jillie's body," Arn said.

Wooly Hank looked sideways at Arn. "Did the Association hire you to solve Jillie's murder?"

"They did not," Arn answered, his head out the window looking for anything the killer might have dropped from his truck. "So as of now—with none of your sheep missing—I'm officially off the Association's time clock. Just accept it that I wish to spend my free time looking at what happened."

"No offense, Arn, but that seems a little … sick, wanting to get wrapped up in a murder investigation."

"Can't argue there." Arn wanted to explain that after years of looking at murder victims, there was a profound satisfaction in bringing a killer to justice. Even if it meant wading knee-deep into the sinister side of life and imagining how a victim died. "Stop there." He pointed to where Slade had driven stakes into the ground to cordon off the murder scene.

They stopped and Arn looked at the tracks, obliterated up to that point by sheriff's office vehicles. Past the tape all the way to the edge of the pasture, tracks stood out sharply in the afternoon light. "Way the grass is smeared, he must have been hauling butt last night."

Wooly Hank nodded. "He flew off that hill like he was racing in one of those off-road rallies. No way was I going to follow him down there." He turned red. "But if I'd knowed he was a killer, by gawd I would have chased after him."

Arn patted the old man's shoulder. "I'm certain you would have. Now let's go see what the killer saw." He walked bent over, looking into the sun. When he got to the edge of the field, he spotted scuffed shoe prints of undetermined size and kind. And something else—the paw prints of a dog. Wooly Hank spotted it, too. He grabbed his cell phone and started punching numbers. "I'll call Slade. Bet he didn't cast that print."

Arn reached over and closed Hank's phone. "Don't waste your time. Casting this paw print would be about as useful as trying to lift a fingerprint off a rock. The only thing it tells us is that someone squatted here with a dog alongside them." He started for the truck. "Let's drive down there and see what Slade's evidence tech found."

Wooly Hank said the hill was too steep to drive down in his old Dodge, so he drove a meandering trail he regularly used that skirted the steep hill. When they reached bottom, Arn pointed out the impression in the dirt where the evidence technician had set his frame to pour the plaster of Paris–like concoction over a tire impression. Dots of hardened white casting material had balled up when it dropped into the fine dust.

Arn walked around the pasture that had been cropped flat by sheep. "What do you make of this?" He pointed to a flat scrape mark several feet wide. It started close to the bottom of the hillside and continued all the way to Hank's gate.

"Looks to me like they were dragging something," Hank said.

Arn thought so too. With no sheep missing, and the tracks indicating the truck had driven out of the pasture at a high speed, he could only think of one explanation. "We know the Midnight Sheepherder's been using dogs. And with a trailer big enough to hold thirty or thirty-five head, a good dog can gather them up and the rustler can be gone within minutes." He knelt and ran his hand over the scrape mark. "I think Slade's way off base thinking Jillie and the killer were in the rustling game together."

Wooly Hank wiped tobacco juice off his stubble with his shirt-sleeve. "What you getting at?"

"You're not missing any sheep."

"I told you that first."

Arn closed his eyes, reconstructing the murder scene as he often did throughout his years as a homicide detective. "The trailer ramp is down. The rustler has his dog out and is ready to gather your flock. But I think he's interrupted by the killer." Arn motioned topside to Wooly Hank's upper pasture. "He scrambles up the bank with his dog. Sees the killer strangling Jillie Reilly. The killer spots him, and the rustler flees so fast he doesn't even bother to raise the ramp."

"So that's why the rustler didn't steal my sheep?"

"That what I figure."

Wooly Hank picked at his whiskers with a chipped fingernail. "If what you say is true, then the Midnight Sheepherder is the only witness to Jillie's murder. That makes sense, but—no offense, Arn—you ain't had any luck locating the rustler yet. How you going to find him now?"

"With that." Arn squatted next to the gate. Paint transfer from a fender, perhaps the box of a pickup, had been smeared on the wooden gatepost as the truck passed. Arn opened his pocket knife and dug around the wood until he could pull the paint chip free. He tore a sheet from his pocket notebook and fashioned a mini-envelope to put the paint chip in. "We now know the color of the rustler's truck."

"Whoa," Wooly Hank said. "I followed you up until you came up with that cockamamie notion. Maybe that paint chip came from the killer's truck."

"It didn't. Look." Arn broke off a piece of sagebrush and circled a tire track. "When I looked at one of the tire tracks topside, I noticed the killer's truck has a chunk of sidewall missing. This one that brushed the gate and left this paint mark doesn't."

"But Deputy Slade said you can't see tire tracks in the grass."

"Slade knows just enough about police work to be dangerous." Arn stood and stretched. "If he'd looked closer, he would have spotted them as well."

"Maybe the witness left these, too." Wooly Hank kneeled by the gate. He brushed dirt away and picked up two slivers of plastic that he handed to Arn.

"Good eye." Arn turned the plastic shards over in his hand. It looked like a piece of broken taillight or a side marker light—not enough to determine what make or even type of vehicle. But now he had one more thing to look for: a navy blue truck with a broken marker or taillight.

"That's just great." Wooly Hank threw his hands up. "Now you'll be trying to find Jillie's killer rather than investigate our sheep thefts."

Arn clamped a hand on Wooly Hank's shoulder. "I'll still be at the Association's beck and call. Except now I have something to do between those calls." He started for Wooly Hank's truck, then stopped and turned back to where he'd picked up the shard of plastic.

"Now what'd you find?"

Arn squatted in the dirt and ran his hand through tiny mounds. He stood and arched his back. "It's what I don't find. I don't find the rest of this marker lens."

"So maybe it didn't fall out of the truck when it hit the gate," Wooly Hank said. "Maybe it's still stuck in the fender."

Arn turned the broken plastic over in his hand. Ridges showed that the light's base had broken. "It broke off, all right. And it's not here."

"So?"

"So, if it's not here, I'm certain by these tracks the person that hit the gate didn't dawdle long enough to pick it up." Arn looked up the hill, envisioning what kind of killer would be after the witness. "That means the killer stopped and picked the lens up. And is probably looking for a match to it right now."

Four

DANNY SPOTTED ELK SLID an omelet onto Arn and Ana Maria Villa-rreal's plates. He set his own poached egg atop a biscuit before sitting across from them at a table he'd scored from Goodwill.

"You outdid yourself," Ana Maria said. She sliced a corner of her omelet off and let it ferment on her palate for a moment before swallowing. "New recipe?"

"Rancid sausage." Danny patted his mouth with a napkin. "Dug it out of the dumpster down at the homeless shelter."

Ana Maria gagged and dropped her fork on the table.

"Relax." Danny smiled. "Just joking. It is the same sausage we always buy."

Ana Maria broke into a grin then. "You got me there." She nudged Arn, who hadn't smiled at the joke. "You feeling all right?"

Arn swirled a spoon around in his coffee cup.

"You want to get involved in Jillie Reilly's murder," Ana Maria said. "I can tell by the way your lip is dragging on the floor."

Ana Maria had perfected her people skills from years as a television reporter: first in Denver, fresh off of working as an auto mechanic, and then here in Cheyenne. Between that and her time spent investigating—honing her bullshit detector—Arn knew he couldn't fool her. But it didn't stop him from trying. "Jillie Reilly's murder is none of my business."

"Of course it isn't," Danny said. He took a small bite of egg and laid the fork on his plate. "The last thing you should do is stick your great big Norwegian nose into it."

Arn nodded.

"Especially when that nice sheriff deputy Mike Slade can handle it." Danny daintily dabbed his mouth with a napkin. "Before you know it, he'll have the killer bagged."

Arn dropped his spoon on the table. "Slade couldn't find his own shoelaces."

"Nothing left to do then"—Ana Maria winked at Danny—"but go out every night and sit on some rancher's pasture hoping to catch the Midnight Sheepherder. Pretty wild and exciting work there. Bet talk radio gets real interesting about daybreak. *Coast to Coast AM*, is it?"

Arn pushed his plate away. "Just what would you have me do?"

"Offer your services for free," Danny said. "At least you wouldn't be moping around here getting in *my* way."

"Slade would rather eat ground glass than take my advice," Arn said. "Besides, I'm a mercenary. Show me the money first."

Ana Maria grabbed the coffee pot and refilled her and Danny's cups. Arn hadn't touched his since he sat down. "How about if I told you DeAngelo will call you today and offer you a consulting fee to find Jillie's killer? Would you turn it down?"

"I've got a job—catching sheep thieves. Besides … " Arn waved his arm around the half-finished kitchen that had been his mother's pride when she was alive. "I've got work to do here. I think I'll hang some drywall today."

DeAngelo Damos, the crotchety television station owner and Ana Maria's boss, had hired Arn last winter to solve the decade-old murder of police detective Butch Spangler. Having the money to finally restore his boyhood home, Arn had moved back to Cheyenne, taken the consulting money DeAngelo offered, and then struck a deal with Danny for the home repairs.

Danny leaned his elbows on the table. "Do us both a favor—leave the remodeling to me. I get more work done if I don't have to go back and fix your mistakes."

"You implying my work is bad?"

"I'm not implying anything," Danny answered. "I'm stating a fact— you're a poor carpenter and a worse plumber. And you'll burn the house down if you try rewiring the place again. Take DeAngelo's offer when he calls and do what you do best—hunting down bad guys."

Arn started to speak, but he kept quiet. He had no argument for Danny. Ever since he'd first allowed the emaciated-looking old homeless man to live in the house in exchange for repairing it, Danny had worked miracles. He'd restored the structure along with some cosmetics. Wiring and plumbing and heating had been upgraded, and the one-time engineer had turned the house from one the city intended to condemn to one on its way to restoration glory. And they both knew that Arn couldn't have afforded a contractor for what Danny had done so far.

Ana Maria finished her coffee and stood. "I'm off to the station. I'll tell DeAngelo you're not interested."

"Why would he even want to put me on the payroll again?" Arn asked cautiously.

"Why else?" Ana Maria said. "He desperately wants Sheriff Grimes to lose the next election. He doesn't like the sheriff's politics or the way he runs his agency. If some outsider solved Jillie's murder before Slade did, it'd make DeAngelo's day." She paused in the doorway. "As soon as I returned from talking to Slade, DeAngelo briefed me. He's got a contact at the sheriff's office who feels there just isn't enough evidence to solve Jillie's murder."

"What did Slade tell you?" Arn found himself asking. Another consulting gig with DeAngelo would enable him to purchase material needed to finish the renovation.

Ana Maria grinned. "He said he knows you and I are friends, and he alluded to us being *more* than friends with me living in your spare room upstairs."

Danny chuckled. "Arn's old enough to be your dad."

"Thanks," Arn said. "What else?"

"He gave me a not-so-veiled threat to pass along to you to keep your nose out of his investigation: 'Maybe us yokels don't have the resources the big city boys do, but we always manage to solve our cases.' I don't think he likes you much."

"I'm hurt." Arn suddenly felt famished and dug into his omelet. "Does he have any leads?"

Ana Maria walked to the coffee pot and dumped the old grounds into the garbage. "His theory is a little different than yours. He's sticking by his belief that Jillie and her killer were in cahoots rustling sheep."

"That's a boneheaded theory," Arn said. "I read the tracks at Wooly Hanks, and they indicate the rustler spotted the killer strangling Jillie and ran away."

"Slade's adamant they had a falling out which culminated in her partner strangling her," Ana Maria said. "He'll appeal to the public for any information. But you know how successful that's been in the past." She turned on Mr. Coffee. "You want to hear Slade, news at seven tonight? You can catch all his inflated ego in action."

"Sergeant Slade will be 'On the Case with Ana Maria' tonight?"

"He will," Ana Maria answered. "Suit and all. A natural ham I suspect."

"Good luck getting anything substantial out of him."

"Don't count me out yet. Besides having a head too big to get through that doorway, he asked me to dinner."

"I thought I saw a wedding ring on his finger," Arn said.

Ana Maria shrugged. "Guess it doesn't make any difference to him. Sounds like he and his missus have an open marriage."

"Great." Danny winked at Arn. "Now I got to set another plate for dinner one night soon."

Ana Maria scowled at him. "Don't bet on it." She turned to Arn. "So, you'll take DeAngelo up on his offer."

"I don't know. I still need to go out nights and catch the rustler." Arn finished his breakfast and held his cup for Ana Maria to refill. "If I accept DeAngelo's offer, I'll need your help."

"I thought as much," she said.

As a seasoned reporter, Ana Maria had a way of getting people to open up to her. When working at the CBS affiliate in Denver while Arn was at Metro, she could extract information from people quicker than a police interrogator. Arn knew he would need that acumen if he hoped to find Jillie's killer. "Did you find out any more about Jillie?" he asked.

"Jillie was the secretary, receptionist, and call center operator for Dr. Maury Oakert, Psychiatrist," Ana Maria said. "His practice is down by the hospital."

"The one the police send their officers to when they have psychological issues?" Danny said.

They looked at Danny. "How do you know that?" Ana Maria asked.

"As many times as I raided the dumpster down there—in my homeless days—and saw officers go into a shrink's office, I put two and two together."

They just stared at him.

"Don't say it." Danny held up his hand. "I *am* astute."

Arn began clearing the table of paper plates and Styrofoam cups. He hadn't found the money for a dishwasher yet, and Danny said that some things, like clearing tables, were above a chef of his caliber. "The police mandate that their officers visit a psychiatrist whenever they're involved in a shooting," he explained. "The city and county pay for officers to see the psychiatrist if they have personal issues that might affect their job."

"Anyways," Ana Maria said, "Jillie worked for Dr. Oakert ever since he opened his practice three years ago."

"Why is it doctors never get it right?" Danny asked.

Ana Maria looked at him for an explanation.

"Doctors and lawyers always *practice*," Danny clarified. "They never *get it right*."

"It seems like Dr. Oakert got it right." Ana Maria passed the coffee pot and Danny refilled their cups. "I called one of my contacts at the police department, and all I heard were good things about him."

"Then I need to talk with him," Arn said. "*If* I accept DeAngelo's offer."

"I forgot to tell you." Ana Marie smiled. "I actually confirmed to DeAngelo that you'd take the consulting gig."

"What if I wanted to turn him down?" Arn held up his hand. "Don't say anything other than 'it's the shits when someone knows you so well.'"

"Call it predictability." Ana Maria sat at the table and leaned back. "I talked with Dr. Oakert briefly yesterday afternoon at his home. He was pretty upset and could only give me a few minutes." She took a long reporter's notebook from her shoulder bag and turned to a dog-eared page. "Jillie was a partier. Dr. Oakert said she came in late most Mondays looking like she'd been on an all-night bender. Shame. She was a pretty girl." Ana Maria grabbed her cell phone and punched up her photos. She handed the phone to Arn. "I took that pic from a photo on her desk."

The picture showed a woman somewhere north of thirty. Her long, wind-swept hair partially obscured her face as she sat a sorrel mare herding steers while a dog ran beside her. "I got the impression that Dr. Oakert wanted to date her."

Arn's hackles stood at attention like they usually did when something wasn't quite right. "That might pose some ethical dilemmas, dating his employee. And how old is this doctor?"

"He says he's forty-six, but he looks older. He's got a toupee that fits like he stuck his head in a blender. But maybe he just looked older because he'd been crying."

"I would, if I lost my secretary of three years," Danny said. "Maybe he's just an emotional person."

"That's what I thought," Ana Maria said. "I gave him the benefit of the doubt, even though it appears he's a born-again bachelor. Has an ex-wife somewhere around San Francisco." She chuckled. "And I don't blame her splitting up with him if he was as big a horn dog then as he is now."

"How so?"

Ana Maria pocketed her notebook. "Where Slade was subtle, almost smooth when he came on to me, Maury—that's what he insisted

I call him—was clumsy. I can see why Jillie never took him up on his offer. *If* he tried dating her."

Danny nudged her. "Maybe you ought to take one for the team and date him. Maybe he'd open up a bit if you get a little … kissy-face."

Ana Maria slapped Danny on the back. "I think Dr. Oakert's just cagey enough not to open up on anything. But he did tell me some things. Like that Jillie was his only employee. She answered the phones and transcribed all his taped clinic notes. When he showed me her desk, it was neat. Organized. Not like someone who dragged ass on Monday mornings. The only thing he critiqued about her"—she took her notebook out again—"was, and I quote, 'I had to reprimand her several times for jumping on dating sites.' He even had a block put on her office computer so she couldn't troll the internet."

"Those dating sites aren't a big thing anymore," Danny said. "I'd get on some myself and find a little lady if some cheapskate"—he exaggerated a nod at Arn—"would spring for the net."

"Why would Arn do that when I research things whenever he wants?" Ana Maria asked. "But that's right—it shouldn't have been a big deal if she went on the internet during her lunch break." She stood and started out the door. "Mark my word: DeAngelo is going to call. He should, too. The piker conned me into doing a valve job on his old International truck."

"Where you gonna to do that?" Danny asked.

"Right out in what we lovingly call a yard. Among the tall weeds, I'm going to tear into that beater truck this weekend unless I get a tip about Jillie's case. But I'll be lucky if DeAngelo reimburses me for materials."

Arn's cell phone buzzed and he took the call, Danny and Ana Maria eavesdropping expectantly. DeAngelo Damos offered him a sizeable consulting fee to work with the television station to find Jillie

Reilly's murderer. When DeAngelo disconnected, Arn pocketed the phone and dropped his napkin in the garbage. "It's official—we'll be working together again," he told Ana Maria.

She held her hand up for a high five. "We'll talk more about the case when I get home tonight." She leaned closer. "And you realize you'll have to get in front of my camera now and again, just to talk about this case. Generate some excitement."

"I wish I was an enthusiastic as you," Arn said as he headed for the door. "Looks like the first people I need to talk with are the ones at the courthouse who know Jillie's father."

"Why the courthouse?" Ana Maria asked.

"If you want to know something about a person here in Cheyenne, you go to the courthouse. Those ladies know *everything* there is about a person." A sadness overcame Arn. "Then I'll talk with Little Jim. Nothing like talking to a man about his murdered daughter."

Five

ARN TURNED OFF TERRY Bison Ranch Road and drove six miles west to the Reilly Ranch. Ladies at the courthouse had told him that Little Jim kept to himself ever since his wife died thirty years ago. "He's pleasant enough," one lady at the Treasurer's Office told him. "Whenever he comes in to renew his plates or pay his property taxes, he's polite. But ..." She paused and looked around. "His size is a little intimidating." They described the Reilly Ranch as a modest place by Wyoming standards—a thousand acres, most of it pasture land. And up until her death four days ago, Jim had shared the ranch responsibilities with his only daughter, Jillie.

Arn passed a small feedlot with fifteen head of buffalo that Little Jim raised to sell every year, with another hundred head of registered Black White-Face heifers in a pasture beside the feedlot. A flock of sheep helped with his ranch expenses, the busybodies at the courthouse said, and Jim always had a few large-breed Lincoln ewes that he loaned out to the Little Britches Rodeo for the Laramie County Fair each year.

When Arn had spoken with Jim on the phone earlier, the man sounded neither pleased nor antagonistic that he was coming. He just sounded like most parents of recently deceased children—going through the motions of life while they sorted through memories of a lifetime with their child.

When Arn drove into the yard, Jim Reilly was sitting on the porch swing that overlooked the feedlot where he kept the buffalo. A Border collie sat at his feet, tongue lolling to one side. Little Jim watched Arn drive the long road into the yard and park in front of the porch.

Arn used the A pillar to extricate himself from his 4-4-2 and arched his back, stretching. "Hell of a thing to be driving on gravel," Little Jim said as he looked askance at the car. "Ought to be driving it on the drag strip instead of navigating these roads."

"I can't argue there," Arn said. "But it's all I have."

Little Jim motioned for Arn to join him on the porch.

As Arn mounted the steps, he realized Little Jim was even bigger than he remembered. Although he was only four inches taller than Arn, he appeared taller and much heavier in his dusty ranch clothes. His overalls strained at the seams as if they were a size too small. Arn guessed Little Jim had him by thirty pounds. No small feat.

"No offense," the man said, "but you look thinner on TV. And younger."

Arn grinned. "Old stock photos the station insists on using."

"I still recognized you. You asked me to come into the police station that July ... " He broke it off and turned his head away. When he turned back, his eyes had watered. "I miss Doris every day. You have a wife, Mr. Anderson?"

"I did," Arn answered. "Cailee died twelve years ago. Cancer." He forced a smile. "And I miss her every day too."

Little Jim offered Arn a seat in a wicker chair on one side of a round metal table and poured glasses of lemonade. Arn sipped, and held the cold glass against his temple. "Fresh-squeezed?"

"Crystal Light."

The dog lay down beside Little Jim's chair. "This is—was—Jillie's dog. She raised her since she was a puppy. Now with Jillie gone ... " He looked away and paused. "Jillie used to help me on weekends. Not that I really needed it, but it was an excuse for us to spend some time together." He stroked the dog's muzzle. "With Jillie gone, the dog seems to know she's not coming back. She follows me everywhere."

They sat in silence for long moments. Arn was in no hurry to ask questions and dredge up more pain for Little Jim.

"I saw that Villarreal woman's special last night," he said at last. "And I remembered you from when you told me about Doris. And last year, when you solved the murder of that Cheyenne detective, you were on TV a few times."

Arn wanted to tell Little Jim it ended up not being a murder, but he let it go. "My mug was pasted across the TV screen quite often last winter."

Little Jim leaned forward in his chair. The wicker creaked under his weight and his eyes locked on Arn's. "Point is, you have a reputation as an astute investigator. That's one of those ten dollar words I learned in college that I rarely use."

Arn shrugged. "Sometime I just get lucky."

"More than sometimes," Little Jim said as he sat back. "I've checked you out since you called yesterday. You solved every homicide assigned to you when you were in Metro Denver."

"Like I said, I'm lucky now and again."

"Well, Mr. Anderson, you get lucky this time—give me Jillie's killer—and your bank account will get lucky, too."

Arn sipped his lemonade. Little Jim wasn't the first man to request that a relative's murderer be turned over to him. "I'm afraid I can't do that. If and when I help the sheriff's office find your daughter's killer, I'll have to turn him over for prosecution."

Little Jim reached into his vest pocket and withdrew an envelope. He tossed it on the table where the sweating pitcher soaked the edge of the envelope. Arn clearly saw paper money inside. "There's five thousand dollars. Take it for expenses." He held up his hand. "Consider it helping to find the son-of-a-bitch."

Arn hefted the envelope. For a moment, all he saw was central air for his old house before he handed it back to Little Jim. "The television station is paying my expenses. I can't take this. But I'll do whatever I can to find your daughter's killer."

"Had to try." Little Jim nodded but put the envelope on the table again. "What can I do to help?"

Arn crossed his legs and laid his notebook across his lap. "Just some basic questions—"

"Like those questions that sheriff's deputy already asked, that smart-ass Mike Slade? I damned near put a boot in his rectum for accusing Jillie of being a sheep rustler."

Arn's gaze automatically went to the sheep pasture, and Little Jim caught it. "I'd know if any sheep that didn't belong to me suddenly appeared on this place."

"Unless she had another holding pen somewhere. Someplace to graze them until she could ship them out of the area."

Little Jim tensed. "That's what Slade said. You *really* believe Jillie was involved in rustling? Hell, all she ever did was work and help me on the weekends."

Arn debated telling Little Jim about his theory that there was a witness to Jillie's murder—that the rustler-witness was at Wooly Hanks to steal sheep when Jillie and her killer drove into the pasture. He decided that for now, he'd keep his theories to himself and Ana Maria.

Arn began doodling. He didn't need to refer to the notebook, but it took people's minds off him as they answered questions, thinking that he was writing everything down. "Jillie's employer, Dr. Oakert, claims she partied quite a bit."

"That pompous ass would say that after trying to get her in bed as many times as he did." Little Jim spit a string of tobacco juice that cleared the porch steps. *World class.*

"You think Dr. Oakert was lying about Jillie's partying?"

Little Jim looked toward the lot holding the buffalo so long that Arn wasn't sure he'd heard him. "Jillie was always a little wild," he began. "Sure, she liked to bend elbows at the bar on weekends. She worked hard all week and helped out here on weekends. She relaxed a little with a brewski or two, but that was okay by me. Didn't make her a bad person." He swiped a hand across his eyes. "Fact was she was just about the best person I know. Sounds biased, huh?"

"It sounds like a father who had the utmost respect for his daughter." Arn doodled. "Dr. Oakert said Jillie went on dating sites quite a bit. Didn't she have a computer at home?"

"We have crappy service out this far, and we never bought one. Deputy Slade asked the same thing."

Arn refilled their lemonade glasses and sat back down with his pen in hand. "Did anyone hold a grudge against your daughter? Anyone she didn't get along with?"

"Eddie Glass," Little Jim answered immediately. "Jillie had a fling with him last year. I had to step in and put the run on that bastard.

Last thing I wanted was my daughter to become involved with a married man."

Arn wrote and underlined Eddie's name. And *married man*. "Did he leave her alone after that?"

"Damn well better have," Little Jim answered, his voice faltering just talking about it. "Or I'd have put the boots to him."

"Did Jillie have a favorite watering hole?"

"Boot Hill. She always went there 'cause they have live music on weekends, and she loved to dance. And because there were fewer lounge lizards trying to pick her up."

"Did she mention any problems at the bar?"

"Not there." Little Jim looked back to the buffalo as if the answer were on the backs of those shaggy, shedding beasts. "She came home early from work one day last week upset big time. Something at work frightened her. I told her I'd be more than happy to pay that Dr. Oakert a visit and make sure she never came home like that again."

"But you didn't?"

Little Jim took off his Stetson and wiped the sweat off the inside band with a paisley bandana. "She said it had nothing to do with Dr. Oakert trying to put the moves on her. She just said it was something she couldn't talk about. That's all she'd tell me."

Little Jim stood and hooked his thumbs into the straps of his bib overalls as he looked at his south pasture. "She was going to help me gather some heifers from the south range. She always helped me around the place. She was a good girl, Mr. Anderson." He stepped off the porch. "Now I better get used to doing it alone."

"You got a horse I can sit?"

Little Jim looked skeptical. "Jillie's sorrel mare is in the corral. Why?"

Arn laid his pen and notebook on the table. "In my younger days I was a passable cowboy. You let me use her horse, and I'll help you gather up those heifers."

Arn followed Little Jim to the corral. If all he had to do to help a grieving father was help gather heifers, Arn would do it every day.

Six

I LAY THE MORNING edition of the *Wyoming Tribune Eagle* on the table
beside bills and letters and a US map with locations of potential dates. The
lead article was a rehash of what Ana Maria Villarreal said on air last night.
She interviewed Sergeant Slade, who believes Jillie's killer was her partner in
a sheep rustling ring. Slade speculated she and her partner had a falling out,
which resulted in her death in Wooly Hank's pasture. Slade cited no more
thefts since Jillie's death as supporting his belief that she was half of the
Midnight Sheepherder. Damned fool. If he remains the lead investigator on
the case I'll never get caught.

Unless that witness got a good look at me.

Now, that old retired Denver Metro investigator ... is something else.
When she put him on air after Slade, Anderson said little, but the tone of his
voice, his confident manner, showed him to be a possible danger to me. Worse,
when I hopped on the internet to talk with babes tonight, I got sidetracked
and researched Anderson. He was some kind of legend in Metro Denver, solv-
ing every homicide assigned. "A born predator" is how the Denver Post

referred to him. But I'm not worried. I've fooled the law all these years since being released, and I'll continue to fool them.

And fool some washed-up range detective.

I've been a born predator all these years as well.

I check my watch and turn the TV on. Ana Maria's noon update has already begun. She wraps up Jillie's murder update with Slade's theory and goes right into a story about working dogs. She explains how rustlers are using herding dogs to gather sheep and cattle quickly, making their escape long before anyone even knows they are there. This is not the first time I've heard this. "Within the space of a few minutes," she says, "a dog can herd thirty head of sheep into a trailer, and the rustler's away before the rancher has a chance to put his pants on."

She asks for the public's help: anyone knowing Jillie's partner in crime— her killer—needs to call the Laramie County Sheriff's Office.

For the briefest of moments, that old retired Denver cop's face flashes across the screen again like he's some secret weapon or something. But I've endured everything the law could send against me before. Sure, I spent some time in that retirement home for the criminally insane in Napa. But I look at it as time well spent, talking with loonies crazier than I ever was, who taught me to think things through before I act. Even crazies can have good ideas. Like planning your move down to the tiniest detail to avoid exposure.

The one departure from my flawless routine all these years was Jillie Reilly. With her, I had to act quickly or everyone within earshot in the bar would have known about me. And if Anderson believes Sergeant Slade's theory, I never will get caught without the public's help. But then I always knew that this time, I never will get caught. Perhaps I'll send the cops a little note. Just a one-line zinger or something to let them know I'm still out here and alive. And of course I'll send it from out of state like I always have. That'll be a nice touch.

I start to turn off the noon news when I stop and stare. It just hit me that Ana Maria looks like the others: dark eyes, dark complexion, a little chunky. Except for her hair—dark brown and longer than the others—she could fit right in with them.

I quickly turn off the TV. The last thing I need to do now is get distracted by someone local when there are so many others within driving distance. "Don't shit in your own nest," Dad once told me, a few days before I killed him and stuffed his body into that abandoned water well.

I slip on my jeans and pull one boot on, caked with cow dung and sheep shit, and I pause. In the back of my mind, I worry my time may be running out even though I often think I'm untouchable. I know it's just a matter of time before the witness that fled Wooly Hank's gets a case of conscience and goes to the law. At some point he'll take a rustling rap rather than live with the guilt of seeing Jillie's murder. And the guilt that her killer will go free.

I tug on the mule ears of my other boot and my foot slides in. How good a look did the Midnight Sheepherder get? In the full moon, and illuminated by the headlights for a brief moment, he might have gotten a very good look.

Or not.

I just can't take the chance. I must find that witness.

I pick up the broken piece of taillight and stuff it in my vest pocket. I need to go to town today, and it'll give me a good excuse to look for the match for this piece of plastic. Ana Maria talked about the dog class put on by the county extension office starting at the Archer Complex. I didn't plan to be there, but I'm thinking it would be a good place to start my search. Where else would the Midnight Sheepherder want to be other than in a class of sheep-herding dogs?

Seven

ARN ENTERED THE BOOT Hill saloon and stood to one side of the door. He waited until his eyes adjusted to the dim light and wished his nose would adjust to the stale smoke of cigarettes, the retching odor of spilt beer too slow in being cleaned up. The Boot Hill was the place to go for a cheap drunk, dating back to the days when Arn worked for the Cheyenne police department. The owner, Flo Martin, had outlasted her eighty-year-old husband to run the bar herself. She'd recently committed to live music every weekend and made sure everything sticky was mopped from the dance floor. So at least the dance floor was clean. And she advertised door prizes for anyone testing over a .20 on her alcohol machine hanging by the exit door.

"What you say, sugar?" Flo Martin wheezed as she walked across the empty dance floor. She stopped in front of Arn, one hand resting seductively on her bony hip, all ninety pounds of her. Her other hand waved the air with a cigarette jammed into a silver holder as she spoke. Ashes flicked onto the floor as she sucked deeply. Her lips pursed in the vertically-lined indents consistent with a woman who has smoked all her long life. "You want a drink?"

"Not at noon."

"That only means you'll get a late start." She tilted her head back and laughed heartily. Which quickly deteriorated into a coughing fit violent enough that Arn worried she'd keel over right there. A passing thought caused him to retch; the last thing he wanted right after lunch was to perform CPR on Flo Martin.

He waited until he was certain she'd live another day before he motioned to the alcohol testing machine. "Is that right? You give door prizes to anyone getting blasted enough to register a .20 BA?"

She nodded and hit her chest with a fist. "We bribe folks with a blender or a toaster, just like the banks do. We want people to test themselves before they leave, make sure they know how wasted they are. Wouldn't want anyone driving drunk."

"What about the .20 testers that leave the bar alone? Don't you worry about them?"

Flo crossed herself. "I worry about all of them, sugar. We *tell* them not to drive. But what they do when they leave here is none of my business." She snubbed her butt out in a chipped Grain Belt ashtray and stuck another one into her filter in one practiced motion. She caught Arn eying it. "Filter keeps carcinogens out of these lungs." She coughed again and lit up. "Gotta stay healthy. Now what can I do for you if you're not here to drink?" She winked.

"I understand Jillie Reilly hung out here," Arn said, changing the subject. "She might have been drinking here the night she was murdered."

"She did." Flo crossed herself again with a wrinkled hand. "This was her place."

"Can we sit?"

Flo led Arn to a booth. He sat and she nudged him over to sit next to him. "Married, sugar?"

Arn held up his hand, where a worn wedding ring glinted in the dim light. Although Cailee had been dead for years now, he still wore the ring in her memory. And sometimes—like now, with Flo—it proved useful in other ways. "I'm spoken for."

"Shame," Flo said as she took in another long draw of smoke. "What you need to know?"

Arn opened his notebook and took out his pen as if he intended to write. He'd jot his notes down later in the car. For now, he'd sit and listen and judge Flo's body language, her voice inflections, to see if she was truthful. "Tell me, what was Jillie like last Saturday night?"

Flo looked at the *Miller High Life* beer sign with broken neons that flashed *Mil e High*. It made Arn think he was back in Denver. "She waltzed in drunker than usual. But then she usually got snockered-up and wild. It was what made her charming, and attracted cowboys to her."

"Any cowboy in particular that night?"

Flo chin-pointed to the stage with the instruments still assembled awaiting the musicians gig next Saturday night. "Eddie Glass. He and Jillie danced so many tunes I thought they'd wear their legs out."

"Her father said Eddie was an old flame?"

Flo shrugged. "Jillie had a fling with Eddie last summer. But then a lot of women around Cheyenne had a fling with him, much to the chagrin of his wife."

"So, she knew?"

Flo blew smoke upward. It lingered over the booth and she waved the air. "Karen stormed in here one night last month. Got someone to watch their baby while she went out looking for Eddie. I don't hold to messing around on your wife—it was none of my business. But when she came in raising hell and ragging on Eddie, I told the bouncer to show her the door."

"Did Karen come in last Saturday?"

"I didn't see her, but my bartender might have." Flo craned her neck around and yelled, "Hey Karl, did Eddie Glass's old lady come in here last Saturday?"

Karl stood from behind the bar, but Arn barely saw him. When he walked around the end of the bar, a towel was draped over his muscular shoulders. Shoulders less than half as large as Arn's—Karl was a little person. He had a stogie stuck in his mouth that looked way too big for him, and a muscle shirt that showed off his physique. For a wee man, Karl was put together mighty well. "What the hell you want now?"

"This is Mr. Anderson. He's helping the police find Jillie Reilly's killer."

Karl tipped his pork pie hat. "Howdy, old timer."

"Mr. Anderson wants to know if Karen Glass came in here last Saturday night."

"Early." Karl nodded. "She looked around for a minute and then left. I never saw her again. Now is that it, 'cause I got a ton of shit I gotta do before we start getting drinkers tonight."

Flo waved him off, and Karl returned to his chores behind the bar.

"Got him an attitude," Arn said.

"He's the best bartender I ever had, or I'd can him."

"How about your bouncer? Maybe he saw Eddie's wife—"

"Karl *is* my bouncer," Flo said, and she must have read the surprise etched on Arn's face. "Karl's a tough little bastard. You ought to see him compete in dwarf-tossing."

Arn grabbed his pen, as much to get the thought out of his head of Karl sailing through the air like one of the Flying Wallendas and landing on a stained and filthy mattress on the floor of the bar. "Let me get this straight: Eddie and Jillie danced all night?"

Flo lit another cigarette and held the holder away from Arn. "Not all night. Don Whales and the Dolphins had just started their first break—"

"Odd name for a Wyoming band."

Flo patted Arn's hand. "We like to think it a … quaint name. Anyways, Bonnie Johns came in and sat in the corner. When Jillie went to the crapper, Bonnie grabbed Eddie as he was sitting catching his breath. They cut a rug, they did, clearing the dance floor, until Jillie came out and tried to cut in. Bonnie shoved Jillie and she fell to the floor. Karl had to give Bonnie the bum's rush."

Flo waved her hand, and Karl came over with a mug of draft beer. "You want one, old timer?"

"You got one with a Geritol chaser?"

"A what?"

"Never mind," Arn said. "I'm fine."

"And that was the last of Jillie and Eddie for the night?" Arn asked after Karl had disappeared behind the bar.

"Eddie dancing with Bonnie didn't sit well with Jillie, and she latched onto some other dude sitting at the bar. Then Eddie wanted to make her jealous so he grabbed some woman sitting with her old man. They started dancing, and Eddie was rubbing again' her pretty seductively. Well, it was Katie bar the door then. Her old man jumped Eddie for dancing with his wife, and Karl ushered them both outside. Eddie came back in a few minutes all bloodied. Said he made the husband wish he'd let him dance with his old lady."

"And you let Eddie back in after that?"

Flo blew the head off the mug of beer, and it hit the floor with a nasty *plop*. "What happens outside is none of my business. Besides,

Eddie gets pretty crazy when he's drunk. I didn't know if Karl could even handle him."

Arn let that pass. "So how long did Jillie stay? I'm trying to get a fix on her timeline for Saturday night."

Flo looked at the ceiling fan wafting smoke around the room. "Jillie didn't stay long. While Eddie and the husband were duking it out outside, Jillie spotted some guy I never seen before drinking by his lonesome in the corner. I figured she wanted to score with the guy just to make Eddie jealous, but all she did was stand by his booth and taunt him. 'I'm going to tell,' she said. 'Just wait until this gets out.'"

"Wait until what gets out?"

Flo shrugged. "I'm guessing he was another married man that Jillie had a one-night stand with at one time. She was known for that."

"And she hung around taunting him?"

"I figured she was waiting for Eddie to come back so he could see she was interested in the guy." Flo took a huge gulp of the beer. Some froth spilled onto her chin and ran down her chest. She winked at Arn. "Want to wipe it dry?"

Arn held up his ring finger, and her smile faded as she grabbed a napkin. "The guy tried to make himself small, but Jillie kept pestering him. Embarrassing, if the guy was married. Anyways, when Eddie came in, he saw Jillie leaning over the guy's table and he started for him. The husband of the woman he'd danced with burst back into the bar then for round two. Between the fight and Karl breaking them up, it gave the poor bastard time to escape Jillie's nagging. He ran out in the confusion with Jillie right on his heels. Eddie turned to catch up with her, but it wasn't until he'd waylaid the husband on the dance floor that he could run outside after Jillie and the dude."

"Did Eddie catch up with them?"

"He might have, 'cause he never came back in. Or else Karen was waiting for him outside." Flo leaned closer than Arn liked. "If you talk with Karen, you watch your backside. That girl's got a temper as bad as her old man's. She'd as likely clear out a bar as Eddie would."

"I'll remember that." Arn jotted down what Flo had told him and tapped on his notebook with his pen. "What did the guy look like that Jillie was harassing?"

Flo paused, her cigarette halfway to her puckered lips. "Don't rightly know, except he was … plain. Sure, that's the word I'm looking for, just plain. Not like most guys who wander in here for a beer and a babe." She chuckled. "He wasn't flashy like Eddie. Certainly not at all the kind of man Jillie usually took home." Flo lowered her voice as if Karl were eavesdropping. "She was a looker, Jillie was. She could have most any man she sashayed her cute little ass in front of."

Arn put his pen and notebook away and gently nudged Flo. "If you think of anything else, please let me know." She reluctantly slid out to allow Arn to get out of the booth. "One other thing—do you know where I could find Eddie?"

She looked at her watch. "Sometimes he drops into the Fairgrounds to help with the dog class. You might catch him there."

Eight

MY ASS GETS SORE sitting on these hard metal bleachers these many hours. Why the hell can't they hold a dog class in some comfort? Guess that's why the class is small. I ought not complain—the other people filling these bleachers aren't. And I sure don't want to call attention to myself.

As I look out over the students sitting below me on the bleachers, holding their dogs, I suspect one of them is the witness I'm looking for. The class was offered for beginners through experienced handlers, but most people here have worked dogs most of their lives and want to perfect the dog-handler team. I just want to find the witness so I can get on with my life without worry. Somewhere among these nine students, I'm betting, is the Midnight Sheepherder. All I have to do is watch and figure who has enough skill to be the rustler.

Beverly Johns shuffles her lesson plan until she finds the paper she's looking for. "It's going to be a little awkward this first class," *she says.* "My sister Bonnie twisted her ankle, and she usually gives this first lesson. Please bear with me while I go over her notes."

That's quite all right, I want to tell her. It gives me more time to look this class over and size everyone up. Like the fat guy in the bib overalls helping with the class. I saw him last Saturday at the Boot Hill. Don Whales was the lead singer of that motley foursome that was less than melodious, but adequate enough for the drunks that stagger into the Boot Hill.

I look away lest he sees the contempt I have for him. When Jillie started cussing me Saturday night, Whales could have excused himself long enough to break us up. He could have. But he sat fiddling with that steel guitar of his. If he'd intervened, perhaps she would be alive.

Or not.

Maybe I ought to give him the benefit of the doubt—Jillie was cussing most people in the bar even before she spotted me. The evils of alcohol.

I glance to either side of me. Ranchers and dog trainers and people just wanting to see a good show watch Beverly as she runs her dog through the paces. Her Border collie threads a ewe through a series of pylons set up in the arena. "By the end of the class," she says, "your dogs will be at the same skill level."

I couldn't care less. All I want to know is whose dog is capable of rounding up sheep right now. Today. When I find that person, I might find a broken marker light.

And I'll rid myself of the little problem of a witness.

Nine

ARN PULLED OFF I-80 and into the Archer Complex where the fair-grounds were now located. When he'd competed at the rodeo as a boy, he'd been able to walk the couple miles to the fairgrounds in Frontier Park, in town. Now with the Archer Complex up and running ten miles east, there was more room for special classes. Like the handler-herding dog class being put on by Bonnie and Beverly Johns.

He walked through the arena doors and stood to one side of the bleachers. The class of nine sat with their dogs, a mix of Australian shepherds and Border collies and one Belgian Malinois. Arn stood beside the bleachers packed with people who'd come to watch the class unfold.

A man not quite as tall as Arn but rangy like the Marlboro Man, with blond hair that flowed past his collar, stood from the bleachers. He talked briefly with the class before sending his Border collie out onto the floor. The dog moved toward four ewes at the far side of the arena. She carried her head low, her hindquarters high. The dog's tail was tucked between her legs as she stared intently at the sheep, intimidating them. She barked softly and began herding the sheep through orange pylons before pushing them around the arena—gently, so as not to frighten them—and over a makeshift ramp into a holding pen. When a heavyset man in bib overalls shut the gate, the dog ran to the blond man and sat quietly at his feet. He reached into his vest pocket and gave the dog a bone.

"You don't *need* to give the dog a treat when she's finished," he told the class. "The dog gets pleasure from doing the one thing it loves—herding livestock. And when you're done, your dogs will each be able to do what Britches just did."

A man sitting with the other spectators raised his hand and stood. He was as raw-boned as any Wyoming rancher Arn had met. Forty or so, average in stature, yet with power in the way he held on to the bleacher railing. "They say you're some kind of authority on herding dogs."

The man with the Border collie looked at the woman conducting the class, and she cleared her throat. She appeared to be in her mid-thirties, though it was sometimes difficult to age ranch women with the hard life they led. She introduced herself as Beverly Johns and faced the man. "You must be new to these parts."

The man took off his hat. His hair was clipped short and he wore a silk bandana around his neck. Sweat dripped down his face, and he wiped it away with another bandana he'd produced from a back pocket. He gestured with holey work gloves that had seen better days. "I've been working for the Potts for a couple years now. Scott Wallace, ma'am."

"The veterinarian," a woman at the far end of the bleachers said.

"You're a vet?" Beverly asked.

Scott smiled. "I'm not a real vet. I just picked up doctorin' critters from working with them over the years. It comes in handy now and again when critters take ill. My day job it to shear those miserable beasts." He nodded to the sheep. "Though I'm more inclined to work cows if I got a choice."

Beverly motioned to the blond man with the Border collie sitting beside him. "In answer to your question, Eddie Glass is *the* recognized expert in training and raising herding dogs. He's won the Meeker Classic in Colorado twice—no small feat for all the dogs and handlers that compete, and more regional competitions than you'll ever attend. And his dogs have been sold in six countries. We're fortunate he dropped in for a minute." She smiled warmly at Eddie. "It was a pleasant surprise, though he does this often."

Scott held up his hand. "No offense."

"None taken," Eddie said. "But you should have done your homework more carefully, Mr. Wallace." He faced the class. "I won't be teaching today. Prior commitments take me out of town. Bev and her sister Bonnie—whenever she recuperates—will be teaching you." He smirked at the portly man in the bib overalls. "With Don Whales assisting."

Don waved at the class as he let the sheep out of the pen.

"Now you folks take a fifteen minute break," Beverly said. "When you return, we'll start your dogs singling. By the end of the day, he—or she—will be able to single out a particular sheep from the rest of the flock."

Arn made his way toward Eddie Glass, but students circled him asking for autographs. "You going to get his autograph?" Arn asked Scott Wallace.

"Don't believe I will." Scott took out a tin of Altoids and offered Arn one of the breath mints, but he waved it away. "It shames me enough not knowing that he is *the* authority on herding dogs."

Arn slapped Scott on the back. "Don't feel bad," he whispered. "I didn't know either."

"You just moved here too?"

Arn shook his head and waited for the class to finish crowding Eddie. "I lived in Denver the last thirty years, but just moved back to Cheyenne last year." He leaned against the bleachers and used a piece of stiff straw to pry fresh sheep shit off his boots.

"It's a losing proposition," Scott said, motioning to his own boots. "Best thing you can do is get used to the aroma." He exaggerated drawing in air.

"So, you work for the Circle Trot?"

"Just a ranch hand," Scott said, stroking the muzzle of a dog sitting beside one of the students in front of the bleachers.

"I hired out to the Potts one summer when I was a kid," Arn said. "How're Hubert and Henrietta doing?"

Scott laughed. "Feisty. I hope I'm that active when I'm eighty."

"Still working their tails off. Amazing. And did I hear you right you make money on the side shearing sheep?" Arn was killing time until the people around Eddie dispersed.

"I do all right picking up money hereabouts during shearing season. But now things are a little slow at the ranch, so I came into town to pick up cake at the feed store. I heard they started a dog class, and didn't figure it'd hurt none watching for a bit." He snapped his fingers. "Now I recognize you. You're the one—"

"That the TV station hired to work Jillie Reilly's murder."

Scott shrugged. "Don't know anything about that. I was going to say, you're the feller the Association hired to catch that Midnight Sheepherder. Hubert mentioned you. Any luck finding him?"

"Not yet," Arn answered. "But the law of averages—"

"Understood."

Arn saw an opening. He started toward Eddie, but a young woman in tight Wranglers and a low-cut top approached him before Arn could. She lowered her voice, and the two laughed about some private joke.

Beverly approached them. "If you want to talk with him you might have a long wait," she said. "As you can see, he's sort of a rock star in the agility dog world."

"A regular Elvis," Arn answered.

"Or a Fabio," Scott said and tipped his hat. "Got to get to the feed store."

Beverly sat next to Arn on the bleachers as he waited for the woman to leave Eddie alone. "I recognize you from the TV." She looked him over. "But you look a little—"

"Older and larger in person?"

"Exactly."

"Old photo they're using."

Beverly motioned to Eddie. "This is about Jillie, isn't it?"

Arn nodded. "Among other things. Did you know her?"

"Vaguely. I'd run into her now and again at the fair. Or while she was sniffing around Eddie. My sister knew her quite well at one time. Competed in barrel racing together, went to the movies and hung out. But they had a falling out right out of high school over a man and haven't really spoken since." Beverly looked away. "Seems like all the local meat hangs out in the same bars trying to pick up their one-night stands."

Arn grabbed his pocket notebook and flipped to a blank page. "I understand your sister and Jillie got into a fight at the Boot Hill this last Saturday night."

Beverly took out a can of Copenhagen and stuffed her lip before putting it back in her pocket. "Bonnie never said squat about it. When Eddie came to the morning class and told me what happened, he was pretty upset. He'd danced with Jillie Saturday, and now she's dead. He said that except for some guy she knew at the bar she was hitting on, he was about the last person to see her alive." She nodded toward Eddie. "That's all he knows. But you mentioned you're here for other things."

Arn tapped the pocket notebook with his pen. "The Wool Growers Association hired me to catch the Midnight Sheepherder."

"And you think you might find the culprit here?" Beverly motioned to the students.

"That would be the most efficient way to steal sheep—using a trained dog. Like Eddie's. Or, I would wager, most dogs here."

Bev pointed to two dogs held by women huddled at the far end of the bleachers comparing Eddie's autograph. "Those two are Border collies. This is their second class and they may be capable of it. That Australian shepherd the man's got beside him is a new student, so probably not. The rest of the class"—Beverly motioned to the Belgian Malinois and the five remaining students, all with Border collies—"are advanced students. Their dogs would be able to herd sheep into a trailer in minutes. But you're not implying one of these folks is the rustler?"

"I'm just covering all the angles. All I'm saying is that anyone with trained dogs and a knowledge of livestock could be the Midnight Sheepherder." Arn pointed to Don Whales's Australian shepherd. "Like your assistant's dog would be capable, I suspect. And your own."

"Now see here, Mr. Anderson—"

"It's Arn." He laid on the charm, which, even if he tried hard, was still pretty lame. "I'm not accusing anybody. I'm just keeping an open mind."

The woman talking with Eddie looked to be wrapping it up, and Arn saw his opening. He started toward Eddie and then turned back. "You say your sister sprained her ankle?"

Beverly nodded slowly.

"I'd like to talk with her as soon as I'm finished with Eddie."

Beverly looked away.

"Bonnie didn't sprain her ankle, did she?"

"You psychic?" Beverly lowered her voice and looked around at the students within earshot. "She dragged back to her house Sunday afternoon. She was still drunk enough that I threatened to haul her to the ER to get her stomach pumped. She couldn't make the class 'cause she's still hung over." Beverly looked around again. "Bonnie's got a drinking problem."

"You mean a stopping problem."

"That, too. When I left her on the couch, she'd just finished off her second can of tomato juice and Tabasco sauce."

"Family recipe?"

"Not really, but she doesn't know that. I figure if she's forced to drink something nasty like that, it might make her think twice about getting knee-walking drunk again."

The woman who'd been talking to Eddie walked away, looking over her shoulder, smiling seductively. Eddie smiled back until he noticed Arn standing in front of him. He held out his hand. "What you need signed, old timer?"

Arn bristled. At not quite sixty, he resented this salutation. Even his granddad at ninety-two had fought any man who called him that. He felt like taking Eddie out back and showing him what an old timer could do, like he'd wanted to when Flo's bartender Karl called him that. At least he thought he could take Eddie, although he wasn't so sure about Karl—it's hard to beat a dwarf-tossing champion. But Arn held his pride and handed Eddie a business card.

"Arn Anderson Investigations. This supposed to mean something?"

"I've been hired to look into Jillie Reilly's murder."

"I already told Sergeant Slade about Saturday night. How I danced with Jillie until she found some other dude to go home with."

"Did you tell Slade you and Jillie were once an item?"

Eddie kept quiet.

"*Did* you mention it, even though you're a married man?"

"I don't have to listen to this bullshit."

"Would you rather have your dirty knickers aired on Ana Maria Villarreal's nightly special? I assume your wife watches television."

Eddie stepped closer, his jaw muscles working overtime, his fists clenched. Arn had him by twenty pounds and a few inches, but by the looks of it, Eddie Glass would be a handful and would never back down. Normally.

"I have half-a-notion to put a boot in your ass," Eddie snarled.

"Make sure it's just half-a-notion," Arn said, blading himself, preparing for Eddie to throw a punch.

Eddie's eyes narrowed for a moment and he backed away. He must have seen something in Arn that he didn't feel was worth tangling with. "I'll talk with you. But God help you if my relationship with Jillie gets on TV."

"I can't promise anything. Ana Maria is her own woman, but I'll ask that she not mention it if possible." He motioned to the top of the bleachers where no one sat.

Below them, Beverly called commands and the students lined up with their dogs to begin an agility course. Arn sat down and looked at the class with interest. "Makes you want to go out and correct some bad habits, I suspect."

Eddie nodded. "They got to develop their own style."

"And what's *your* style?" Arn asked. "Just now I got you riled up with a mere mention of your relationship with Jillie. How riled up did you get Saturday night when she started hitting on other guys?"

"You know about that?"

Arn tapped his notebook. "Lot of people saw how upset you became," he lied.

Eddie shucked out a Camel and lit it. "So I got a few temper issues."

"More than a few, considering you beat that husband at the Boot Hill."

Eddie smiled as if enjoying the retelling of it. "All's I was doing was dancing with his old lady and he got pissed. Of course, I had to defend myself." He blew smoke rings upwards. Stalling. "You think I had something to do with Jillie's death?"

"Did you?"

"You sound like that goofy deputy. He came right out and said as much. But I figured if he had some evidence, he'd haul me in for a formal interview. Or arrest me. He's got nothing."

Arn leaned closer. "Put yourself in his shoes. In my shoes. You and Jillie were an item last summer. You don't want your wife to find out, and I'd bet Jillie and you had some agreement."

"Jillie promised she wouldn't say anything. And she never did."

Arn stood from the hard bleachers and arched his back before sitting back down. "For the sake of argument, suppose you were worried she would spill the beans." He tapped his notebook again as if it contained some secret information that would indict Eddie. "And when you ran outside, the guy Jillie followed out was gone, and she was left standing on the sidewalk. And for the sake of argument, maybe you offered her a ride home. Things got a little heated when she threatened to expose you ... so you see where all this speculation could lead."

"It wasn't me she threatened to expose. It was the guy she chased outside. Besides, when I got out it was too late—she and this feller had already driven off. So I just went home."

Arn let that digest. There was logic to Eddie's argument. "Which brings up what the guy looked like, 'cause I found no one who could give a good description of him."

"How the hell should I know," Eddie said. "I wasn't there to look at guys. And when she followed him out, I was just a little busy taking some fists from that woman's old man. I have no idea what he looked like. Can't recall ever seeing him before."

"What if I told you there was a witness to Jillie's murder?"

Eddie shrugged. "I'd say that's good news. Who was the witness?"

Arn tapped his notebook again. "Just someone I need to talk with. If I can find him."

He pocketed his notebook and started down the bleachers when Eddie stopped him. "Look, I don't appreciate you coming in here implying I had anything to do with Jillie's murder. Fact is, we talked recently about me leaving my wife. The last thing I'd do was want to hurt her. I loved Jillie."

How many domestic abuse calls had Arn been on as a policeman where the husband had said the same thing: *"But I love her."*

Ten

BEVERLY GAVE ARN DIRECTIONS to the small ranch that their father had left them ten years ago in his will. Arn turned off I-25 onto the county road four miles north of Cheyenne and followed directions to the dirt driveway. He'd learned that Mr. Johns built a guest house across the yard from the main ranch house some years before he died; Bonnie had inherited the guest house, while Beverly got the ranch house her father had lived in.

"My house will be the one that looks like a home in a Currier and Ives postcard," Beverly told him. "Fresh coat of beige paint set off by forest-green window shutters. A white picket fence, and hanging flower baskets lining the walkway to the door." She described Bonnie's house in more colorful terms: the shade of gray found on old photos of Hiroshima after the bomb, with the rest of the house looking just as depressing and eerie. There was apparently one shutter left hanging at a crooked angle, and the porch had drooped in disrepair at some point after one of Bonnie's month-long benders. "And if she invites you in," Beverly advised, "make sure you have a bottle of hand sanitizer with you. You'll need it. I love my sister, but a homemaker she's not."

Beverly, Arn realized as he pulled into the yard, was one for extreme understatements. Bonnie's house was everything she'd said it was. And less. A trailer made out of a pickup box sat piled high with garbage that Bonnie needed to take to the dump. Pizza boxes and beer cans overflowed as evidence that she was, indeed, professional drinker material. A beige truck was parked in the barn situated between Bonnie's shack and Beverly's house, at the far end beside some farm implements. From Arn's vantage point as he passed the open barn door, the truck looked as if it had been in a dozen minor wrecks—crumpled fenders, the paint scuffed off the box from past injustices at the hands of a drunken Bonnie Johns.

To one side of Bonnie's front door, a lawn mower sat disassembled where water could get to it and ruin the motor—something Bonnie could point to when explaining why the weeds around the house were two feet tall. At one time there'd been a gate across the curved entryway, which was now missing. Like at one time there'd been a picket fence surrounding the yard. On closer inspection, Arn saw the gate on the ground, buried and obscured by the weeds.

He cautiously walked up the rickety steps, the bottom one broken through, onto the porch that creaked under his weight. He stood at the door and picked a spot that wasn't splintered. After a minute of knocking and getting no response, he went to a window on one side of the front door. He peeked around duct tape covering the broken pane and cupped his hands against the sun. No light shone inside the house. No music. No sounds of a television or other sign of life.

Arn was turning to leave when the door cracked an inch. "If you're the Watkins salesman, my sister's the one that buys your tit salve."

He slipped a business card through the crack in the door. "Your sister said you'd be home. Can we talk?"

Bonnie opened the door wider. Bags drooping under her eyes and her frizzled hair made her look older than her big sister. Sloppy pajamas dragged on the stained shag carpeting and her tank top was stretched to the point that Arn was forced to look away. She stuck her head out, looked around the yard, and stepped aside to allow Arn to enter. She shut the door quickly after him.

Without another word, she led Arn through a long hallway lined with old newspapers and magazines, which made walking dicey. She stumbled into the kitchen and picked up two beer cans from the table. She tossed them into the garbage, but both cans rolled off the overflowing pile. She looked at them but she made no attempt to pick them up.

"What does Arn Anderson Investigations investigate?" Bonnie asked, then held up her hand. "You want something to drink?" She looked around. "I got no soda or coffee, but I think there's still some Budweiser in the fridge."

"Bladder issues," Arn said, and Bonnie sighed knowingly.

"Mind if I do?" Without waiting for an answer, she pulled a can of beer out of the fridge. While she popped the top, Arn stood admiring the lovely little Shangri-La. Dishes were stacked in the sink waiting to be washed. Sometime this year, perhaps. A pan with old and crusted mac-and-cheese sat on the stove waiting, like the dishes, for the Dish Fairy to wash it. A box of plastic forks lay open on the counter. Easier than washing normal utensils.

Bonnie eased herself into a kitchen chair and grabbed a tall glass of tomato juice. She motioned to a chair across from her, and Beverly's warning echoed in Arn's head. He had no hand sanitizer. "Been sitting all day. I think I'll stand."

"Suit yourself." Bonnie took a drink of tomato juice and washed it down with a swallow of beer. "Beverly said some old guy would be coming around to talk with me."

"That's me." Arn forced a smile. "The old guy."

She used Arn's business card as a coaster for her beer can and sat back. "She said you were looking into Jillie's death."

"I am."

"You a cop, 'cause—no offense—you seem a little long in the tooth to be stopping people and giving them tickets and shit like that?"

"I'm retired, like the card says."

"Good, 'cause right now I don't want to talk to no cops."

"They'll come around sooner or later."

"One already has," Bonnie said, drinking more beer chaser than tomato juice. "Some tall drink of water stopped here yesterday. He stood outside banging on the door until he got tired and left. Didn't much want to talk with him anyhow."

"Why'd you open it for me?"

Bonnie grabbed a bottle of aspirin and shook out three. "Got to trust my big sister's judgment sometime. Like when she told me I ought to quit drinking." She groaned and downed the aspirin with a swallow of Bud. "I should take her advice."

"But of course, you won't."

Bonnie polished off her tomato juice and sat looking at her beer can. "I'll have to see what I feel like once my hangover goes away. Now what do you think I know about Jillie's murder?"

"I'm not sure you know *anything* about it." Arn took out his notebook and pen. "But I do know you were in the Boot Hill last Saturday and picked a fight with her."

Bonnie hung her head, and Arn wondered what was going on in there. Jillie and Bonnie had been close friends once, Beverly had said.

Even if the two didn't interact much anymore, something had caused Bonnie to want to fight Jillie on Saturday night. Arn looked at Bonnie's corded arms. Even though she hit the sauce, she was a ranch girl, rough and strong and used to hard work.

When she was sober.

He was certain Bonnie had enough strength to strangle Jillie. But if he was right in his theory—that the killer strangled Jillie and the Midnight Sheepherder was witness to it—then Bonnie was nothing more than someone who'd picked a fight with her former best friend the night she was murdered. But he didn't believe in coincidences.

"Why did you start that fight?" he asked.

"Why else? A man. Jillie wanted to dance with Eddie again and I just lost it."

"You and Eddie were ... lovers, too?"

Bonnie chuckled. "And half the women in Cheyenne. Sure, we dated for a time. When I went into the Boot Hill and saw Eddie and Jillie dancing, I got pissed. Booze made me do it." She laughed. "I waited until Jillie went to pee before I grabbed Eddie and drug him onto the dance floor."

"Where'd you go after Karl tossed you out of the Boot Hill?"

Bonnie waved the air. "Everywhere. I had a few beers at the Eagles Nest. A couple Jägermeisters at the Outlaw Saloon. I finished up at the Green Door. I think."

"You went to a strip bar?"

"About the only place in town I hadn't been that night." She laughed again.

"Anyone vouch for you at any of those places?"

"Do I need anyone to vouch for me?"

Arn shrugged. "You tell me. It's your story."

"I can't say…" Bonnie went to the fridge and grabbed another can of tomato juice. Then, for good measure, another beer. She blew dust out of a glass on the counter and offered Arn some. He declined. "I was pretty wasted. I was there until closing, but I don't rightly know who I ran into."

"How'd you get home?"

Bonnie dribbled Tabasco sauce into her juice. She scrunched her nose up as she drank it. "Some guy I wanted to go home with, I think. He was decent enough to have one of his friends follow us here in my truck. But I think I might have hit something in town earlier."

"You *think* you hit something?"

"My truck's all bunged up."

"Sure it wasn't the guy who drove it home?"

"I just don't know." She held her head and grabbed the bottle of aspirin again. "Have you heard of any hit-and-runs Saturday night?"

"I'm out of the loop, but I'll talk to a friend. Where's your truck now?"

"Parked in back of the barn. It's all messed up, and I parked it in there until the deputy left." She laid her hand on his arm. "If you can find out—discreetly—if I hit someone's vehicle, give me the name and I'll make it right."

Arn had no obligation to report Bonnie's hit-and-run accident. But if she was intent on making it right with the other owner, that was more than he could say for most drunks.

He was about to leave when Bonnie stopped him. "You are going to help the law find Jillie's killer, right?"

"I'll do my best."

She brushed bangs out of her eyes. "I just feel responsible. Maybe if I hadn't picked that fight with her, maybe I could have talked her into bar hopping with me. At least she'd have been safe."

Until you got behind the wheel, Arn thought. He headed for the door. "I'll see myself out," he said. "And whenever the deputy comes around again to talk to you, I would. You can't put it off forever."

———

Arn walked across the yard and stepped inside the barn. Wind whipping through the door created a venturi effect, and he spit out a piece of straw that had blown into his mouth. The scent of fresh cow dung—courtesy of two Holstein milk cows in stalls at the near end of the barn—drifted past Arn's nose. They chewed their cuds and paid him only scant attention before going back to munching alfalfa.

Arn walked past the cows to the far end of the barn. Out back of the barn, Bonnie and Beverly, like many ranchers, kept a slew of trucks and implements that had broken down over the years. A dark-colored truck was up on cinder blocks, partially covered by a tarp that shared its duties with a rusty Farmall H tractor sitting at an acute angle on the ground with a broken axle.

Bonnie's beige Dodge truck was parked next to a pull-behind rake. The passenger-side fender had been knocked clean of paint where Bonnie—or someone—had hit something, and Arn bent to study the damage. Paint had peeled off down the side where the truck had scraped against something, leaving deep gouges that had begun to rust months ago.

Arn stood and his knees popped, so he rubbed them as he looked over the rest of the truck. The extended-cab pickup had hit something significant, by the extent of the damage. It had been a sideswipe accident—but the front end and back, not to mention the driver's side, were intact. Bonnie could drive it anywhere she wanted. Arn could understand why she should be worried: this amount of damage should have been reported.

He opened the door, and it *pinged*—the key had been left in the ignition. But that was nothing new. As protective as ranch folks were, most never thought anyone would mosey onto their property and steal their rides. And certainly not the fine piece of automotive iron that sat wrecked inside the Johns' barn.

Arn shut the door and took his cell phone out. He snapped pictures from different angles and pocketed his phone. He'd talk with Ana Maria tonight and find out if any hit-and-runs had come over the police blotter. And he'd have to bite his tongue and ask Chief Oblanski for another favor.

Eleven

*I KEEP MY DISTANCE behind Don Whales as he follows Beverly Johns.
Lucky for me—unlucky for Don —I overheard him volunteer to fix Beverly's
old Farmall H. Why these ranchers continue making due on a shoestring and
patching equipment up when it should have been trashed decades ago is be-
yond me. But then I've never been a cheapskate.*

*They turn off Highway 85 onto the county road, and the dust kicked up
masks my presence. By the time they finally turn into Beverly's ranch drive,
my truck is coated with fine Wyoming dust. But that's okay. I'll buy another
one soon.*

*I back under the trees of a shelter belt across the road a quarter mile away
and grab my spotting scope. I clamp it to my side glass, positioning the truck
so I can watch the house. Don stops in front of the barn and climbs out, his
dog bounding beside him. He grabs a large red toolbox from the back of his
truck and waddles toward the barn. Even in dirty work clothes, he still wears
the "Army" pin on the strap of his overalls.*

I uncork my Thermos bottle and pour myself a cup before settling back. I don't know if Don is the Midnight Sheepherder, but I've survived this long by trusting nothing to chance. After all, he knows just enough about dog handling to be a threat to me. In class, he gave a demonstration with his dog. It proved it possessed enough herding skills that Don could be the witness. But if he is, why hasn't he come forward by now? Either he's scared of me—which I doubt, if the man survived two tours in the Army motor pool in Iraq—or he didn't recognize me. Perhaps he can identify me from the brief time I passed across my headlights.

I begin to question whether this plodding man about to work on Beverly's tractor is the witness. I conclude that yes, I believe he is. He is single and can come and go whenever he wants. How convenient for someone who goes out nights stealing sheep: no woman to come home to and explain where the hell he's been.

Then there's Don's money. When I asked if he ever went to the Veteran's Affairs Medical Center here in town, he said he was ineligible. Said he wasn't disabled. That means he's living on a meager pension from the Army and what he makes turning a wrench on the side, and, as crappy as their music is, I'm sure he makes little from his bar gigs. But—I am certain—he makes enough money from the sale of stolen sheep to afford that new truck of his. During the past year, Don must have saved most of the money he got from his Midnight Sheepherder activities to buy that Dodge one-ton. They don't come cheap.

I start up my truck. I've decided to take a chance that Don will not go to the law by tomorrow. According to the website for Don Whales and the Dolphins, they're playing a wedding reception Saturday night at the state park. I'll show up there. Maybe I'll dance once or twice. For certain, I will save the last dance for Don.

Twelve

A **POLICE CADET IN** a crisp blue uniform escorted Arn to the second floor of the new public safety building the Cheyenne police department had just moved into. It housed all emergency services except the sheriff's office, and Arn was glad for an escort. It would look foolish to get lost in the building.

The cadet led Arn to Ned Oblanski's office. The lady-wrestler-turned-secretary-to-the-chief, the always hirsute Gorilla Legs, stood guard outside Oblanski's office. She frowned at Arn when she motioned him in. "Be quick," she said. "The chief's got a budgetary meeting with the town council in twenty minutes." Arn and Gorilla Legs had never bonded, but at least he thought she'd be glad to see him after these many months away. He was wrong.

When Arn stepped into the office, he was impressed by the size of the room: it was fully twice as large as the chief's office had been in the old telephone building. Oblanski even looked small sitting behind his oversized mahogany desk. He looked up from studying a spread sheet and dropped his glasses on the desk. "Thank God you're here."

Arn looked around to see if Oblanski was talking to someone else. "Why, thank you."

"Don't get a big head, Anderson. Only thing I meant was that you give me an excuse to push these damned figures aside. Shut the door." Oblanski walked to a new coffee bar at the other end of the room. Arn almost missed the old pot, with its quaint odor of scalded coffee that smelled like old feet from sitting on the burner all day. The chief turned to Arn. "Latte?"

"Don't you have just coffee?"

"We're expanding our horizons," Oblanski said. "Think yuppie."

"Okay then, Americano if it'll make it."

Oblanski punched a button. "It will. It's an amazing piece of technology. Fresh-brewed will be ready in a moment." He nodded for Arn to sit on a chair and said, "I saw Ana Maria's special last night." He walked back to his desk and sat on the edge. "I thought you were done with consulting. Rumor has it that you're positively orgasmic about being a range detective. Now why would you want to get back into the consulting business?"

"If all I wanted to do was smell cow crap and sheep shit all night while listening to them whine, I'd be thrilled. I'm out there nights doing anything I can to stay awake. Even listening to nighttime talk radio. No, I'm about as happy being a stock detective as you will be cleaning up that mess."

"What mess?"

"That mess." Arn pointed to the espresso machine. It had filled Arn's cup and kept running. And running. Oblanski sprang to the machine and unplugged it, but not before it had soaked the new beige carpeting. He frantically tore paper towels off a roll and squatted beside the spill, patting the carpet.

"Why not just call your lovely secretary out there to clean up?" Arn said with a grin.

A look of terror crossed Oblanski's face. "Lower your voice. She'd have my nuts in her pocket if she found out I messed up this carpet."

After two rolls of Bounty, the spot was nearly invisible, and Oblanski wiped sweat off his forehead and nearly bald head with the last paper towel. He tossed the wet mess in the trash can and sat in his chair. "You were going to tell me how you got roped into another consulting gig," Oblanski said, one eye on his office door, the other on the evil coffee machine.

"DeAngelo Damos made me an offer I couldn't refuse. I'll be able to put central air in with what he's paying me."

"*If* you solve Jillie Reilly's murder," Oblanski said. "And before Sergeant Slade does, I'll bet." He walked to the machine. He eyed it warily as he plugged it in again, the sound of water heating cutting through the air. As if it would actually work this time. "It's no secret the pissing match between DeAngelo and Sheriff Grimes goes back years." He smiled. "My guess is that's why Slade will give you inside info—'cause rumor has it that big SOB intends to challenge Grimes the next election."

"I heard that scuttlebutt too," Arn said. "And have you heard any scuttlebutt about the Reilly homicide?"

"You know I can't say anything"—Oblanski looked past Arn to the door—"officially. Unofficially, Slade went to the county and asked that a ten thousand dollar reward be offered for information. He'll go on air and publicly once again say that Jillie was one half of a duo the ranchers have dubbed the Midnight Sheepherder."

69

"That'll devastate her father." Arn stood and paced in front of Oblanski's desk. "Little Jim doted on her. Spoiled her, from what the ladies at the courthouse say. And it didn't matter to him that she partied too heavily and too often." He faced Oblanski. "I don't think Jillie had anything to do with the rustling. Slade will just muck things up. Make it harder to ferret out the real killer."

"And this is not because you haven't been able to catch the rustler after all these months?"

"No," Arn said. "It would make it easy for me if Jillie was the thief. But I don't get the feeling she was, at this point. So what *can* you tell me?"

Oblanski grabbed a pencil and began chewing the end. "I might be able to confirm or refute a guess. Give me your best shot, and I'll tell you if you're full of it."

"Okay," Arn began. "Here's what I found out so far: Jillie danced with Eddie Glass that night at the Boot Hill, then she went to the crapper. When she came back, Bonnie Johns was dancing with Eddie, and the fight was on. Evict one Bonnie. That soured Jillie and she started coming on to some other guy sitting by himself, and Eddie retaliated by dancing with some married woman just to make Jillie jealous."

"I don't see anything there that contradicts Sergeant Slade's theory."

"And nothing that supports it," Arn said. "Jillie taunted the guy she was talking with. Threatening to tell on him. Followed him outside." Arn held up his hand. "Before you ask, believe me when I say I haven't been able to find out what it was she was going to rat him out about. Flo Martin believes Jillie had an affair with the guy and had decided to expose him that night. But Flo figures it was the booze talking."

"And Flo would know about that," Oblanski said. "So you're saying Jillie chased the guy outside—"

"She chased the guy out of the bar while Eddie was fighting with the husband of the woman he'd danced with. After he waylaid the guy he ran after Jillie. Eddie claims he never saw her outside the bar. But he never came back in the bar that night, either."

Oblanski rifled through daily call sheets and settled on Saturday's police calls. "We never got a fight call to the Boot Hill Saturday."

"If I recall from working here, bars in Cheyenne usually take care of their own problems. I bet you rarely get fight calls to any of them."

Oblanski laughed. "Especially with that mean little midget Karl bouncing for Flo." He flicked the coffee machine on and off again and lorded over it. Just in case. "Again, how does all this dispute Slade's theory about Jillie being one of the rustlers?"

Arn fished the envelope with the paint chip out of his pocket. "Because of this. I found it embedded in the wooden gatepost at Wooly Hank's after a truck had fled the pasture—and the truck wasn't the killer's." Arn sat back in his chair and took off his hat. He unwrapped the sliver of side marker light and showed it to Oblanski. "It's my belief that either Eddie or the guy Jillie chased out of the bar killed her. I think the Midnight Sheepherder witnessed the murder while he was in the process of stealing sheep, and he fled before the killer could catch him."

"Run that by me again."

"The guy that Jillie chased out may have grabbed her and drove off to Wooly Hank's. Or, Eddie caught up with her outside the bar after the other guy motored away, and he drove her to the pasture. Either way, we know the outcome."

"She *was* a wild one. Never had much sense when she was drinking, if I remember my rookie days." Oblanski searched his desk for another victim-pencil to chew on. "But I hoped she'd settled down after she started working for Dr. Oakert."

"Any rumor there that the doctor was ... bedding her?"

"For all I know he's as pure as the driven snow," Oblanski said. "When he first set up his practice, he presented the council with a proposal whereby he would treat officers needing counseling. Before you knew it, we and the sheriff's office were sending all our officers to him when there was a shooting. Or when officers just had emotional or psychological problems with work, or problems at home. He came with unusually good credentials for a town this small."

"How good?"

Oblanski handed Arn his coffee. "Oakert used to be in charge of a big mental hospital in California." He punched more buttons on the espresso machine and remained beside it, still not trusting such an amazing piece of technology. "Jillie Reilly worked for him from the first day he opened his practice here. She did everything in his office. Made things kind of homey. I saw her when I met him there initially, about his services. She remembered me arresting her once for public intox, but she was still friendly. Professional. But you know how rumors spread. A few of our officers even dated her, but she was too wild for them."

Oblanski spit a piece of eraser into the garbage can by the coffee bar. "Nothing explains why she was killed," he said. "How about if neither Eddie Glass *nor* the guy she confronted killed her? How about it was some other guy Jillie picked up at one of the other bars? You can damn well bet if it wasn't closing time, Jillie would have continued bar hopping."

"Maybe she took a ride with one of the guys," Arn said. "I just don't have enough information right now to do much more than speculate." He turned his Stetson over in his hands.

"You got nothing.," Oblanski said. "You don't even have enough to speculate. Maybe if you knew what Jillie was going to rat that guy out about—whatever the hell she had on him—it might help."

"Believe me, I laid awake half the night thinking just that." Arn added sweetener and crème to his Americano and stirred. "Here's my last … speculation," he said. "A long shot is that Jillie transcribed all of Dr. Oakert's notes. She knew what the doctor knew, and she threatened the guy in the bar to 'tell on him.'"

"But she was bound by the same ethical standards that Dr. Oakert is. She wouldn't dare reveal anything about one of his patients."

"Except it was the booze talking," Arn said. "She may have gotten way over her head with one of the patients—one of Oakert's dangerous and volatile patients—and threatened to expose him. But he couldn't chance it getting out."

Oblanski tossed his pencil stub in the trash can. "That's some tinfoil theory you've concocted. I liked it better when Eddie Glass was your prime suspect. He's pure mean when he's drunk, and an SOB that our officers have to fight every time he's arrested. Either way, you have your hands full."

"Don't you mean 'we'?"

"Not this time. Jillie's death is so far out in the county, my department will never get involved."

Oblanski could say nothing more about it, and he and Arn talked about the Cowboys' last season and who they might field in the fall. Oblanski had been a running back for Wyoming before dropping out to take a job with the police department, and Arn had played high school ball before a horse threw him and sidelined him with a busted leg.

Arn had finished his coffee and was starting to leave when Oblanski stopped him. "By the way, I checked hit-and-runs for this weekend like you asked. We had two and the county had one. All more damage than you described."

"Thanks," Arn said. Perhaps Bonnie was so drunk that she'd even got the date wrong on her accident. Or maybe it was the guy driving her truck home from the bar who'd run into something.

———

Arn walked a block down the street to the sheriff's office. The midday sun reflected intense heat from the pavement, and he wiped the inside of his hat band with his bandana. He stepped into the lobby of the SO and asked for Sergeant Slade. After a forty-five-minute wait, in which Arn was forced to read year-old copies of *The Smithsonian* and *Woman's World*, Slade came into the waiting area. "You could have called first, Anderson."

"I did. Three times. I even left a message. I just assumed you would rather see my smiling face in person."

"So call me busy with this homicide. What bullshit you after now?"

"Jillie's murder—what can you tell me about it?"

"Nothing. You're a civilian." Slade smiled. "Or should I say you're a range detective."

"Sheriff Grimes says otherwise," Arn bluffed, hoping Slade hadn't talked with his boss lately. With rumors of Slade running against Grimes for sheriff this next election, the chance they'd spoken recently was slim. "He said if you failed to cooperate to call him. Immediately."

Slade rubbed his forehead and checked the clock. It was a quarter past noon, and Arn knew Grimes would be down at the Eagles Nest for lunch and a highball. If it hadn't been lunchtime, Slade would probably have called Grimes and given Arn the bum's rush when he found out Arn had just lied to him.

"I'd hate for you to get in trouble"—Arn saw his opening—"right before the election."

Slade sighed and rubbed his forehead. "All right, mercenary bastard. What do you need to know?"

"Out here? Perhaps we better speak more privately."

The deputy led Arn into a side office stacked with desks and chairs and office supplies and closed the door. "All right. Again, what do you want to know?"

"That theory of yours about Jillie Reilly being half a rustling team—any traction on that?"

"Not yet. We put out the reward just yesterday."

"I'll bet if you talked with the TV station, got more exposure on air—"

"Sheriff Grimes and DeAngelo Damos don't exactly swap spit. I was lucky to get on Ana Maria's special one night."

"But you could be above that fray. Solve the case, and next election you'll be a leg up with the voters. What do you say—want me to put a word in with Ana Maria and see if she can give you additional air time?"

"The sheriff won't be happy."

"But the case might just get solved."

Slade mulled it over. "Give her my office number, and I'll go on air however many times it takes. Anything else?"

"What did you find out at autopsy?"

"Jillie had a blood alcohol of .22."

"Qualified her for a toaster at the Boot Hill."

"What's that?"

"Nothing," Arn said. "Just something Flo Martin likes to do. Anything else?"

Slade remained silent, as if debating giving Arn more information.

"What's the worst I could do—help you solve the murder?" Arn asked.

"You're not going to solve it with what little we found at autopsy." Slade wiped his sweaty palms on his trousers. "But we did find one thing that has us stumped. Jillie was strangled with some type of thin rope. Leather thong. Electrical cord perhaps. That will be easy enough to determine once we find a suspect. But the ligature marks on her neck clearly show the killer tried several times to strangle her."

"And you wonder if she fought hard enough that the killer lost his grip on the cord?"

"Something like that."

"Can I take a look at the photos?"

"You're going to bug my ass until I show them to you."

Arn shrugged.

Slade kept silent. "Follow me to my office," he said at last.

He led Arn through the sheriff's office into a small room occupied by a gun-metal gray desk, two straight-backed chairs, and a dilapidated office chair with one arm. He sat in the chair and opened his desk drawer. "I never showed these to you. Deal?"

"Deal," Arn said. He pulled up a chair across from Slade.

Arn opened the manila folder and spread the autopsy photos out on top of Slade's desk. When he came to one showing the marks around Jillie's throat, Slade traced the marks with the back of his pen. "There were these three distinct marks encircling her neck that pooled blood. Three times, like she was fighting him."

Arn picked up the photo and held it to the light. The quality was less than he was accustomed to from working Denver Metro, but the photo was clear enough. "He wanted her to suffer."

"How's that?"

"Jillie's killer wanted her to suffer, and he prolonged her agony so he could enjoy it." Arn put the photo back on the desk and began to pace the room. "I investigated a case in Denver some years back where a man abducted his former wife and locked her in his basement. Every day when he'd come home from work he'd go down there and—just for an evening's pleasure—strangle her to the point of death. Then he'd back off. He ultimately went too far one time and she died. Thank God for nosy neighbors. One called in that she hadn't seen the husband for weeks. Newspapers stacked on the porch. Junk mail overflowing the mail box. You know, everything you're taught not to do when you kill someone and flee. Anyway, patrol officers made entry and found her." Arn took a deep breath. "At autopsy, it looked like he'd made numerous attempts to strangle her but changed his mind. He was captured in Austin and extradited back to Colorado. When I interrogated him, I asked if he'd had a change of heart all those times he let her live. 'No,' he said, 'I got off watching her come so close to death before I let up. You'd think the bitch would be grateful that I let her live all those times. But she never was.'"

"So we're looking for someone who enjoys watching people suffer?"

"That's about it. Prisons are full of them," Arn said. "And some asylums. How much struggle did Jillie put up?"

"Considerable. She wasn't big, but she was a born ranch girl and tougher than boiled whale shit. She bit her attacker, and the lab is working up DNA on blood the ME recovered from the back of her teeth and from one tiny piece of flesh she ripped out." Slade flipped through the papers. "And tissue samples were taken from under her fingernails. But that'll only be helpful if the killer had his DNA sample taken somewhere."

"Let's hope so," Arn said. "Before he kills again."

Slade placed the folder with the autopsy pictures back in his desk.

"I don't expect to look at your incident report," Arn said, "but maybe you can enlighten me on some things."

Slade leaned back in his tattered office chair, and it creaked loud enough Arn thought it would break. "What things? And you're right—if you want to see official reports, the sheriff himself will have to approve it. Even I can't go over the old man's head."

"Fair enough." Arn nodded. "But you can tell me if you learned anything from the bar patrons about that night?"

"That I can," Slade said. "Only because there's nothing there you don't already know about. They all recalled the fight with Eddie and the married guy, but nobody remembers Jillie chasing some dude out the bar."

"And Karen Glass?" Arn asked. "From what Flo Martin's bartender said, Karen came in earlier in the evening looking for Eddie. Have you talked with her?"

Slade shrugged. "No reason to. She waltzed into the bar long before Eddie arrived for a night of drinking. And long before the fight with that married dude. I can't see her sticking around and waiting for Eddie to *maybe* come to that bar when there were so many others in town he could be at."

Arn jotted Karen's name down even though Slade didn't think it important that she be interviewed. He'd learned through the years at Metro that people only remotely connected to a case should be talked to. It had paid off more times than not for him. "I think I'll visit with her."

Slade shook his head. "You watch yourself. Karen can be a nightmare when she's got a temper on. "

"That's what Flo told me."

"And it's good advice. Karen's been arrested for drunk driving. Fighting in public. She pulled a shiv on another woman at a bar in Ft. Collins a few years ago. That was before she settled down and had a baby. But she's still as mean as she always was. You watch yourself. That woman's a holy terror."

Arn checked his watch. The afternoon was early: he had time to visit Karen Glass and see just what a holy terror looked like.

Thirteen

ARN DROVE THE TWELVE miles to the Frosty March ranch. He'd gone to school with Frosty's son, Mather, who'd gone to Alaska after high school to work offshore oil rigs. He'd done well, too, until an accident took his life early. The last time Arn had seen Frosty was at Mather's funeral. Was that how the rest of his life was going to be: hanging around his home town, going to funerals of people he barely remembered?

He spotted Frosty bent over, holding the leg of a Chestnut gelding, hoof nipper hammer in one hand and horseshoe in the other, a mouthful of hoof nails dangling from his lips. He glanced up at Arn's car and went back to shoeing his horse. When he finished fitting the shoe to the hoof, he spit the nails into a bucket and walked across the yard to Arn. "I recollect Mather saying you never had much common sense." He rapped on the top of Arn's Olds. "Who the hell drives something like this on these gawd-awful roads?"

"Someone who can't afford to buy a truck right now," Arn answered.

Frosty smiled and offered his hand. "Been a while. 'Bout the only time I see you is on the television. Getting too famous to come around?"

"Been busy remodeling mom's old house."

"Ah," Frosty said knowingly. "What brings you out here?"

"I wanted to talk with Karen Glass."

Frosty squinted. "TV says you're looking into Jillie Reilly's murder. Anything to do with Karen?"

"Just establishing times is all."

Frosty pointed to a road that veered off toward the back of the main ranch house. "Couple hundred yards back thataway is where Karen and Eddie live. Karen ought to be there." He checked his watch. "But Eddie's on his way back from town about now. Talk to her quick and skedaddle. Eddie is the jealous type, and I'd not like to see one of Mather's friends get tuned up on my own property."

"I'll be brief," Arn said as he started the Oldsmobile.

"And buy a truck," Frosty called after him.

Arn drove a hundred yards along the road and around a horseshoe bend to a small house nestled among some cottonwoods. Clothes flapped on a clothesline. A woman in men's bib overalls and a tattered work shirt bent over a wicker basket. A covered stroller was parked at the end of the line, and Arn saw movement under the baby blanket. The woman looked up as Arn parked beside the house and got out.

"You Karen Glass?"

She straightened. For all Eddie's catting around, Arn expected to see a frumpy, unattractive woman more at home on the ranch than in the bedroom. But Karen was anything but. She stood nearly as tall as Arn, with a lithe figure and short brown hair. She wore no makeup, but then she needed none—her olive skin smooth, taut. She was, Arn concluded, a striking figure of a woman.

She hung her canvas bag containing the clothespins on the line and met him beside his car. "I'm Karen. And you are?"

Arn handed her a business card, and she held it to the light before slipping it into the pocket of her apron. "What does Arn Anderson investigate?"

"Right now I'm working for the Wool Growers Association trying to catch their rustler. And I'm looking into the murder of Jillie Reilly for the television station."

Karen's face and neck turned red, and the veins stood out in her forehead as she fought to control herself. "I heard about that ... vamp's murder. Hate to speak ill of the dead, but she had her sights on Eddie until I put the run on her last summer."

"Did it come to blows?"

"If it had, it wouldn't have lasted long. One thing I can't abide is a woman hustling another's man." She stepped closer. "Now what's Jillie's death got to do with me?"

Arn grabbed his notepad from atop the dash and flipped pages. "You went to the Boot Hill last Saturday looking for Eddie."

"So?"

"That was an hour before Jillie ran out the bar."

"And you think I had something to do with it?"

"Ms. Glass—"

"Karen. I might be a West Coast gal, but I'm no damned citified woman."

"Okay then, Karen—did you hang around the Boot Hill waiting for Eddie?"

"And did I wait until Jillie came out? Not hardly. I'm not even sure she was in there when I was. I went to the bar looking for him, not her."

"If you didn't find him at the Boot Hill, did you run into him at some other bar?"

Karen paused. "Maybe I did. Why?"

"Because Eddie ran out the bar only moments after Jillie did," Arn said. "And no one saw her alive after that."

Karen wiped the clothesline with her apron and grabbed a pair of damp dungarees from the basket. Arn watched from the end of the line. His mother had used a clothesline. Made things smell fresh, she often said.

"I found Eddie later that night."

"Where?"

"The Outlaw," Karen answered.

"What time?"

"How the hell should I know," she said as she clipped clothespins on the jeans. "Maybe an hour or so after I left the Boot Hill," she said at last, and faced Arn. "If you're trying to pin Jillie's murder on Eddie, he's got an airtight alibi—I was dragging him out of the Outlaw by his ear. Now if there's nothing else—"

"Just one thing," Arn said. "That would have been about ten o'clock at night?"

"About."

Arn nodded to the baby carriage. "You seem a responsible mother—"

"Where is this going?"

"Who was taking care of your baby while you were checking bars? 'Cause I doubt you left the baby to fend for herself."

Karen turned back to the clothesline and hung a pair of trousers. "I got work to do. Good day, Mr. Anderson."

As Arn walked back to his car a truck approached on the road, coming on fast, sliding sideways, kicking up dirt and gravel. Eddie skidded to a stop in front of Arn's Oldsmobile. He jammed his truck into park and jumped out of the cab before it stopped rolling.

"What the hell you doing here?" Eddie threw his sunglasses onto the hood of the truck and stomped toward Arn.

Arn took off his hat and laid it on the top of the car while he bladed himself. He prepared for a direct assault and wondered if Eddie was as tough as folks said. "I'm here checking times."

Eddie halted within punching range of Arn. "You didn't believe me when I said I came home after I left the Boot Hill?" His fists clenched and spittle flew from his mouth.

Karen ran toward Eddie and stepped between him and Arn. "This is not the time and place," she said to her husband.

"Better listen to her," Arn said, "before you're arrested for assaulting somebody who just stopped at your place."

"He's right." Karen took hold of Eddie's arm, but he jerked away.

"What did he ask you?" Eddie said.

"He wanted to know where I found you Saturday night."

"She's right," Arn said. "That's all I was here to find out. And while we're at it, just where *did* she find you?"

Eddie looked to Karen.

"Don't look at her. Tell me where she found you?"

"I told you," Karen said, "the Outlaw."

"That's right," Eddie said. "The Outlaw."

Arn was pretty sure they were lying. But whether or not there was a sinister reason—like Eddie and Jillie taking a fateful drive that night—he didn't know. But he vowed to find out.

Fourteen

DANNY TURNED THE VOLUME down on the remote when Ana Maria came into the living room. Arn had been doing the pecking bird, dozing while he watched reruns of *Family Feud* with Danny, and he rubbed his face to wake up.

"Watch the show tonight?" she asked as she dropped into a bean bag chair Danny had "found" somewhere. Tiny pellets poofed out of a rip in the seam and she batted them out of her hair. "Sergeant Slade was a ham, just like I said he'd be once he got a taste of on-air fame."

Danny laughed. "It was like he was already running for sheriff."

Arn turned in his one-armed recliner. "He might have been a ham, but I don't think he came across as competent. He kept pushing that cockamamie theory that Jillie was one of the sheep rustlers."

Ana Maria's stomach growled and Danny stood. "Might be a good time to grab a snack," he said.

She dropped her purse on the floor and settled back. "I haven't eaten since this morning. Been fielding odd ball calls on the tip line."

"Then cake and homemade ice cream might help?" Danny asked.

"It might be the perfect cure," Ana Maria answered. She watched Danny as he left the room. "We're getting nowhere with that tip line. Bunch of loonies that have nothing better to do than call and air their bullshit."

"And that took you all day—listening to citizens' rants?" Arn motioned around the room. "At least I got some painting done between naps."

Danny returned with two bowls of ice cream with a piece of cake on the side. He handed Ana Maria one and sat in his chair in front of the television.

"Where's mine?" Arn asked.

"You said you're trying to get in shape. Cutting down for your blood sugar." Danny licked melting ice cream off his hand. "Something about folks thinking you look too old and too big. I'm just doing my part to help. Besides, you'll get a sugar dump and won't be able to stay awake tonight watching for that rustler."

Ana Maria put her bowl on the floor and opened her notebook. "I accomplished a lot besides listening to the tip line." She flipped pages. "I talked with the bartender at the Outlaw the other day. He didn't work Saturday night, but he doubts Eddie was there. And he's sure Karen wasn't there looking for him, either. They've both been eighty-sixed there for fighting."

"Both?"

"Both," Ana Maria answered. "Last summer Karen caught Jillie and Eddie drinking there and proceeded to put a hurt on her. It took the bartender and two other guys to drag Karen outside. Eddie jumped in, and the cops showed up and dragged him away. The bar owner even filed a restraining order on them to stay away."

Arn thought back to Karen telling him she'd found Eddie at the Outlaw. There had been looks between them when he'd asked Eddie the same question. And Karen didn't strike Arn as one who would drag her infant along to bars while she was looking for her husband. He'd been almost certain they were lying, before. Now he was sure of it. "Only one reason Karen said she found Eddie at the Outlaw—to give him an alibi."

"So, we're back to Eddie running out the door of the Boot Hill moments after Jillie did," Ana Maria said.

"Sounds like your Eddie is back on the suspect list," Danny said, licking the last of the ice cream and patting his belly. "Damn that was good."

Arn ignored him and faced Ana Maria. "I checked Eddie's arrest record at the courthouse. His last arrest was more than two years ago."

Ana Maria smiled. "You got to have charm. That's the other thing I did this afternoon—went on a date with a clerk from the courthouse. He clued me in that Eddie copped a plea to an assault *last* year and got a deferred sentence."

"That's why I didn't find that arrest," Arn said. "He must have kept his nose clean since." A deferred sentence allowed defendants to plead guilty but not suffer consequences for a specified period of time— usually a year—if they kept out of trouble. If the defendant got in no more trouble after that, their arrest was expunged from public record and their case sealed. Provided they jumped through all the hoops. "Did your contact agree with the deferred sentence?" he asked.

Ana Maria guffawed. "Not hardly. Eddie's been an a-hole to cops and deputies for years. My ... contact thought Eddie would blow it with the shrink."

"Shrink?"

Ana Maria nodded. "Eddie was court-ordered to see a police psychiatrist for his anger issues. Maury Oakert. Jillie Reilly's boss."

Fifteen

ARN DRAGGED INTO THE house and threw his windbreaker at the bentwood coat rack beside the front door. It fell a foot short, but he merely looked at it and made no attempt to pick it up. Later. When he had more energy to spare, he'd hang it up. He'd watched a sheep pasture all night and fought to stay awake, listening to people on talk radio claiming to have seen aliens in their backyards. Now that was an explanation he'd love to give the Association.

He'd used the same nonsense to keep himself awake the last two fruitless nights. Between driving around town looking for a broken marker that might match the lens he'd found at Wooly Hanks' a week ago and hustling across the county sitting in different pastures to catch the Midnight Sheepherder, he'd just about broke the fun barrier. He wasn't sure he could take any more wasted weeks like he'd just had.

And even before Arn made it to the kitchen and a bite of breakfast, Danny the Work Nazi jumped him like a nickel whore. He proceeded to shame Arn into sanding the drywall taping he'd just finished in the sitting room, and it was noon by the time Arn finished slinging mud. He dropped bone-tired into a kitchen chair as his cell phone buzzed. Brushing drywall dust off his hands, he welcomed the brief break.

"You'll want to get to Curt Gowdy Park," Ana Maria's voice said.

"I'd love to. Take a leisurely stroll. Maybe hike to the waterfall—"

"Or drive out here because there's been another homicide. Don Whales has been murdered by the Hynds Lodge. At the amphitheater where bands play."

"I hate to ask, but who's the investigating deputy?"

"Your new bestest friend," Ana Maria answered. "Sergeant Slade."

"Well, don't tell him I'm coming or he'll set me up for a traffic stop or something to keep me occupied."

"Right now," Ana Maria said, "the only thing he's concerned with is Don."

———

Thirty minutes west of Cheyenne sits Curt Gowdy State Park. It offers hiking trails and fishing holes, camping spots and other places just to relax. Named for the famous sportscaster and Wyoming native, it was commissioned a state park in 1971. Hynds Lodge, within the park, was built and donated to the Boy Scouts by Cheyenne philanthropist Harry P. Hynds in 1922. It's known for hosting functions and civic meetings and being a popular place for weddings. Situated among spruce and cedar trees that grow beside its famous granite formations, the lodge is a scenic spot to be married, with the wedding party enjoying the historic building by reservation. Arn was certain Harry Hynds had never intended for the area around the lodge to be used as a killing ground.

He pulled off Happy Jack Road onto the gravel trail that led to the lodge. The gate across the road blocked him but he didn't have to go to the lodge itself, just to an area close to it. He parked in a small gravel area beside a coroner's van and a sheriff's office Expedition. A deputy approached him and Arn rolled down his window. "I'm here working with the press," he said, nodding toward a TV station van beside the Expedition.

The deputy pointed to a narrow trail. "The TV lady is down that-away with her cameraman." He stepped aside to allow Arn to get out of his car.

Arn walked the well-worn dirt path between huge granite boulders, the forty-foot-high rock formations that attracted tourists to the area. When he'd gone a hundred yards, the dirt turned to a series of wide concrete steps that descended to an amphitheater fifty feet below. The amphitheater was large enough to host a good-sized band. He spotted Ana Maria standing by the uppermost concrete bench, taping that night's show with the amphitheater as her backdrop. When she finished and pocketed the microphone, she waved Arn over.

Next to her was yellow evidence tape that cordoned off the crime scene in the amphitheater below. Arn strained, but he couldn't see the victim. Men in gray overalls with *Police* stamped on the back bent over what he presumed to be a corpse. He caught a glimpse of Sergeant Slade before the deputy turned to one of his evidence technicians and said something Arn couldn't hear at that distance.

"Don's body is down in the amphitheater. Off to one side like he was making a grand exit," Ana Maria said.

"Doesn't get any grander than that, apparently," Arn replied. "Give me the headline version."

"I'm going for sodas," Ana Maria's cameraman said to them as he drifted off along the pathway.

"Bobbie is always looking for free stuff."

Arn smiled. In his police days, he'd done the same thing whenever a government van pulled up supplying emergency workers with beverages and snacks. He knew Bobbie would soon score free soda and chips and finger food offered to the crime scene workers and anyone else with their hand out.

He joined Ana Maria at the bench. She sat and laid her purse on the concrete. "Don and his band played a wedding here last night," she said.

The cameraman came back, bringing extra soda and chips for them. "Is the soda diet?" Arn asked.

"Bite your tongue," Bobbie answered.

"I'm only drinking diet nowadays." Arn patted his belly. "Getting back in shape."

"Too late," the cameraman said. He walked to the far bench to eat by himself.

"Who's Mr. Charm," Arn asked, "thinking it's too late for me to get back in shape?"

Ana Maria shrugged. "New guy. Bobbie. Someone who is quite perceptive." She exaggerated a look at Arn's mid-section, then took a big gulp of soda and came up for air as she pointed at the festivities below with the soda bottle. "One who is going to record you in the best light possible in a few moments."

"I don't feel like being on TV tonight."

Ana Maria shrugged. "Comes with you taking DeAngelo's money."

"But why me?"

"You see them getting anywhere?" Ana Maria jerked her thumb at Slade and the others working the crime scene. "They've come up with nothing on Jillie's murder. A little publicity with the famous Metro Denver Homicide investigator might jar some people's memories about seeing something last night."

"Might jar the killer into acting against said famous homicide detective."

"I've never known you to back down from a challenge."

"I'm not," Arn said. "But remember the last time we pushed a little too hard? You damned near lost your life."

Ana Maria nodded. In the Butch Spangler investigation—which had evolved into something far larger—the killer had felt Arn was getting too close to solving the case and had abducted Ana Maria. But she remained unfazed. "I can handle whatever comes my way," she reminded him now, patting her purse. Arn had loaned her one of his pistols—a lightweight .38—and she'd hung on to it all these months.

"Tell me a little more about Don while we're waiting for Inspector Clouseau down there to wrap up," he requested.

"Like I said," Ana Maria began between mouthfuls of chips, "Don's group played the reception. Lots of folks like this area. Makes for a memorable wedding."

"Just what I'd like to tell my grandkids: 'I was one of the last to hear Don Whales of Don Whales and the Dolphins play before he was murdered.' Probably nothing as simple as a fight that went too far?"

"Ah." Ana Maria finished her soda. "Calories." She winked at Arn. "No, the wedding-goers had a good time by all accounts. The band played the old standbys, plus some new blue grass songs that Don wrote. A few danced." She pointed to a concrete slab in front of the amphitheater only large enough for half-a-dozen couples. "They quit at one o'clock this morning when things started winding down. Some drunks invited the band to a shivaree of the newlyweds at the Hynds Lodge. Don wasn't a drinker, so he volunteered to stay and take down the instruments for the other three band members. He was killed sometime between then and this morning, when two hikers found his body slumped by his banjo."

"Gives new meaning to 'hearing banjo music,' I suppose," Arn said.

Sergeant Slade stood from where he'd been kneeling beside the body on the stage. He shaded his eyes with his hand when he spotted Arn, then bent and said something to one of the techs before starting up the amphitheater steps two at a time. When he reached the top, he stepped over the crime scene tape and glared down at Arn. "I thought that was you nosing around. What do you want, Anderson? Looking for stolen sheep hereabouts?"

Arn nodded to the evidence techs working the crime scene. "What's with Don?"

"That's no concern of the not-so-successful stock detective. Now scat!"

Arn looked around the spot, with its concrete benches, its meandering dirt trails that disappeared among the rocks and granite outcroppings, and shrugged. "This looks like a public place to me. I think I'll just stay and catch some morning air. If it's okay with the sheriff's office."

Slade's pale face grew red and he rose up a mite higher to intimidate Arn. It didn't work.

"I'm not your enemy, Sergeant. I've been hired to help find Jillie's killer. But you know that already—"

"What's that got to do with Don Whales?"

"That's just what I was thinking driving out here," Arn answered. "Why would Don Whales's death even be connected to Jillie Reilly's?" He offered Slade some chips but the deputy waved it away. "Then I said, 'Arn, you're being awfully dense. Don Whales helped with the dog classes and has a dog capable of loading sheep into a trailer very quickly. I'm thinking that Jillie's partner—if your theory's right about her being part of the Midnight Sheepherder—was getting worried she'd go to the law, and it came to a head last Saturday night. It's plausible Don trained the dog Jillie used to steal sheep, and her partner didn't want Don getting a case of conscience and turning her in." Arn crumpled the empty chip bag and lobbed it into a nearby trash receptacle. "So what do you say, Deputy Slade? You got some information to pass along to a concerned citizen?"

The coroner yelled to Slade then, and he started down into the amphitheater but stopped and turned back for a moment. "Let me chew on it for a bit. Being a working man, I got some law duties to attend. I don't have the luxury of a retired man to do whatever I please with my time."

Ana Maria watched Slade's backside as he descended the concrete steps. "You haven't changed your mind and started believing his lame theory that Jillie had a falling out with her rustler partner that night she was killed?"

"If I did, I wouldn't admit it to Slade. That's all I need to do: blow up his ego even more."

"But the murders still *have* to be connected in some way," Ana Maria said. "I just haven't come up with a logical explanation."

"I just gave it to you." Arn reached over and brushed corn chip crumbs off her cheek. "Don saw Jillie's killer that night when he and the Dolphins played at the Boot Hill—he just didn't realize it was the killer at the time. But he could as easily woke up any morning in the last few days and had an epiphany and remembered who was in the bar that night Jillie was ragging on. And Don would have been able to ID the killer."

"That lets Eddie Glass off the hook. Don would know Eddie right away from the dog classes. You're back to your line of reasoning that the guy Jillie chased out of the bar killed her."

Arn sipped his soda and looked at Slade bending over Don's corpse once again. "I don't *want* to let Eddie go as a suspect, as big an SOB as he is. But right now, it looks like I got no choice."

Slade helped the coroner zip the body bag up and grunted as they hefted the dead man onto a gurney. They slowly ascended the steps of the amphitheater, each struggling with one end of the rolling cart holding Don Whale's body strapped to it. Sweat dripped off the coroner, yet he cheerily whistled "Zip-a-Dee-Doo-Dah" as he wheeled the cart along the dirt path toward his van. Slade yelled directions to the coroner's assistant, who was backing up the van before they loaded Don's body into it.

Slade walked back to Arn and Ana Maria. "I will tell you *one* thing, Anderson." He was breathing heavily and nodded to Ana Maria. "Alone."

Ana Maria rolled her eyes. "Sergeant, if you say you want it off the record, it stays off the record."

"All right," Slade said at last, looking at the evidence techs still in the amphitheater gathering samples. He lowered his voice as if they could hear. "I guess you're telling her everything anyway." He paused for dramatic effect, like he was already running for sheriff. "Don Whales was tortured."

"In what way?"

"He wasn't strangled just the once. He was strangled repeatedly. Numerous marks on his neck showed the killer made several strangulations before finally killing him."

"Like Jillie Reilly?" Ana Maria asked.

"Just like her," Slade said.

"And it wasn't because Don put up a good fight?" Arn asked.

Slade shrugged. "He's just as dead either way."

"How heavy was Don?"

Slade thought a moment. "We'll probably have to take him to the port of entry and weigh him on a truck scale, but I'm guessing two-eighty if he's an ounce."

"And an Army vet."

"I see where you're going," Slade said. "If Don fought with his attacker—"

"—which we assume he must have—"

"—the killer must be one big bastard."

"Or one strong bastard," Arn said.

Ana Maria had left the scene to file her story, while Arn waited on the concrete bench until the evidence technicians left in their van with boxes of samples to be delivered to the crime lab. Slade came over to him yet again. "What the hell you still want from me? I've told you about all I can for now."

Arn rubbed his back, sore from sitting on the cold concrete. "I just wanted to hear it from you—away from any witnesses—that you think Don and Jillie's murders are unrelated."

Slade looked away. "Sheriff Grimes thinks they're not..."

"But *you* think they are connected? After all, this is a town of only sixty thousand. Hard for two homicides, two Saturday nights in a row, *not* to be connected."

"What do you want from me? I may be planning to challenge Grimes in the next election, but right now I work for the man."

"And you ride for the brand, is that it?" Arn said.

"Something like that."

"Why not start by opening your mind a little," Arn said. "Think that there might be a theory about Jillie's case other than yours."

Slade sat on the bench beside Arn and ran his fingers through his sweaty hair. "The coroner tossed around the notion that Don and Jillie were in cahoots as sheep thieves—"

"But you don't really believe that?"

"Don Whales's murder *might* point to that. But no, I think there's some other explanation why the big man was killed."

"So where *does* that leave Don in your mind?"

"I've known Don for years. Even had him fix my car when the head gasket went to hell last summer. I'd never imagine that he'd be connected with the sheep thefts." Slade took off the lid of his Copenhagen can and stuffed his lip. "I'm thinking he might have seen something at the Boot Hill that night Jillie was killed. Something that the killer is afraid Don might have eventually remembered."

Arn nodded. "My thoughts too. So, we're dealing with a killer who doesn't leave anything to chance."

"It would appear so." Slade brushed loose snus off on his uniform shirt. "I'm thinking we got a list of turds to look at. They're floating on the surface of the water just waiting for me to pull the handle and see what one floats to the top."

"Eddie and that guy Jillie chased out of the bar that night might be the prime turds."

Slade dropped his head. "You might be right. My theory that Jillie was a rustler might be a load of horse shit."

"Or sheep shit, as the case might be." Arn smiled. He'd been just where Slade was on various cases, blinded by his own ideas before sorting through all the facts. "Or the rustler got a good look at Jillie's killer."

"Not that tired old theory again," Slade said.

Arn remained quiet. Nothing he could say would convince this bonehead of the rustler-witness possibility. "Were you able to interview Dr. Oakert?"

"Not at length," Slade said. "He was major upset that his secretary and gatekeeper was murdered. Poor bastard was shaking and bawling in his office, he was so upset when I stopped there."

"I'm betting the doctor might be able to shed some light on things."

"How?" Slade asked.

"Jillie knew what the doctor knew, typing his transcribed notes for him. She threatened the guy in the Boot Hill by saying she'd rat on him. About what? Speculation is that she threatened to tell on the guy for having an affair with her, but we really have no clue. She also knew whatever it was that Oakert and his patients talked about, including Eddie Glass when he was court-ordered to see Oakert."

"How do you know about that? Eddie's files are sealed."

Arn slapped Slade on the back. "Just good old-fashioned police work. The kind any over-the-hill range detective would know how to do."

Sixteen

ARN PARKED OUTSIDE THE Pie Lady and followed Danny into the café. As soon as they entered, the sweet odor of fresh baked pie of every persuasion wafted past their noses. The shop offered other menu items, mostly a lunch variety. But they specialized in pie. The place was crowded, the noon customers hanging around long after they'd finished their meals. Arn motioned to an open corner booth, and Danny sat while Arn talked with the waitress. Soon she delivered coffee and pecan pie to their table.

"Not much variety left," she said. "We had a run on pie today."

Danny glanced around the room. "I'd take any pie that Mr. Cheapskate bought." He craned his neck to look over Arn's shoulder as the waitress went to another table. "As old as I am, I'm about the youngest one here besides you. Kind of looks like *Night of the Living Dead* at the old folks' home."

Arn gestured to the other diners. "They do tend to get an older crowd in here."

Danny took the first tiny bite and closed his eyes. "Damn that's good." He leaned over the table. "Just about as good as my pie. But you didn't bring ol' Danny here out of the goodness of your frugal heart."

"You know me too well." Arn finished his piece before Danny had taken another miniscule bite of his. "I wanted to run some things by you without you getting distracted by home improvement." Ever since trading Danny work for a place to live last winter, Arn had often used the old man as a sounding board. Even though he looked like an emaciated old Indian who couldn't find his way back to the reservation, Danny was—as Arn had quickly learned—an educated and deep thinker. He'd bounced things off Danny and know he wouldn't tell anyone. Hell, Arn thought, Ana Maria and I are his only friends. Who could he tell anyway?

Two men in black suits carrying clipboards entered the café. Arn lowered his voice as he explained what he'd learned about Don Whales that morning. He'd concluded there were two possibilities: one, that Don was the Midnight Sheepherder and had seen Jillie's killer that night—a theory Arn discounted. The other explanation was that Don saw the killer in the Boot Hill as he was playing in his band, and that the killer thought Don would eventually realize it.

"Slade knew Don, and was sure he wasn't the Midnight Sheepherder. If Don was the rustler, he would have recognized Eddie that night in Wooly Hank's pasture and come forward. But if I believe how adamant Slade is, Don couldn't have been the rustler."

"For giggles and shits, let's say Don *was* the rustler," Danny said, daintily sipping his coffee. "And he saw the killer strangle Jillie—and it was someone other than Eddie."

"I don't know—"

"You'd just like Eddie to be a suspect."

"Can't deny that. The asshole's such a ... perfect suspect."

"Okay, so maybe Eddie—if he is the killer—might have *thought* Don got a look at him that night. *If* Don was the witness." Danny held up his coffee cup for a refill. "What did Don say when you interviewed him?"

"He was always out doing some mechanic job. I wanted to interview him, but we never could find a good time to connect, so I'm relying on Slade's interview. His report says Don wasn't the least bit nervous that he might have seen Jillie's killer that night in the bar. He was so busy playing that he paid no attention to the man Jillie chased out of the Boot Hill."

"The killer wouldn't have known that."

"So we're back to the strangler *fearing* that Don recognized him?"

Danny finished his pie and nudged Arn. "Maybe a scoop of ice cream would be nice."

"It doesn't come with ice cream."

"What doesn't come with ice cream?"

"Your pie," Arn answered. "Let's stay on topic here. If Eddie did catch up with Jillie outside the bar, he could have driven her to Wooly Hank's—"

"Unless that other guy she chased out of the bar motored away with her first," Danny said. "That's if what Eddie said was true—that Jillie was gone by the time he ran outside."

The waitress came to their table and refilled their cups. "They'll get to your table in a moment." She winked.

"What's she talking about?"

Arn shrugged and continued. "Can you think of another possibility with Eddie?"

"You really got a case for him." Danny sat back. "How about this: the Midnight Sheepherder is more than one or even two thieves. Even a ... herd of thieves."

"We don't call a gang of thieves a 'herd' around here."

Danny waved it off. "Just hear me out. Maybe Slade is on to something with his theory."

"Go on."

"There's been a lot of livestock stolen this last year," Danny explained. "What if there's a whole herd ... gang of thieves. And what if Eddie and the other man in the bar were part of the ring. At some point, the light bulb would have gone off over Don's head, and he might have connected them. You said yourself, Jillie ragged on the guy, saying she intended to tell about *something*. Everyone's assuming she'd dime him out over an affair. But how about there was actually no affair between them? What if Jillie knew about the ring of thieves? They would be compromised if she outed the guy. So maybe Eddie did take Don out, if that light bulb went on over his big gomby head."

"But he was a big man. It'd take someone powerful to get the best of him."

"Remember last winter when you were hanging by that rope in Pieter Spangler's basement?" Danny said.

Arn's hand went instinctively to his neck. He'd worn a silk neckerchief for weeks until the deep ligature marks disappeared. Last thing he wanted was anyone thinking that he was suicidal. "How could I forget?"

"And how long after you got hung there did it take you to begin to pass out?"

Arn thought back, though he'd just as soon forget. "Just a few moments." And his own light bulb went off. "If someone smaller, but still powerful, got the drop on Don—"

"They might be in for a real rodeo until he went unconscious. But he *would* go unconscious within a few moments. Just like you."

Arn remembered the rope encircling his neck, recalled fighting his attacker, clawing and coming away with flesh from the man's arm just before Danny saved him. "I'll make it a point to ask Slade if there was any tissue under Don's nails."

"And one other wrinkle to your case: what if Little Jim Reilly killed Don? That man's as big and powerful as anyone I've seen. He offered you money to turn his daughter's killer over to him. If he thought Don was in cahoots with the Midnight Sheepherder to kill Jillie—"

"I see what you're getting at."

"Now wasn't that little piece of logic worth every bit of the pie you paid for?"

Arn finished his coffee, and Danny started to stand but Arn stopped him. "I think we're expected to stay for a few minutes."

"What are you talking about?"

Arn motioned to the empty pie plates. "I didn't pay for this."

"What?"

"The pie and coffee are complimentary." Arn took out a crumpled-up newspaper clipping and handed it to Danny: *Free Coffee and Slice of Pie, Just for Listening to our Presentation. Lakeside Funeral Home*

Arn nodded to the two men in dark suits approaching the table. "We—or as the case may be, you—are expected to sit for a sales pitch."

"This?" Danny held up the clipping.

Before Arn could answer, the two men stopped at their table and solemnly handed Danny a brochure from Lakeside Funeral Home. For the next fifteen minutes, Danny sat fuming, glaring at Arn as the men explained their pre-paid funeral plans, complete with a plot over the lake that *might* one day be built. "Most people here signed up for our EasyPay Plan," one of the men told Danny. "Which do you prefer?"

He motioned to Arn. "It'll be like this pie and coffee—whatever Mr. Cheapskate there wants to spring for when I'm worm food."

Seventeen

THE NOTICE SCRAWLED ON Maury Oakert's office door announced he had closed for the day. But a pile of mail and newspapers on the stoop indicated he hadn't been to work for at least a week. A sign that read *Closed for Mourning* had been taped to the door.

Arn called Ana Maria to find out the doctor's home address, and drove across town to his home on the avenues. This part of Cheyenne had historically been home to bankers and lawyers, railroaders and business tycoons wanting to live close to Millionaire's Row on Carey that was established after the Union Pacific adopted Cheyenne in the 1860s. The area was situated right where the Cheyenne-to-Deadwood stage travelled, back during Cheyenne's rowdy and formative years. Arn was sure it was no more rowdy and dangerous than Cheyenne had been recently: two murders in two weeks. He was certain that would match the wild town back in the day.

Arn drove the tree-lined streets, and a red-fiery sky shone through the pine and blue spruce and cottonwoods, courtesy of recent forest fires in Colorado drifting north. Parking was at a premium on these narrow old streets, and Arn stopped down the block. He walked to the doctor's home and took the three steps to the front door, then rang the bell. Repeatedly.

He got no answer, and if the curtain to one side of a bay window hadn't moved, he would have left. *Dr. Oakert was home*, and Arn banged more aggressively. After five minutes of scraping his knuckles on the solid mahogany door, Dr. Oakert cracked it an inch. "I've said all I'm going to tell you people," he said and slammed it shut.

Arn rapped again, this time harder and more persistent. The stained glass in the center of the door threatened to break until the chain rattled across the door. Dr. Oakert cracked it open again. "I said I told you cops—"

"I'm not the police." Arn slipped a business card through the crack and Oakert closed the door. Within a moment, he opened the door again. He stuck his head out and hurriedly looked both ways along the street before stepping aside to let Arn in.

"You're that private detective Ana Maria is working with on Jillie's murder?"

"We're both employed by the TV station, if that's what you mean."

"You and she aren't … an item by any chance?"

Arn forced a smile. "At my age?"

As soon as Arn was inside, Dr. Oakert looked a last time outside before slamming the door. He threw a dead bolt and chain across the door. "Can't be too careful with kids breaking into houses around the neighborhood."

"I'm thinking you're not afraid of some juvies breaking in to swipe a stereo or rifle through your underwear drawer."

Dr. Oakert stood with his hands on his hips. "What's that supposed to mean?"

"You're scared to death of something, Dr. Oakert."

When he started to object, Arn continued. "A dead bolt and chain in the middle of the day? And you keep it so dark that it's hard to even walk in here. May we talk somewhere where there's light, Doctor?"

Dr. Oakert led Arn into a study lined with medical books and publications dealing with the criminally insane. There were books on case studies of famous serial killers and those cheating the penal system through mental asylums. Arn took a book from the shelf dealing with Jeffrey Dahmer. "My guess is you're afraid of someone just like him"—he handed the doctor the book—"to have closed your office."

"It's just temporary until Jillie's funeral. I do have *some* respect for the dead, Mr. Anderson."

Arn let the comment pass. "I think Jillie's killer struck again Saturday night."

The doctor flicked a desk lamp on, and Arn was taken aback. Ana Maria had described Maury Oakert as a self-styled playboy: impeccably dressed, impeccably groomed. Yet here behind the desk sat a man who had neither shaved nor put on fresh clothes recently. He was attired in baggy sweatpants and a USC jersey with food stains down the front.

Dr. Oakert opened a drawer and took out a pack of Winstons. With hands trembling, he shook one out, but four more tumbled onto the desktop. When he tried lighting the cigarette, his hands shook and the flame missed its target. Arn reached over and took the lighter-disguised-as-a-hand-grenade and held it to the doctor's cigarette. "Do you have a gun handy, Dr. Oakert?"

The man blew smoke toward the ceiling. "Of course not. I've never had any use for them before, and I certainly don't now. Why?"

"I'd consider getting one."

Dr. Oakert took a bottle of Southern Comfort from a desk drawer and poured three fingers. He put it back without offering Arn a drink.

"You said Jillie's killer struck again?" he said after downing half the whisky.

"An Iraq war veteran," Arn said. "Murdered in precisely the same way she was."

"Strangulation?"

Arn nodded.

"That's none of my business."

"It is if Jillie knew her killer. And like you told Ana Maria, Jillie transcribed all your clinical notes. She knew the type of people who come to see you. More importantly, she knew all the dark, dirty secrets about your patients. Just like you did."

Arn sat down on an overstuffed couch and set his Stetson on a coffee table that had deer legs for legs. He envisioned Freud using a divan just like this one to get into the heads of his patients. Perhaps Dr. Oakert had, too. "Here's what I'm thinking—and stop me if I'm too far off base here. I think that one of the sets of clinical notes that Jillie transcribed genuinely frightened her. Little Jim said she came home the week of her death scared as hell. Maybe of someone who would pose a serious threat the next time he had a therapy session with you."

Dr. Oakert sipped his whisky without objection and Arn continued. "Maybe Jillie found the patient that Saturday night at the bar and confronted him. Folks said she was reckless like that when she drank. Or perhaps the patient just got to stalking her, and picked that Saturday night as the ideal time to kill her." Arn leaned over to look in the doctor's rheumy eyes. "You got any patients capable of that?"

Dr. Oakert lit a fresh cigarette with the smoldering filter of his first one. He sat staring at the bookcase, and Arn wondered if he was considering answering him. When he'd first seen Dr. Oakert at the door, the man had been shaking worse than a dog passing a peach pit, he was so frightened. Now he'd regained his composure, and he looked at Arn defiantly. "You know I can't reveal that information."

Standing, Arn walked to the doctor's I Love Me wall, plastered with diplomas and certificates and community awards he'd received since entering psychiatry. He tapped one certificate. "Governor's certificate of appreciation. Impressive."

"Governor Jerry Brown thought the work I'd done to get the bill passed was due an award."

"What type of legislation?" Arn knew the more the doctor talked, the more likely it was he'd open up.

"Governor Brown signed into law a bill I pushed for, one that isolated the most dangerous psychiatric patients within California mental facilities."

"Isolated as in *Silence of the Lambs?*"

"Not that severe." Dr. Oakert waved the air with his cigarette. "Prior to that legislation, dangerous—and I'm talking about extremely dangerous, psychotic patients here—were free to mingle with lesser patients. And with the hospital staff." He stood and walked to the window, staying to one side as he cracked the blinds to look out. "I worked the Napa State Hospital in scenic Napa, California. Home to the criminally insane. Home to a patient who strangled a psychiatric technician to death one day before that law was implemented."

"Didn't you have guards to prevent that?"

Dr. Oakert's head snapped around and he glared at Arn. "Mr. Anderson, those people were patients. Not inmates. Sure, we had security available if we needed it. We even wore personal monitors around our necks in case we had problems. But security never quite responded quickly enough." He snubbed out his cigarette and looked at the pack as if he needed another pick-me-up. "We had upward of two thousand assaults a year against other patients and hospital staff, mostly by the most violent patients. And still they were not isolated."

"You mean confined?"

Dr. Oakert nodded. "I myself was cut with a homemade shank, and would have been ripped to death if another patient hadn't come to my rescue." He slid the pack of Winstons into his top drawer and shut it. "After that I made it my mission to get legislation passed that would prevent another incident like that. To ensure the violent patients were isolated from the nonviolent ones in wings where they wouldn't harm others. And, being isolated, they were afforded the best treatment we could give them. It took me four years, but I got it done."

Arn studied the framed certificate with the seal of California embossed in one corner. "You were a psychiatrist working for the state at the time?"

"I was a clinical analyst. I often evaluated prisoners to determine their state of mind at the time of their crime. If my finding showed NGRI—Not Guilty by Reason of Insanity—they were remanded to Napa State where I or one of my staff was assigned their case." He looked at Arn and began trembling again. "But you said the second murder is similar to Jillie's?"

Arn took out his pocket notebook and flipped pages. "Local man named Don Whales. Headed an amateur band that played bars and private gigs. Retired Army. Did mechanic work on the side, as well as helped with dog classes at the fairgrounds."

"There's hardly a connection to Jillie. She was neither in the military nor did she train dogs." Dr. Oakert laughed nervously. "And I'd know if she had any musical abilities."

"Don and his band played at the Boot Hill the night Jillie was murdered," Arn continued. "And, like I said, he was strangled like she was." He turned to where he'd had Slade sketch ligature marks from both victims and slid it across Dr. Oakert's desk. The man's eyes widened for a micro-second—just long enough to tell Arn that he had seen those marks before. Dr. Oakert handed Arn back the notebook, but Arn left it open, atop the desk, where the doctor could see it. "It takes a special person to kill like that. Bringing the victim to the point of death only to let up and do it again, moments later."

Dr. Oakert looked away.

"If you were analyzing a patient who killed like that, what would you discern just from their method of killing?"

The doctor glanced at the sketch. He didn't pick the notebook up, as if in doing so it would be an admission that he recognized the marks. "I'd say the person thoroughly enjoyed bringing his victim just to the point of death so that he—or she—could exert control over them all over again."

"You've seen those exact markings before."

"Nonsense."

Arn stood from the couch and leaned across the desk. "Just now, when I showed you the sketch of the ligature marks, you *knew* who the killer was."

"I had a patient some years ago ..." Dr. Oakert began slowly, choosing his words carefully. "Name of Rodney Alcala. He murdered people in the '70s in New York. And in California he committed numerous murders."

"The Dating Game killer," Arn said. "Seems like he even murdered a couple people after appearing on the game show. He was your patient?"

Dr. Oakert lit another Winston and leaned back in his chair as if he were once again analyzing the killer. "In a manner. He was sentenced to the electric chair in California when I was chief psychiatrist for the state. And I will never forget my initial interview of Rodney." The doctor leaned across his desk and lowered his voice. "The man was pure evil. He would use a ligature—a sash cord, an electrical cord, a belt, whatever was handy—to strangle his victims to the point of death. Then let them live. And he'd do it again. And again, until he finally decided he wanted them dead."

"Just like a case I had in Denver," Arn said. "But I understand Alcala is still on death row."

Dr. Oakert nodded.

"Then he couldn't have murdered Jillie Reilly or Don Whales. But what you're saying is someone equally evil—with the same propensity for death and suffering as Alcala has—killed Don and Jillie."

Dr. Oakert looked away, and Arn pressed. "You *know* the killer. He's a patient of yours now?"

The doctor's head nodded faintly in the affirmative, but he denied it. "I do not know—"

"One of your patients is the killer, and he's murdered long before Jillie Reilly." Arn laid his hand on Dr. Oakert's arm. "And she knew the man's identity. Knew about him, didn't she?"

Tears formed in the doctor's eyes. "She did. She knew all his grisly crimes, which he came to me for help with."

"You say he came to you seeking your help?"

Oakert nodded. "He's a conflicted soul. Like many ... patients I've seen through the years, this one wanted help. Wanted some reason to stay straight. And yet his dark side tugged at him so much harder. It frightened her like nothing else."

"Who is it, Doctor? What is the patient's name?"

He looked away.

"Who is it!" Arn slammed his hand on the desk top. "Who the hell is the patient? 'Cause he killed them both and may very well kill again."

Dr. Oakert dropped his cigarette butt in his tumbler of whisky and it hissed angrily. "I cannot tell you," he whispered.

"What do you mean you can't tell me? You know the man's identity—"

"I cannot even verify it's a *man*, though I will continue referring to the patient as 'he.'" Dr. Oakert stood and paced in front of his desk. "Don't you think I *want* to tell you, and Sergeant Slade, and everyone else who will listen?" He slapped his whisky glass and it crashed against the wall of his study. "Damned patient-doctor confidentiality."

"And you could live with him killing again knowing you could have stopped it?"

"Let's say, for argument's sake, that my special patient is *not* your killer. Do you know the harm it would do to him if I alerted law enforcement, betrayed my oath, and it *wasn't* him? All the progress we made would be nullified. He'd go off on law enforcement and would have a tremendous setback in his program."

Arn backed away and sat on the couch. He was angry enough that he was fearful he'd beat the doctor senseless. He took in deep, calming breaths. "Okay, so there's the confidentiality thing. But surely there are some things you can tell me that wouldn't violate your oath."

Dr. Oakert ran his fingers through his hair and nodded. "The special patient I'm seeing in my practice has killed before—"

"Has he been caught for his crimes?"

"I cannot divulge that," Dr. Oakert said. "If he was insane at the time, there was no ... crime involved."

"Go on, then."

"What I can say is that I think my patient is making progress. That he hasn't killed in years, ever since he's been involved in ... intense therapy. But he may not be the person you're looking for. If I outed him and it wasn't him, I'd lose my license."

"That's better than some other father losing his daughter like Little Jim Reilly did," Arn said. "But what if your patient *is* him?"

Dr. Oakert remained silent, nudging a piece of lint with the toe of his slipper.

"You want me to catch him," Arn said. "Just to see if the killings stop."

The doctor clutched Arn's arm. "No, I *need* you to catch him."

"Then help me." Arn eased Dr. Oakert onto the couch. "Give me something before he kills again."

"He's a troller-hunter," the doctor blurted out.

"A what?"

"A troller," Dr. Oakert explained. "He trolls his domain looking for that perfect victim. And he'll go far afield to find her."

"You mean he drives around looking for his next victim?"

"Or scours the internet," Dr. Oakert said. "Like most serial rapists and serial killers, he has certain parameters, certain requirements he desires in his victims. And he'll go to great lengths to find the perfect victim who fits those parameters." He started trembling again. Arn opened the desk drawer and grabbed the pack of smokes. He lit another cigarette and handed it to the doctor.

"Look for someone who drives," Dr. Oakert said as he blew smoke toward the ceiling. "A lot. Which is why I don't think my patient is the killer. Can you imagine killing two people in a small town like Cheyenne? You'd stick out like a sore thumb. My patient would go out of town to hunt."

"Doctor," Arn said, "three summers ago during Cheyenne Frontier Days someone walked into the Coin Shop here in town. It's only blocks from where they hold their free pancake breakfast for folks attending the rodeos, and there were a thousand people there. Someone shot and killed the owner and his friend. Then just vanished. At nine thirty in the morning, for God's sake. And you can't believe your patient could get away with murder in his own town?"

"Jillie and this Don Whales didn't fit his profile."

"What are—were—the parameters of his victims?"

"I've said too much already," Dr. Oakert replied. "But what I can say is that the killer—if he's my special patient—does not want to be caught. None of this 'please catch me before I kill again' attitude. He'll do what it takes to keep from getting caught. The last thing he wants is to be sent back to an asylum."

"So, your patient has been institutionalized?"

"I just can't say any more." Dr. Oakert led Arn to the door.

"One other thing, Doctor," Arn said. "What kind of patient was Eddie Glass?"

The doctor stopped mid-stride. "What do you know about Eddie?"

Arn shrugged. "Not much, except he was your court-ordered patient. Anger management issues, was it? Did he ever overcome his urges?"

The doctor ignored Arn, throwing back the dead bolt and peering outside before fully opening the door. "Just find my patient, Mr. Anderson. In case it *is* him."

Eighteen

I JUST MAKE IT back to my truck when Anderson pulls into the parking lot beside Maury's clinic, and I doubt he's there because he needs psychiatric help. He checks the door, as I did. I want to yell at him that the good doctor hasn't been to his clinic since Jillie and I danced at Wooly Hank's pasture that Saturday night. I'm disappointed in Maury—he's always been there when I needed to talk to him. Like now.

I scoot down in the seat, even though this truck is like a hundred others around town and I blend in well. I don't know where Maury lives, but I have a hunch Anderson's got his ways of finding out. If I stay with him, Anderson will lead me to Maury's place.

Anderson climbs into that neat old car of his, and I let him get a block down the street before falling in behind him.

I wake up when Maury opens the door and lets Anderson out. I rub the sleepers out of my eyes. For a moment I feel a twinge of panic, not unlike when I was nearly caught that night in Flagstaff when the husband almost caught me in his house dancing my special soft shoe with his cute wife. But sleeping in my truck on a public street near Maury's house was stupid, no matter how many late-night hours I keep. Any neighbor in this historic part of town could have called the law. That would have drawn Anderson's attention, and I can't afford that. Still, it's gotten dark since Anderson went inside the doctor's house, and I doubt anyone saw me sleeping in my truck.

I take off my glove ever so carefully. A human bite is worse than a dog's, and I grab my first aid kit. I grit my teeth and tear the bandage from my hand. It's healing too slowly where Jillie bit me. Thank goodness for Neosporin, though. Another few days and my hand will be fine. I wish I could say the same about my neck. As much ointment as I've smeared over the deep scratches, I'd have thought it would heal sooner. Maybe mechanics have shit under their nails that is infectious.

Don Whales put up even more of a struggle than I thought he would. He isn't the first one who's resorted to clawing his attacker. But I hold no grudge against ol' Don. I'd have done the same thing if someone was strangling me with a stout boot string.

I check my watch. Anderson talked with Maury nearly an hour—a long time if Maury refused to give any information about me. Up until now, I've doubted Maury would tell anyone. After all, we've been through so much over the years, Maury and me. When Anderson drives off, I'll catch a few more winks. And as soon as it gets totally dark, I'll visit with the doctor. Find out what he told Anderson. And I'll ask Maury why I've fallen off the wagon.

As if I was ever on the wagon.

Nineteen

ARN PULLED OUT OF Dr. Oakert's house, digesting what the psychiatrist told him. And more importantly, what he didn't. Dr. Oakert had jumped at every sound, every unexpected movement of the curtains when the central air kicked on. He knew Jillie's killer, or at least he suspected. Why else close your practice and barricade yourself in your house, sitting in fear of your special patient coming to visit you?

As Arn started out of the historic district, headlights a block away flicked on. The vehicle neared, the same cobalt-colored truck he'd spotted two blocks behind him when he'd left Dr. Oakert's office. "You're getting paranoid," he said aloud. But it wasn't paranoia: it was his cop instinct kicking in, instinct that had saved his butt more times than he could recall when he worked the street. His cop DNA was ingrained in his soul. *Thank God.*

Arn made two more turns, and the truck stayed with him. He punched in Oblanski's number but then quickly disconnected. Even if a police cruiser was in the area, the stalker might be alerted and he'd rabbit.

Arn headed for Frontier Park a few blocks away. With the sun setting, the cool night air prevented joggers from using the park. An elderly couple strolled bundled-up, hanging on to a German Shepherd that was walking them on the sidewalk. They were the park's only occupants; Arn and his stalker would have the area to themselves. With his muscle car, Arn could easily outrun anyone tailing him. But he didn't want to lose the stalker. He wanted quality time alone with whoever was tailing him.

He drove slowly through the park. The truck waited for a moment before following him in. When he cleared the Botanic Gardens building, he doused his headlights and used the emergency brake to stop. He scrambled out of the car, shutting the door before the stalker could see the Oldsmobile's dome light.

He ducked behind the building and stripped off his light blue shirt. The air chilled him, but he knew he didn't have to stay in shirtsleeves long. He waited until the truck neared and for a brief moment allowed the truck's headlight to illuminate him: a man in a white T-shirt running around the building.

Arn sprinted—as much as a two-hundred-thirty-pound man can sprint—toward a row of bushes. He draped his shirt over a lilac bush obvious enough so that even Ray Charles would have spotted it fluttering in the wind, and hunkered down on the far side of a nearby spruce tree. He drew his .38 snubbie from his boot holster and waited for the stalker.

Would the man put up a fight, like Jillie and Don had? Or would he be subdued meekly, come to the authorities quietly, only to one day kill again? Arn didn't have long to wait for his answer, as the man's hulking form ducked under overhanging tree limbs on a bee-line toward Arn's shirt. When he reached the bush, he snatched the shirt and looked frantically around.

"How about you keep your hands where I can see them." Arn stepped from behind the tree as he leveled his gun at the stalker. "I'd hate for this little gun to go off accidentally and ventilate you."

"I'm not armed," the man said, and Arn immediately recognized the rough, gravelly voice born from a lifetime of grueling work.

"That you, Little Jim?"

"It is."

Arn lowered his gun but kept it beside his leg as he approached Little Jim Reilly. "Why the hell you following me?"

Little Jim remained silent.

"I want to know why you've been tailing me, or I'll call the law and have your ass tossed in the hoosegow."

Jim's hand went to his back pocket and Arn raised his gun, tensing. But Little Jim only retrieved his can of Copenhagen and took a dip. "Jillie's killer," he said at last.

"That's the only explanation you're going to give me when I damn near shot you just now?"

Little Jim leaned against a tree. "I figure you'd eventually lead me to Jillie's killer."

Arn snatched his shirt from Little Jim and put it on. "How long you been following me?"

"All day," Jim answered. "From when you left your house this morning."

Arn cursed himself. In his police days, he would have detected a tail right away. Little Jim had been on his case all day and he hadn't noticed it.

"What did Dr. Oakert say?"

Arn holstered his gun. "Not enough that would help me."

"You thought any more about that money?" Little Jim sat on a stump. "It's all yours just for turning her killer over to me."

"I told you before, my client is the television station. Now you stay away from me or I'll slap stalking papers on you."

"Bet you never threatened the other guy with stalking," Little Jim said.

The hair on Arn's neck stood up as he turned slowly to face Little Jim. "What other guy?"

"Some guy that's been tailing you. I didn't recognize him or his truck, but then I'm working the ranch a lot. Don't get to town a lot nowadays."

"What did his truck look like?"

"It was a Chevy truck like mine. About the same color." Little Jim chuckled. "But feel free to look—it was like half the other trucks in Cheyenne."

"How you know he was tailing me?"

"Wherever you went, he went," Little Jim said. "I figure it was some plainclothes cop assigned to make sure you don't wind up like Jillie and Don Whales."

"Where was he parked?"

Little Jim spit tobacco juice. "About a block down from the doctor's house. East side. Can't miss the spot. Guy must be a chainsmoker, as many butts as he tossed out." He stood from the stump. "You swearing out a complaint on me?"

Even if Little Jim hadn't just lost his only daughter, Arn wouldn't complain to the police. He should be thanking Little Jim—who had just sent him a warning that he better be more aware of his surroundings. The killer might be the man in the truck. "I'm letting this pass," Arn said. "Just stay out of my way."

When Little Jim left, Arn drove back to Dr. Oakert's house and pulled to the curb. He grabbed a flashlight and began walking the block surrounding the doctor's house. Little Jim had seen the man flicking his butts out the window. Those might lead Arn to the man's identity.

In the next block down, Arn's flashlight picked up six cigarette butts. He imagined the smoker sitting behind the wheel, tossing his butts out the window as he watched the house. He turned and looked at the doctor's house. The smoker had had a good view of the front door, and the butts were in the exact spot Arn figured they ought to be.

He bent to the smokes. All the butts had burned down to the filter, the brand unidentifiable. But DNA would be all over them. He took out his pocket notebook. After folding a page of notebook into a tiny envelope, he collected the butts and pocketed them. Maybe this would prod Slade into seeing things his way.

———————

Before he pulled away from the curb, Arn called Slade. "Make it quick, Anderson. I got to meet with Sheriff Grimes and explain what's going on with these murders."

Arn explained about Little Jim following him from Dr. Oakert's house and spotting the man in the truck. "Someone in a Chevy pickup followed me from Dr. Oakert's office to his home. Have you put a tail on me?"

"Don't know why I would." Slade chuckled. "You're not that important."

"That's what I thought," Arn said. "Then it's got to be the doctor's special patient he won't tell me about."

"It's just Little Jim imagining things. The last time I talked with him he wasn't exactly rational."

"Think that has something to do with losing his daughter?"

"What is it you want, Anderson?"

"Put a man on Dr. Oakert's office and his home. If it was the patient watching the house, it's just a matter of time before he pays the doctor a visit."

"Doesn't mean it was the killer."

"But it *could* be."

"You want me to tie up an officer on some bullshit surveillance? We got odd things here—like budget constraints. Surveillance takes a bunch of overtime. We're already working overtime on these two murders, and I can't spare a single officer to watch the doctor's place. Grimes would never authorize it."

"Then do this. I picked up butts belonging to the driver. If you'd send them to the crime lab, the DNA database might come up with a match."

Slade sighed heavily over the other end of the phone. "It *has* been a long time since you worked for a small agency. Our state lab is just a little overtaxed. We've been sending samples down to a lab in Colorado. But only for things that might pan out."

Arn resisted the urge to smash the phone against the dashboard. Perhaps Little Jim had imagined the truck following him. But he hadn't imagined the driver sitting, watching, flicking butts out the window in view of Dr. Oakert's house. If Little Jim was right, it might be the only break he'd get in catching Jillie and Don's killer. If he could watch for the rustler and the special patient at the same time, he would be a happy man.

Twenty

"**WHEN ARE YOU EVER** going to get a real car?" Arn asked as Ana Maria helped him out of her shoebox Volkswagen. "Why can't you drive DeAngelo's old truck?"

"Because I'm waiting for the machine shop to call and tell me the heads are finished," she replied. "I'm having new valves and seats installed in it. Besides, while this VW may be tiny, it's not like your Olds"—Ana Maria pulled her skirt down—"that gets crappy mileage and can't make it a block in the snow come winter. Now quit your bitchin'."

But Arn *was* bitching. Ana Maria had conned him into going with her to interview people at the Boot Hill for her show that night. The last time he was there, the odor of cigarettes and beer farts had nearly gagged him. Arn had even warned Ana Maria and her cameraman to wear a respirator the moment they crossed the threshold. But Bobbie had other things in mind now. "They got some food there?" he asked.

"I wouldn't recommend eating the popcorn," Arn answered. "And I suspect Flo sucks the chocolate off the covered peanuts." He got little reaction except a lazy shrug from the cameraman. Quite a different reaction from the one he'd offered Ana Maria when she'd asked him to accompany her there. "Why do you need me to go along?" he'd asked over supper.

"Because every drunk in the bar will be hitting on me unless they think I'm spoken for."

"If Arn goes as your partner," Danny had chimed in, "folks will think you're trolling retirement homes for dates."

"Thanks, Danny," Arn had said. "But I'm not quite ready to swap dentures and have wheel chair races yet."

Ana Maria leaned against her VW's fender, looking at the tall Boot Hill bar sign leaning to starboard atop the building. "It'll be all right," she said, snapping her compact case shut. She pulled her long hair back and wrapped a tie around it. "Just be here to look intimidating if anyone hits on me."

"We've pretty much mined this dirty little treasure trove of a bar for all the information we can get," Arn argued.

"Maybe not." Ana Maria motioned to her cameraman, who was adjusting his equipment. "You'll be surprised what people will tell me if they think they're going to be on TV. If they think they'll be famous for a night."

Arn knew as much from working with Ana Maria last winter. She could get folks to open up when he'd called the investigation a dead end. People often told her things—all sorts of things—they wouldn't have told a cop. Or a private investigator.

He led the way into the Boot Hill, smoke escaping the moment he opened the door. He nearly gagged as he picked out a table while Ana Maria—with Bobbie in tow—began making the rounds. She talked to drunks in the bar packed with cowboys and oil workers, mechanics just off the job and lounge lizards looking to score for the night.

Arn started to sit on a high stool when he felt the seat. It was sticky with God-knew-what, and he carefully sat on the other side of the round table. He began to settle in and wait for Ana Maria to finish when someone grabbed his arm. He jerked away, but Flo Martin tugged harder. For an anemic-looking ninety-pounder, there was strength in those bony talons. "Let's dance," she said through her toothless grin, dragging him toward the dance floor.

"My wife won't be happy—"

"Not that young women who came in with you?" Flo said, her words slurred, fresh-spilled beer decorating the front of her apron. "She's young enough to be your daughter." She took a long drag from her cigarette as she led Arn to the middle of the dance floor, where two other couples—only slightly drunker than Flo—propped each other up from falling down as they swayed to the jukebox music. "Surely you're not going to pass that girl off as your wife?"

"You were right the first time," Arn said as he tried unsuccessfully to disengage himself from Flo. "She *is* my daughter, and she'll spill the beans to the missus. I'll bribe her with a few drinks, and—"

"—that's the TV lady. Just recognized her." Flo rubbed her blood-shot eyes. "Is she filming in here?" She stopped undulating against Arn and shook her head. "You tried to snooker ol' Flo. That's not your daughter." She pulled Arn tight to her and her meatless hips caressed him. "But I forgive you for bullshitting me."

Then Flo pulled Arn toward a corner of the dance floor where no other couples danced. Suddenly she straightened up and her eyes seemed to clear. And when she spoke, gone was the slur of the inebriated Flo Martin. "Had to get you over here—last thing I want is for my customers thinking I ratted out one of them."

Arn stopped, but Flo swung him around. "Stay moving."

"What's going on?"

She looked over his shoulders, but no one was within earshot. "You wanted me to let you know if I thought of anything else."

"Have you?"

"Not about the night Jillie was killed," Flo answered. "But you might be interested to know that Karen Glass came in here this afternoon. Asking questions."

"What questions?"

Flo stepped on Arn's boot and he jerked it back. "She wanted to know all about when Eddie came in here the night Jillie was murdered. She wanted to know how soon he followed them out, after Jillie ran out after that other guy." Flo put her hand over her heart. "I got me a suspicion."

Arn had worked with enough female officers to know their intuition was often spot-on. He was banking on Flo having just enough female left in her wracked old body to qualify. "What's your suspicion?"

"That she thinks Eddie caught up with Jillie that night. And that they took a drive to Wooly Hank's."

"Did she specifically say that?"

Another couple came close to them and Flo reverted to her drunken partner form before the others sashayed across the floor. "She believes Jillie waited for Eddie outside." Flo stopped and looked seriously at Arn. "And she thinks you believe so, too." She stepped away from him. "You watch yourself. If Karen Glass thinks you suspect her man, believe me, she'll do whatever it takes to protect him."

Flo pulled Arn tight once again. She led while Arn followed, craning his neck around to look for Ana Maria with the hope she would rescue him. But she'd already found someone to talk with, and merely winked at Arn when she spotted him intertwined with Flo. The old woman spun him around, and Arn had to be careful not to step on her frail feet as the music died.

"Shit!" Flo said. "Damned jukebox quit on me again." She patted Arn's cheek. "Don't go anywhere, sugar. I'll be back as soon as I fix this thing."

She staggered toward the jukebox stuffed in the corner of the bar, while Arn, dizzy from the dancing, staggered back to his table and plopped down onto the stool. And he didn't even care if it was a sticky stool.

Ana Maria led a young man through the minefield of drunks on the dance floor to the table and they sat. "This is Mick Flemming," she said, and held her hand high for a waiter. The waiter—a man older than Danny and sporting a chest-length beard just long enough to fall into someone's drink—hobbled over to the table. His *Vietnam Service* hat sat perched on his head and he smiled with a snaggle-tooth grin. Between him and Flo they might have had a full set of choppers. Arn ordered Coke and Ana Maria a Long Island Ice Tea. The drunk kid Ana Maria had brought to the table ordered the exotic stuff since she was buying—Grain Belt on draft.

Ana Maria waited until the bar dog had left to fill their order before leaning across the table. "Mick was here the night Jillie was killed."

"That's right," Mick said. "I was here. Just like I'm here every Saturday night."

"He recalls Jillie," Ana Maria said. "And the guy she followed out."

"That right Mick?" Arn asked.

The bartender returned with their drinks and Arn nodded to Ana Maria. "She'll catch the bar tab," he smirked. "It's on the television station. Just what did you see?" he asked when the bardog left.

Mick slurped the head off the beer and leaned back on his stool. "Jillie was hot that night. But then she usually was. I danced with her a time or two, real close. She rubbed against me like she was trying to start a fire or something. Until Eddie Glass showed up. Then she wanted nothing to do with me. Which was all right. That jealous bastard can be one nasty SOB."

"Tell him about the guy Jillie chased out later," Ana Maria said.

Mick nodded, foam stuck to his mustache before he swiped his shirtsleeve across it. "The guy kept staring at Jillie, checking her out real close when she wasn't looking."

"But you said she looked hot." Arn nursed his Coke. "It'd be natural for some guy to check out a good-lookin' woman."

Mick downed half his beer and ran his tongue across his upper lip. "Weren't nothing natural the way he kept staring at her. Watching her every move." Mick spilled beer on his shirtfront. He grabbed a snotty bandana from around his neck and dabbed at the spill. "She danced with Eddie until she had to go pee, with the guy watching her the whole time. Soon's she went to the crapper, Bonnie Johns came in and grabbed Eddie. Drug him onto the dance floor. They was like that couple in *Saturday Night Fever*. So when Jillie came out of the pisser and saw them, she blew her top. Tried to cut in, but Bonnie shoved her away and she fell over a table. That mean mini Mr. T Flo's got bouncing for her—"

"Karl."

"Yeah, that midget," he answered as he looked nervously around. But luckily for him, it was Karl's night off. "He come from back of the bar and put the habeous grabus on Bonnie. Showed her the door."

Arn sipped his watered-down Coke and marveled how a bartender could screw up something like a cola. "And what was that other guy doing while this was going on?"

"'The weird one? He just kept staring at Jillie." Mick laughed. "By the time Karl broke up the catfight, Eddie had latched onto some dude's old lady and they started dancing. I think that's what set Jillie off."

Arn encountered a long, curly hair in his Coke that looked suspiciously like the waiter's beard, and he spit it out. "Explain what you meant by 'setting Jillie off.'"

Mick held up his hand, and the waiter picked his way through the crowd to the table. "Another round for everyone, Louie," Mick said. "And put it on the TV lady's tab."

Arn held up his glass and Mick clinked it. "Why thanks, Mick. Now, about Jillie—"

"Sure. Jillie. When she saw Eddie and the woman dancing real close, she went on the prod. She looked for someone to dance with, I think, when she finally spied the guy who had been staring at her, drinking all by his lonesome in that corner booth." He pointed across the room. "Well, I'm here to tell you, Jillie ran right up to him. I couldn't make out what she said. I think she wanted to dance, but the guy was having none of it. He tried getting rid of her, but she came right onto him."

"Like she knew him?" Ana Maria asked.

Mick slid off the stool and walked to the bar. He grabbed a bowl of peanuts and sat back down. He offered Arn some, but all Arn could think about was Flo sucking on them, and he passed. "Suit yourself," Mick said, leaning his head back while he tossed a peanut into the air. It failed to land in his gaping mouth and hit the floor. "I moved a little closer to the booth when she started yelling at him."

"Yelling what?"

"Shit like, 'I'm going to spill the beans on you' and shit like that."

"Spill the beans about what?"

Mick tried unsuccessfully to land another peanut in his mouth and gave up. "I never heard what she said, except a lot of cursing. Jillie wasn't exactly a nun. Mattered none to her if she went home with a married guy or not. I got the impression she was going to tell the dude's wife or something."

Arn went to the bar and returned with a small bowl of popcorn, figuring it was safer than the peanuts. It wasn't, he soon learned as he tossed some into his mouth. It was greasy and stale, and he thought he saw another hair matching the one he'd found in his Coke in the middle of it. "I understand Jillie and the guy left together."

"If you call it that with him beat-feeting it to the door and her yelling at his heels."

"You must have gotten a good look at him, then," Ana Maria said.

"'Nother round, Louie," Mick yelled and turned back to Ana Maria. "Sure, I got a good look. He was a little bit bigger than me, maybe five eight, five nine. Stocky guy." Mick snapped his fingers. "And he had cow shit caked on his boots."

Ana Maria paid Louie for Mick's latest glass of panther piss. "It's not unusual for men to have cow crap and horse manure on their boots around here."

Mick slurped the foam from his beer and winked at Ana Maria. "I figured a babe like you would get out more. Be a little more attuned to folks hereabouts."

"If you mean hanging out here"—Ana Maria gestured around the bar—"I don't know how long I'd last before I decked some drunk." She winked back.

Mick tilted his head back and laughed. "You *are* a pistol, lady. But if you got out more, you'd notice things." He waved his hand at men bending elbows at the bar. "See any cow shit caked on any of their boots? I don't."

"I see where you're headed," Arn said. "Cowboys want to clean up before coming to town."

Mick nodded and touched his glass to Ana Maria's drink. "When they come to town snaggin'—as the Indians like to call it—they want to make a good impression. They do that, and they might go home with something besides a hangover."

"Unless that guy just stopped in for just a quick drink." Ana Maria swayed on her stool, her Long Island Ice Tea nearly gone. "Anything else you remember about the guy?"

Mick's foot slipped off the stool rung and Arn caught him before he fell. "I looked at him only once, when I asked a lady in the booth next to his to dance. He looked at me." Mick set his glass on the table. "No, he looked *through* me like I wasn't even there. I said howdy to the dude, but he acted like he didn't even hear me. He just sat there and smoked his Marlboros. But he sure wasn't the Marlboro Man."

"Did you see his face?" Ana Maria pressed.

Mick nodded. "But I can't say exactly what he looked like except he was plain as mud, like damned near everyone else you see in here."

Ana Maria got her cameraman's attention. She ran her finger across her throat, and Bobbie took his camera from his shoulder. He grabbed a last handful of stale popcorn before leaving the bar. Arn helped Ana Maria stand just as Louie brought her the bar tab. She fumbled in her purse before Arn took it and grabbed money to pay the bill.

He led Ana Maria past the alcohol reader. She stopped and read the sign beside the machine. "I think I can qualify for a blender."

"Not tonight," Arn said. He was leading her away from the machine when Mick stopped them

"One other thing," he said as he staggered along behind them. He stopped and used a stool for support. "One other thing I'd do: I'd check the emergency room. 'Cause when Eddie stormed out of here, he had bad intentions written all over his face. Bad as his temper is, once he started beating the guy, I doubt he'd let up."

Twenty-One

ARN PULLED INTO THE parking lot at the Archer Complex in front of the arena that hosted the dog class. He walked into the pole barn and stood by the bleachers, taking in the musty odor of recent sheep dung, the hushed whispers of students as they watched the instructor giving silent commands to her dog. The beginning and intermediate classes sat with their dogs, observing Bonnie's Border collie as she worked sheep in the pen. Bonnie—looking considerably more human now that she was sober and cleaned up—gave commands with her hand.

Beverly sat next to Eddie Glass in the bleachers beside other spectators watching the exhibition. Then Eddie stood and smoothed his jeans, pressed with a crease sharp enough you'd slice your hand on it. He ran his finger under the flowing red silk bandana around his neck as he walked to the center of the arena. His back to the class, he bent and said something to Bonnie before motioning to her dog.

Arn joined Beverly on the bottom row of bleachers.

"He's fine-tweaking Buckwheat," Beverly said as if reading his mind. "The dog needs more work. Eddie's like that—always helping folks with their dogs."

"Fine dog of hers."

"Buckwheat is my dog," Beverly said. "I bought her out of Eddie's litter two years ago. I thought it'd be good for Bonnie to get some working-time with her."

Eddie stepped aside and let Bonnie send the Border collie after three sheep milling together at the far side of the arena. "So how have you been holding up?" Arn asked.

"Holding up?"

"Don. I understand you two were close."

Beverly grabbed a can of Copenhagen from her shirt pocket. "Don thought we were closer than we actually were." She paused and looked away. "That sounded cold, didn't it?"

Arn waved the air as if to dismiss the comment. "I just thought with him helping teach the class …" He trailed off.

"Don was a friend who sometimes helped me around the ranch."

"And with your class, to be close to you, the way it sounds."

"He did." Beverly replaced the can in her pocket. "But we weren't an item if that's what you heard."

"Sometimes I assume things when I shouldn't," Arn said, pulling out his pocket notebook. His prop. "Did Don fight with anyone in the class lately? Maybe someone he'd had a run-in with recently?"

Beverly laughed. "That would take more ambition than he had. No, Don was the easy-going type. You could have spit in his face and he would have just smiled at you before wiping it off."

Eddie moved closer to Bonnie on one side of the arena, and Arn stretched his legs out in front of him. "I thought this was your and Bonnie's class."

"How's that?"

"Eddie," Arn said. "It appears that he's conducting the class."

Beverly smiled and motioned to Eddie. "He had nothing else to do today. He just returned from a show, and he was gracious enough to stop and help. Why?"

Arn shrugged. "Just curious. It looks like it'll be a while before I can visit with him."

"What do you need to talk with him for?"

Arn waited until Bonnie's dog had singled out one sheep with a green X spray-painted on its back and herded it toward her. "I'm trying to piece together that night Bonnie and Jillie had a fight at the Boot Hill. Eddie was there, and I needed some clarification. I thought if I could talk with him—"

"He don't know nothing."

Arn's eyebrows rose. "I didn't realize you were at the bar that night."

"I wasn't," Beverly blurted out. "But I know what my sister told me, and Eddie was nowhere near Jillie when she left."

"Don't mind if I ask him myself?"

"Suit yourself. But it's going to be a while."

"Then I'll be outside getting some fresh air. Tell Eddie I need to speak with him again."

"I will, but be easy on him. His dog just bit him a couple days ago, and he's a little self-conscious about it."

"I'll do nothing to hurt his self-esteem," Arn said, and left the arena.

Fresh horse dung from a recent riding clinic drifted past Arn's nose. He'd ridden all his life, even doing some pleasure riding when he lived in Denver. He often thought about buying another horse, but never did. And buying one for working cows those odd times wasn't an option anymore. His afternoon in the saddle helping Little Jim

Reilly with his heifers had convinced him he was a little over the hill to be riding. Still, it remained a temptation that always tugged at him.

Arn fished the folded envelope containing the paint chip out of its familiar place in his shirt pocket and began walking the parking lot. With a larger chip, and time, a lab could tell him the year range and manufacturer of the vehicle that left the paint transfer on Wooly Hank's fence post. But he had so little a chip to go on—hardly enough to send to the police lab, even if Slade would agree to do it—it seemed futile. The color was like many blue trucks around town, and Arn knew he would have to rely on his eyes.

There were two cars and two pickups in the lot of a similar color to the chip he'd dug out of Wooly Hank's fence post. At each vehicle, Arn bent and ran his hand over the tires. The tire mark he'd seen in the pasture that morning would produce a sizable gouge in a sidewall, yet none of the tires showed anything like that.

"What the hell you doing around my truck?" Eddie Glass half-ran across the parking lot. He stopped within arm's reach of Arn and stood with one fist clenched, the other wrapped in a dirty gauze bandage. Eddie's temper was evident in his piercing eyes and the way his jaw muscles worked overtime suppressing his rage. "I said, what the hell you doing around my truck?"

"I didn't know this was your truck." Arn stood and arched his back, looking around the lot for a way to maneuver should Eddie explode in flailing fists.

"You got no business—"

"If you think I was breaking into your truck, feel free to call the sheriff's office. I'll just wait here." Arn tried to hand Eddie his phone, but he backed away.

"I just want to know why you're looking at my pickup," he snapped.

Arn motioned around the parking lot. "I've been looking at many trucks this last week. Ones with a color like this." He opened his hand to show Eddie the chip.

Eddie didn't look at it, just continued his stare down. "You want to ask me something, ask. Don't sneak around."

"All right then," Arn began. "Let's begin by clearing up the night Jillie was murdered."

"You already know what I did that night."

"Humor me," Arn said.

"What's there to clear up?" Eddie shook out a Pall Mall and lit it. "I told Deputy Slade everything that went on." He smirked. "I'd bet there are ways you can get your hands on that interview."

"I can," Arn lied. Slade would never let him see the video of the interview. All he'd say would be that Eddie's alibi was weak. "The tape showed you had no one to corroborate your statement that Jillie was gone when you ran out of the bar."

"You think I lied?" Eddie stepped closer to Arn.

Arn took a step back and slipped the paint chip into his pocket, fully expecting the Eddie Glass temper to boil to the surface. He would be a handful, and Arn braced himself. "You could have made any outlandish statements, and if there's no one to back you up ... well, you understand why I'm skeptical," he said.

"Like Karen told you the other day, she found me at the Outlaw. Hauled my ass out of there."

"So she claimed." Arn debated telling Eddie he knew he and Karen had been barred from entering the Outlaw Saloon. But he held that pearl of information close to his vest.

"Jillie had already left with that other dude by the time I ran outside," Eddie continued. "If I'd've caught up with him, he'd have been drinking his supper through a straw for a month."

"That how you always handle your affairs?" Arn smiled, taunting. He'd had his butt-full of the smart-ass fuming in front of him. "By beating people?"

"If they need it."

"And you're sure Jillie didn't need a beating that night for coming on to that guy?"

Arn heard Eddie's teeth gnash, his face reddened to the point that he was about to erupt. Arn read his eyes, saw some internal debate about whether or not to attack him. But then Eddie breathed deeply and turned away.

He was heading back to the arena when Arn called after him, "When did you get these tires?"

Eddie stopped and half-turned around. "Recently," he said slowly. "Why?"

"They're new."

"So, I needed tires."

"But this truck is"—Arn bent to the taillight and read the year of manufacture—"only two years old."

"So?"

"So, why would a person need new tires on a two-year-old truck? You're running Coopers. You buy them at Fat Boy's Tire?"

"I bought them somewhere on my last road trip. They were getting threadbare." Eddie walked back to Arn. "Is this going somewhere?"

"You tell me. Jillie's killer may have driven a truck with a huge gouge out of one sidewall and tread. It made a distinctive pattern in the dirt. Would've been trouble, as bad as the gouge was." Arn tapped Eddie's tire with his hand. "Now, when did you decided to replace these—the Monday after Jillie's murder?"

"Listen, Anderson, before I stomp a mudhole in your ass, let it drop. I drive all across the West and Midwest giving seminars. Dog shows. Me and the dog see a lot of road time—"

"I thought you were a ranch hand? Most ranchers wouldn't want to lose their help that many days in a year."

Eddie smiled. "Me and the owner's got an understanding: if I'm not back Monday morning following a seminar or a show, he'll let me make it up. Besides, Karen can help out. She's a dyed-in-the-silk ranch gal."

Arn thought back to Dr. Oakert: his special patient was a troller, ranging far afield just to meet up with that perfect victim. "So how many miles *do* you drive a year?"

Eddie closed his eyes. "Forty thousand. Fifty thousand. What the hell's that got to do with anything?"

"Nothing," Arn answered. *Unless you're meeting your victims far away.*

Twenty-Two

I SEE ANDERSON WALKING around the parking lot. From time to time he looks at something in his hand. I finally notice that he compares what he has to trucks and cars parked outside the arena. A sliver of paint, perhaps? Probably for the same reason I've been checking parking lots looking for a match for that broken marker light I picked up at Wooly Hank's, hoping to find that one vehicle at Walmart or Kmart or the bars in town it belongs to. Is the paint sliver in Anderson's hand mine? I don't recall hitting anything when I drove like a crazy man out of the pasture. But then I was just a little pumped up by the adrenaline, with the rancher coming fast at my back and the witness getting away in front of me. Farm trucks always have dings and scrapes on them. I might have left some paint on that wooden gate of Wooly Hank's, but I doubt it. But if Anderson has a paint chip, that means the law probably doesn't, and I'm not worried. Much.

I've tried to convince myself that Jillie wasn't a mistake. I always plan meticulously, running every scenario over in my head before following through. Isn't that what Dr. Oakert always told me—make sure you follow

142

through with your plans? Of course, he was referring to my treatment goals for any particular session with him. But Jillie had forced the issue, made me act impulsively before she talked her fool head off and the whole world knew about me.

I look at Don Whales as a mistake, then I bite my tongue. He wasn't a mistake: he was just someone who could have been the witness, could have been the Midnight Sheepherder. And even though he wasn't, and I silenced him anyway, he might have broken through his dull fog and remembered me in the Boot Hill that Saturday night. Still, I wish I hadn't had to wrestle with that big bastard. He damn near broke my hip when he fell backwards on me, and he took a years' worth of hide off my neck with those guitarist's fingernails.

But unlike Jillie, Don Whales was different. Listening to the police scanner, I know Slade and the evidence techs were with the coroner for hours looking for anything explaining why he was killed at the amphitheater. They may be small town, but Slade—I suspect—is thorough when he works his crime scenes. They found nothing, I'm certain. It was all in the planning. Dr. Oakert would be proud of me. Of my progress. Like he always has been before.

What would my doctor friend say to me if he had me on his couch? Would he accuse me of relapsing? Would he say I fell off the wagon like a common alcoholic? But the good doctor would be wrong to say that. Relapsing indicates you stopped what you were doing and, in a moment of weakness, started again. I didn't relapse. Except for the years in Napa Hospital, I never stopped. Even those years, I hunted in my mind's eye.

Anderson runs his hand over tires, looking for imperfections. Why else would he be doing that? I know he won't find any obvious ones. It was over-obvious to me the morning I walked around my truck after the tire had caught that fence post and lost a chunk of one sidewall. I almost hadn't heard it over Jillie's screaming as we drove into the field, so I bought a new set that Monday morning.

And now that I'm a free man, I will remain so. Free to find ladies with like-minded attitudes that see things just my way.

But I need to stay off the internet, stay off the road while I find that witness. That TV lady has a way of finding out things, I've heard. Maybe I'm tailing the wrong person—maybe I should see where she goes, who she talks with.

Or it may be time for another therapy session with the good doctor. And a session with Anderson, if the doctor told him about me.

Twenty-Three

ARN LOADED NEW BATTERIES into his flashlight and grabbed the Thermos of coffee from Danny. "I think you ought to rethink burning the flame at both ends," Danny said. "Between staying out nights and working Jillie's case during the day, you're dragging your keister."

Arn patted Danny on the shoulder. "Thanks for the concern. But the one night I'm not sitting on some pasture is when the Midnight Sheepherder will strike. I'll be okay."

He grabbed his binoculars from the nail beside the door and stepped into the cool night. As he started away from the house, he just hoped he'd be able to stay awake. For one more night.

Arn drove through the open gate into the pasture. Sheep munched on grass, glancing only briefly at the gold-colored car driving slowly through the flock. Mike Shaffer, president of the Wool Growers Association, had called him earlier that afternoon. Mike was convinced the rustler would hit either his north field or his neighbor's south sheep pasture. "It's been months since I've had sheep stolen," he told Arn over the phone. "I'm about due." Like most of the wool growers, Mike didn't think that Jillie was half of the Midnight Sheepherder. He didn't think that her death would stop the thefts. And neither did Arn.

He doused his lights and stuck his head out the window, flicking on his flashlight to see where he was going. He drove a hundred yards and came upon a slight rise where he could look over Mike's pasture as well as the neighbor's, so he settled back.

As Arn cupped his hand around a mug of hot coffee, his eyes closed for a moment. Movement outside his window caused him to snap awake. Sheep grazed right outside his window, and he breathed with relief. The Midnight Sheepherder *was* still alive, and Arn was certain it was only a matter of time before he struck again.

He thought about the homicides, and what Slade had said to him: he shouldn't be out here at night. A retired cop sneaking up on sixty ought to be snug in front of a fire, robe wrapped around him, reading his favorite classic. Arn thought so too. Until he recalled officers he'd worked with who did just that: kicked their feet up after retirement. Took it easy. After a few weeks, could name all the popular soap opera stars. And died within a few short years from boredom and inactivity. Arn had no desire to go the way of those retired cops. His grandfather had lived to ninety-two staying active, and Arn was certain his father would have too if a train hadn't highballed through Cheyenne and caught him passed out in his car on the tracks.

Still, he thought as he fought to keep his eyes open, there was something to be said for a warm place to sleep right about now.

He closed his eyes. For just a moment he would rest them, certain any rustler entering Mike's pasture would awaken him.

———

146

Cold steel jammed into Arn's ear woke him. He clawed for his gun, but a familiar female voice standing beside his car door thought otherwise. "Skin that gun I know you carry and toss it out the window or you're a dead man."

Arn carefully brought his leg up and took his gun from his ankle holster. He tossed it out the window.

"Now put your hands on the wheel."

Arn wrapped his fingers around his steering wheel and turned his head ever so slightly. Karen Glass stood next to the car door. She held a Judge in her hand, a behemoth of a revolver capable of firing .45 and .410 shotgun rounds. There was just enough moonlight for Arn to recognize the look on her face: she intended to kill him. "I'm betting this little meeting is about Eddie," he said.

"You're smarter than you look," she replied. "You've been making noise that Eddie murdered Jillie Reilly. He didn't."

"Because he was in the Outlaw Saloon?" Arn inched his hand lower on the wheel. "What if I told you I believe you?"

Karen laughed, but there was no humor in her voice. "I don't believe your cock-and-bull. You've got it in your mind that Eddie murdered Jillie, and nothing I can do will change that."

"And if Sergeant Slade knows what I found out—that you and Eddie weren't in the Outlaw that night? That you've both been barred from entering the bar?"

"You have been busy."

"Where was Eddie that night?" Arn asked, his hand slipping ever so slightly lower on the wheel. "Because he wasn't at the Outlaw. Maybe giving Jillie her last ride. And where was he when Don Whales was murdered?"

Karen shoved the cold muzzle of her gun tight against Arn's cheek. "Eddie was out of town that night," she said between her teeth clenched tight. "At a dog show."

"You don't believe that. I'd bet that even you believe he followed Jillie out the Boot Hill"—hand sliding lower—"and you feel he would be good for Don's death."

"Horseshit—"

"Why else follow me here? Don't you think Slade's going to zero in on you when I'm found dead?" Arn's hand was now close to the door handle.

Karen chuckled again. "Just say good night, Mr. Anderson."

She jammed the muzzle harder into his cheek and cocked the revolver just as he grabbed the door handle. Arn jerked upward and threw his head to one side, away from the muzzle of the gun.

Karen fired, the deafening sound bouncing around the confines of the Oldsmobile as Arn shoved the door with his shoulder. It hit Karen on the hip, and he drove the door open all the way. She reeled back, fighting to regain her composure as she fired again. Shotgun pellets bounced off the windshield and peppered Arn's face as Karen fell to the ground. Arn threw himself on her and pinned the gun to the dirt as bleating sheep scurried in all directions.

Karen bit his ear and tried kneeing him in the groin. "You son-of-a-bitch—"

Arn snatched her gun and tossed it aside. "Just say good night, Karen." He doubled up his fist and laid a right cross square on her jaw.

Twenty-Four

WHEN SOMEONE BANGED ON the front door, Arn missed the drywall nail and nailed his thumb with the hammer. "Now will you listen to me and let me do that?" Danny asked as Arn stuck his thumb in his mouth. "Just see who's here and I'll finish up this sheet."

Dropping his tool belt, Arn answered the door. Sergeant Slade smirked at the thumb stuck in his mouth. "Going through your second childhood?"

"Cute," Arn said. "What do you want?"

"Aren't you going to invite me in?"

Arn stepped aside and Slade entered. He stood with his thumbs hooked in his belt. "Very impressive," he said as he looked around the entryway leading to the living room on one side, the kitchen on the other. "I remember in my patrol days backing up the city on juvie parties in this dump a few times." He motioned to the front lawn. "Don't recall that old Montana Mini Storage—"

"That what?"

149

"Montana Mini Storage. That's what we call junk like that old International truck parked in your weed field you call a lawn. About all it's good for is storing crap in it. Anyways, I always thought this place should have been condemned. It never looked this good, though."

"Tell me you have something besides old memories of my mother's home to share. Like tell me how the interrogation of Karen Glass went."

"In due time," Slade said. "What I have now is a case of the ass. I thought we agreed to share information?"

"I did share." Arn motioned for Slade to follow him to the kitchen.

"Not from what I heard. You paid a visit to Eddie Glass at the Archer Complex during the dog class."

"Let's jaw over coffee."

Slade stopped when he saw Danny bent over a bucket of drywall nails in the hallway. "Didn't I run you in for panhandling a time or two?"

"Once. And once for dumpster diving. But I like to think of this"—he waved his hand around—"as changing my economic situation."

"Slade." Arn motioned to the kitchen.

"What's with the old dude?" Slade stopped in the kitchen. "You running a geriatric daycare out of your home?"

Arn jerked his thumb at Danny walking down the hallway. "That old man can work us both into the ground." He poured each of them a cup of coffee and sat at the table with his notebook.

Slade reached over and flipped Arn's ear lobe. "Looks like she got you good." He grinned.

"Damn lucky she didn't kill me. Bad enough she shot the hell out of my windshield. You know how hard it is to get one for a 1970 Olds?"

"I was wondering where it was. New windshield, huh?"

"Just tell me what Karen said."

Slade stirred sugar into his coffee and crossed his long legs. "That's one tough woman. She refused to say anything without her lawyer."

"Who is?"

"She doesn't have one. Not like she and Eddie are swimming in greenbacks. She'll have a public defender assigned tomorrow at arraignment." Slade scrunched his nose up. "What the hell's this?"

"Chicory," Arn answered as he killed the taste with sugar and creamer. "It's Danny's idea to keep me healthy."

Slade set his cup down and pushed it away. "I did my best to get Karen to open up but she wouldn't take my bait. But when I told her I knew she drew down on you because she was just protecting her husband, that little twitch came on."

Arn forced himself to sip the chicory as he eyed the kitchen door. About one more sip and he'd sneak his cup into the sink and pour it out. "Karen knew Eddie disappeared right after leaving the Boot Hill. And when Eddie didn't come home right after that, she must have thought he was the one who took Jillie for a ride."

Arn made his move to the kitchen sink and poured the chicory out. Slade handed him his cup and Arn tossed that out as well. "If Karen risked it all thinking Eddie's the killer, she must be going on more than just a feeling," Arn said. "You don't set out to kill a man on a damn hunch."

"Which she won't say," Slade replied. "Now, you were going to share what you found out from Eddie after dog class."

"I was going to look you up as soon as I finished hanging drywall." Arn began to explain when Ana Maria plodded into the room, sweatpants riding low, pajama top riding over her belly, rubbing sleepers from her eyes. She paid Slade no mind as she poured herself a cup.

"Well, you old dog, you." Slade grinned as Ana Maria sat at the table and began to butter a piece of bread. "Not even a 'morning, sweetheart'?" he asked.

"Morning, asshole," Ana Maria said, and the smile faded from Slade's face.

Arn flipped notebook pages. "Eddie Glass drives his truck in excess of forty thousand miles a year. Maybe as much as fifty thousand, going to training seminars and dog trials."

"What's your point?"

"I spotted a tire impression—and your evidence tech cast one—in the dirt that showed one of the trucks in Wooly Hank's pasture that night had a sizeable chunk out of the sidewall and tread."

"He did cast one. And you think Eddie's truck has such a tire?"

"No," Arn answered. "Eddie's truck's wearing new skins all around."

Slade shrugged. "So he has a reason to travel a lot. If I did that much driving, I'd need tires periodically too."

Arn flipped to another page. "Dr. Oakert said the killer we're looking for trolls—drives long distances to meet up with that perfect victim."

Slade threw up his hands. "Well, there you go. I'll just go to the County Attorney and tell them to cut a warrant for Eddie Glass because he drives a lot to his dog shows." He stood and looked down at Ana Maria before she pulled her top up, which had fallen south over her shoulder. "Just because Karen thinks he might be Jillie's killer doesn't mean she's right about her husband."

Ana Maria laid her hand lightly on Arn's arm. "I'm sure that Sergeant Slade is working his tail off on Jillie and Don Whales's cases. And by now the teletype he sent probably came back with more matches than he has time to follow up on."

"What teletype?" Slade asked warily.

Arn picked up on Ana Maria's prodding. "The Triple I—the regional teletype—that you sent out asking if agencies had homicides involving a similar MO as our killer."

Slade looked away, and Ana Maria rested her hand on his arm. "I'm sure it's just an oversight on your part. That or you've been so overworked preparing for the election it slipped your mind."

"It's supposed to be sent out this morning."

"Don't you beat all," Arn said. "You didn't send one."

"I was going to," Slade sputtered, "when I had more information to go on."

"And you wonder why I don't trust you when I find shit out."

Slade's face turned red and he blurted out, "I also came here to tell you about the tox report that came back on Jillie. No drugs, but she never was a druggie. And Don was as sober as my priest."

Ana Maria leaned forward. "Is Don's autopsy completed?"

Slade shook his head. "You know I can't talk with a civilian about it."

"Remember that sheriff's race this fall?" Ana Maria said. "I'm in a position to put you in a good light again, if I can get some information now. Off the record until it's releasable."

Slade thought a moment. "All right, here's what we have: Don put up a tremendous struggle the night he was attacked. Drums and guitars scattered and broken all over that amphitheater. But the interesting thing at autopsy was beaucoup amounts of skin under his nails. Whoever strangled Don to death was powerful. But Don also took some hide off his killer."

"How much of this do you want to go to air with?" Ana Maria asked.

Slade misread her and scooted a little closer. "I'm not sure yet. Maybe we'll have to talk about it over dinner."

Ana Maria smiled wide. "That is an excellent idea. Danny!" she yelled. Danny came into the kitchen and took off his earphones. "Now what?"

Ana Maria chin-pointed to Slade. "Sergeant Slade will be our guest for dinner tonight."

Danny smiled knowingly. "Great, deputy. You'll love it. You've never had deer liver and onions like ol' Danny makes it." He chuckled. "With prune pudding for desert."

Twenty-Five

THE LOCK ON THE front door rattled and Arn instinctively reached for the gun in his ankle holster. He forgot he'd left it on the kitchen counter, and he felt foolish. Ana Maria came into the house and walked into the half-finished living room that had once been Arn's mother's sewing room. It was the room in the house that was closest to being completed, and she dropped into the bean bag chair the "chair fairy" had left for Danny. "What you watching?"

Danny paused the recording. "Last year's episodes of *Days of Our Lives*. Aiden just about killed Hope before Bo rescued her." He jerked his thumb at Arn. "And Mr. Congeniality here is brooding."

"I am not brooding," Arn said. He absently smeared polish on his boots and turned to Ana Maria. "I'm just running Jillie and Don's scenarios through my head."

"We saw your special tonight," Danny said. "The high sheriff's going to be miffed with you giving Slade so much air time."

Ana Maria uncapped a water bottle. "I wanted to knee that fool in the jewels tonight. If he keeps up with that baseless theory that Jillie was one of a rustling team, we're never going to get anywhere."

"We saw he was back espousing that crap," Arn said. Under the bright lights of the TV camera, Slade had claimed as proof that Jillie was a member of the rustling ring the fact that no more sheep thefts had occurred since her murder.

"And he believes that the other half of the team fled after killing Don Whales," Ana Maria said. "Just what I need on top of someone following me from work."

Arn set his boots and shoe brush down. "Who followed you?"

Ana Maria didn't answer, but she glanced at the front door.

Arn picked up on it and looked in the direction she did. "You look like you've seen a ghost. One follow you in here or something?"

Ana Maria shuddered. "I didn't actually see anyone following me. I ... felt someone was back there."

Danny turned off the television and stood. "You need something to calm you down."

He left the room, and Arn turned his chair to face Ana Maria. "How do you know you were followed?"

"I just know it. Don't ask me how. Call it women's intuition or something."

Arn knew her feelings were righteous. Back when he worked the street, he'd had several woman patrol partners. He'd learned that whenever they indicated things weren't right, he should listen. And he'd had his butt saved more than a few times heeding their hunches. "When did it start?"

Ana Maria rubbed her temples. "This afternoon. I went to the sheriff's office to meet with Slade about tonight's airing, and as soon as I left, I *felt* it." She held up her hand. "I know it sounds crazy—"

Arn laid his hand on her arm. "No, it doesn't."

Danny returned with bowls of ice cream for all and handed Ana Maria the biggest one. "This will help you."

"It will?"

"Hell if I know," Danny said. "But I've been looking for an excuse to have ice cream all night." He took a small spoonful into his mouth. "Maybe it was Little Jim Reilly following you. He was stalking Arn."

"That's a possibility," Ana Maria said.

"Maybe not." Arn licked ice cream from the side of his bowl. "You say you never saw the person following you?"

Ana Maria waved the air with her spoon. "I'm probably overreacting, what with the killer still on the loose and me the focal point of the TV special. But no, I never actually saw anyone on my tail."

Arn set his ice cream down. "Let's go on the premise that someone *is* following you. If that's the case, it's hard to believe it's Little Jim. Remember me telling you how clumsy he was when he tailed me? I made him right off, and confronted him even easier. That man's not cunning enough to follow someone without being spotted."

"Maybe he learned something when he tailed you," Ana Maria said. "Maybe he got a whole lot cagier once you made him. After all, he wants to find his daughter's killer in the worst way."

"All the same, let's go on the assumption that someone besides Little Jim is following you." Arn motioned to Danny. "Double check all the window locks, and test the alarm."

"I'll get right on it," Danny said and left the room.

"Maybe I'd better pack my revolver from now on," Ana Maria said. "The sooner we catch this killer, the sooner we can all relax." She finished her ice cream and sank lower in the chair. "Slade is convinced that the guy Jillie chased out of the bar might have been one of her

157

rustling partners. That's what she was going to squeal on the guy about."

"Then why confront him that night in the bar?" Arn asked. "And if it was her partner, outing him would be as bad for her."

Ana Maria shrugged. "Slade thinks the booze replaced whatever good judgment she might have had that night." She stood and glanced at the front door as if expecting someone to come busting in. "What did Eddie Glass tell you about his new set of tires?"

Arn explained how Eddie justified buying new tires. "He told me to pack sand when I asked where he bought them. 'You don't believe me, you can kiss my behind,' he told me. 'Figure that out yourself, mister investigator.'"

"Well, I talked with him twice," Ana Maria said, "and each time— besides hitting on me—he got a little too close in my space for my comfort."

"Of course he hit on you. He's a womanizer and you're an attractive lady."

"Then why did he preface it with 'even though you're not exactly my type' before he insisted on shaking hands? I wanted to douse myself in hand sanitizer after that."

"Don't get on his bad side if you talk with him again," Arn said. "The man's got a temper. I'm thinking he needs more anger management therapy with Dr. Oakert. If I'd have pushed a little yesterday, he would have taken a swing at me."

"That's what Slade said. Eddie stomped into the jail today demanding they release Karen. The detention officers had to call in the street deputies to escort him out. Slade says Eddie holds us both accountable for Karen's arrest." She laid her hand on his shoulder. "I'm just glad you were able to get the best of her."

Arn finished his ice cream and set his bowl on the floor. "She'll be waiting a bond hearing, but keep your eyes pasted for Eddie. I'm thinking he's not going to take his woman getting arrested lying down."

"That's what some chick at the bar told me who went home with Eddie just once." Ana Maria wrapped her arms around herself as if she were cold. "'He liked the rough stuff,' this woman said. 'Slapped me around, and pulled a hunk of my hair out.' She said that Saturday night when she spotted Eddie come into the Boot Hill, she lit out the back before he saw her."

The front door alarm chirped and Danny quickly reset it before coming back into the room. "So we got Eddie who is a possessive SOB," he said as he picked up his bowl of melted ice cream. "And we got the guy who Jillie chased out of the bar as suspects."

"And we got the third suspect," Arn said. "What my training officer as a rookie told me. 'There's always that suspect you don't see,' Rolf Vincent used to say, 'and that'll be your real suspect, dummy.'"

"You're suggesting there's a third suspect we haven't thought of?" Ana Maria asked.

"That's just what I'm saying." Arn finished his ice cream and picked up his boots and the brush.

Danny collected the bowls and set them aside. "We still don't know what connects Don Whales to Jillie, except he was playing with his band at the Boot Hill that night."

"Did you find out anything else about Don?" Arn asked.

Ana Maria grabbed a long reporter's notebook from her purse and flipped pages. "Nothing new. Retired Army vet. Worked the motor pool in Iraq. Little disposable income. He formed his band not so much because he had a love of music but because he needed to make some extra money to supplement his mechanic side business."

"I got it. I got it," Danny blurted out. He stood and paced in front of Arn and Ana Maria as if he were addressing a jury. "How about this: Slade might be right—Jillie might have been one part of the Midnight Sheepherder, and her partner might have been Don. Maybe when she ran out the bar that night she never left with anybody, but waited for him until he was done playing for the evening."

Arn nudged Danny. "You just might make an investigator."

"Might." Danny smiled. "How's this—after his nightly gig wrapped up, Don and Jillie took a drive, maybe to steal sheep, and things went south between them." He wrapped his hands around his thin neck. "And that was lights out for Jillie."

Arn held his boots to the light. "I don't know. I'm still convinced Don was murdered because he saw the killer that night in the bar. And it was just a matter of time before he realized it."

"Or that third suspect." Danny smiled. "See, it's practically solved."

Twenty-Six

ARN STOPPED BY STARBUCKS and grabbed coffee with three extra shots. He'd been up all night watching two different pastures, hoping to catch the Midnight Sheepherder after Wooly Hank called and gave him a heads-up. The Wool Growers Association had had an emergency meeting: although sheep hadn't been stolen in the last two weeks, they were concerned that their money spent on a range detective was money down the toilet. They wanted someone prosecuted for the thefts, and they blamed Arn for not catching the rustler. And last night had been no different—he'd had no luck catching the thief, sitting listening to coyotes and seeing the occasional shooting star. He'd been alone with his thoughts surrounding Jillie's murder. It showed him he was missing some things that had been right before him.

He made his rounds to local body shops on the list he'd made last night. He drove to other dealerships and independent repair shops looking for any evidence of someone bringing in a truck with fresh, unexplained damage. The sixth shop—the body shop connected to the Ford dealership—panned out. The shop manager, Roy Bechtholdt, emerged from under a new aluminum-bodied Ford Super Duty and wiped his hands on his trousers. "Dotty said you were looking for someone who might have brought in a truck with front end damage." He waved his hand around the crowded shop that looked like a bone pile from the demolition derby. "We got us a bunch of wrecked trucks. Take your pick."

Arn handed him a business card. Roy took his reading glasses from the top of his head and held the card to the light. "You're that PI the TV station hired."

Arn nodded. "I'm not sure just what kind of damage I'm looking for, but I know it might come across as front end damage about this color." He unwrapped the envelope and showed Roy the paint chip.

"Pretty common-looking blue," Roy said.

"Then what do you make of this." Arn unwrapped the other tiny envelope with the marker or taillight lens he'd recovered from beside Wooly Hank's gate.

Roy carefully took the slivers of plastic and held them to the light. "Ah," he said knowingly. "It's from a 1998 Dodge Ram truck with a Cummins diesel and a five-speed transmission."

"You can tell that from that tiny piece?"

Roy laughed and handed it back. "Of course not. I'm just shittin' you. There's not enough to determine what the hell vehicle this came from."

"Thanks," Arn said. "Call me if anything unusual comes in."

He'd started for the door when Roy stopped him. "Some cowboy came to the dealership last week wanting to trade in a truck."

"Is that odd?"

"No." Roy hitched up his jeans, which were falling a bit south. "The boss wanted me to check it out. See what kind of shape it was in for a trade. The frame was bent, the box catawampus. It had a hundred twenty thousand miles."

"I still don't follow you—"

"The truck was two years old and been in one too many scrapes," Roy said. "Who the hell puts that many miles on a ranch truck? I told the boss it was junk, and he passed on offering a trade to the guy."

"You have a name?"

"Roy."

"I meant the guy with the truck."

"Can't help you there."

"You recall what the guy looked like?"

Roy shrugged. "Looked like you or me. Well, he looked like you anyway—kinda plain." When Arn didn't laugh, Roy continued. "I mean the guy was like a dozen other fellers who come through the shop every day. He was just average height. Average looking. Sorry."

Arn was half-way to his car when Roy called after him. "When the boss turned the guy down for a trade-in, the new kid in the shop—Brandin—said his brother might be interested in buying it outright. Brandin called his brother, and he made a deal over the phone."

"What's his brother's name?" Arn asked as he grabbed his pen.

"Don't know," Roy answered. "Brandin will be back after lunch, and I'll call you with the name."

———

Roy called Arn after lunch and gave him Brandin's brother's cell number. "Floyd is just finishing up his welding class at the college for the day." Arn called Floyd's number, and he agreed to meet at the campus.

When Arn drove onto the campus grounds, he spotted Floyd's truck right off: a Ford three-quarter ton sporting oversize wheels and tires more at home at the Baja than driving the mean streets of Cheyenne. He pulled beside Floyd and craned his neck upwards. "You Floyd?"

"Yes siree," he said, and looked over Arn's car. "Cool ride. For sale?"

"You couldn't afford the gas." Arn rubbed his neck. "Can you parachute down from there so we can talk?"

Floyd used the grab handles to climb down. When he landed on the pavement, he looked up at Arn. Floyd was bigger than Flo's bouncer Karl. But not by much.

"This your new ride?" Arn asked.

Floyd smiled. "A beaut, isn't she?"

"She is," Arn lied, recalling what Roy said was wrong with the truck. The color was right: dark blue metallic. Just like half the trucks in Wyoming.

Arn walked around the truck. He took out the paint chip from his pocket but he wasn't sure if it matched or not. The truck had so many scratches and dings that Arn couldn't tell which damage was recent. "I understand you bought this truck when Ford refused to allow it for a trade-in."

Floyd nodded. "Got it for a song, too, 'cause it has a ton of miles." He grinned. "Don't bother me none, though. It's a real chick magnet." He motioned to Arn's 4-4-2. "Like your ride. Bet you get a bunch of babes hanging all over you when you drive it."

"I have to beat them away. A real curse," Arn said. "What's the guy's name you bought this from?"

"Can't say," Floyd answered. "Dad took care of getting the title signed over, and the new one's coming in the mail. Is it important?"

Arn shook his head and climbed into his car. "I don't think so. The truck I'm looking for had tires near bald, with a chunk out of one sidewall."

"That's why I bought the new set of skins," Floyd said.

Arn shut his car off. "You just bought these tires?"

"And rims, too. I can't testify to the chunk missing, but the tires were near bald. I needed new ones, and I figured I might as well buy tires that a real chick magnet deserves."

"And your dad knows the name of the seller?"

"He's got the bill of sale and all that paperwork."

Arn grabbed his cell phone. "What's your dad's cell?"

"Won't do you any good," Floyd said. "He's an engineer for the Union Pacific railroad and had a run up to Edgemont. Ought to be back in cell range tomorrow night. Maybe."

Arn punched the father's number into his cell. He'd call the dad and leave a voicemail later. "Last thing—where did you buy those monstrosities?"

"Fat Boy's Tire." Floyd grinned. "I'll get a twenty-five buck gift card if you buy a set from them. Make sure you give 'em my name— Floyd Pompolopolis. Common spelling."

———————

Arn stopped at the service desk at Fat Boy's Tire. The service manager was at lunch but his assistant was in. He shook his head when asked where Floyd's old worn-out tires might have been tossed. "Can't say, Mr. Anderson." He opened a door leading to the shop area. "Adam, drag your sorry ass in here."

Adam shuffled through the door. A kid Floyd's age, eighteen or nineteen, he wore his pants south of his plumber's crack and entered the office picking his nose. He rubbed an eye oozing pus from a sore as he focused on the manager.

"This is Mr. Anderson," the assistant said.

Adam thrust out his hand, and all Arn could think of as he shook it was that oozing eye.

"Mr. Anderson wants to know what happened to Floyd's old skins after we put the new set on."

Adam motioned to the back lot. "Tossed them out with the rest of them."

"Then what?" Arn asked.

"They'll be sold later this year. Mostly shredded for road material," Adam said. "Along with all the tires too worn out or too bald to even be sold as trailer tires."

"Then you know where they are?"

"I know *right* where they are if you follow me."

Arn felt as if he'd finally caught a break.

Until the old Arn Anderson shitty luck kicked in as Adam led him outside. A huge pile of old tires—hundreds of them—waited to be picked up by the truck on their way to the shredder. "There they are," Adam said proudly, waving his arm at the pile. "In that mountain of tires somewhere."

"Where, more specifically, in that pile?"

"Can't say." Adam rubbed his runny eye. "Sorry I can't be more help, but we get a *ton* of business. Lot of ranch folks buy tires from us. Floyd's not a ranch hand, but his tires had crappy pasture written all over them, is all I can recall without seeing them again."

"How am I gonna find the ones that came off Floyd's truck?"

"Easy." Adam grinned. "They're Coopers."

Arn sighed. "Cooper Tires. At least we're making progress. Can you tell me where the Coopers are?"

"Sure can," Adam answered. "In that pile. Floyd's might be at the bottom. Might be the first ones you come to. We just toss 'em there when we get junkers"—rubbing his sore eye—"but if you find ones

you think were Floyd's, you let me know and I'll tell you if they are."
He tapped the side of his head. "I'll know. 'Cause I got what they call
a photogenic memory."

Twenty-Seven

NOW WHAT DO YOU suppose Anderson is doing at Fat Boy's Tire? By the looks of that fancy Oldsmobile, he doesn't need tires. And I doubt it's for that beat-to-hell International truck sitting in his front lawn.

As I'm into my second Thermos of coffee, Anderson follows some geek from the tire shop around the back of the store. I maneuver my truck so I can watch them. The kid leads Anderson to an enormous pile of old rubber. He went to six body shops before the Ford dealership, and I followed him as he met with the college student. Now the tire shop? What the hell's he up to?

And then I have my answer. Somehow, Anderson has found out about that one tire I took a chunk out of when I ran over a metal fence post driving into the pasture that night with Jillie. Perhaps he spotted it at Wooly Hank's. Either way, he knows about the huge chunk missing as surely as it were an identifiable fingerprint. While I was being rehabilitated in Napa, the good Dr. Oakert finagled me a job in the hospital library. That had access to the internet. What else did I have to do but study up on methods cops use to tie people to crimes: one being tire impressions. After the fact, I kick myself: I've underestimated him. Anderson tracked down the kid with the truck, and he tracked down where the kid bought new tires and wheels.

Anderson leaves the pile of tires too soon. Without looking for mine. He has not found the ones they took off my truck, and it's odd that he hasn't even looked. But if the Denver Post stories are right about his persistence, Anderson will find them. In time.

I don't want to confront Anderson. I don't want to risk anyone seeing me with him. But between the tires and him talking with Maury, it's a matter of hours, perhaps, before he figures things out.

Damn! I hit the dash, and the bite Jillie gave me radiates pain from my hand all the way to my shoulder. Damn! I'll have to take care of Anderson sooner than later. But where? He's far too cautious. A retired cop will be too hard to get to while he's out here in the public, so that leaves his house. As many times as I've successfully entered homes unnoticed, I've learned that most people feel safe and secure in their castles. They drop their guard. Will Anderson relax at home? He has to, as it's the only place he can relax. And the only place he'll let his guard down.

I put the binos away and break off following him. Tonight, Mr. Anderson. Tonight, we dance like Don Whales and I danced last Saturday night.

Twenty-Eight

"WHAT DO YOU MEAN you're giving me the day off?" Danny asked. "I got a suspicious feeling that it won't actually be time off."

"Why do you say that?"

Danny patted drywall dust off his sleeve. "Because you told me to stay in grubbies. You must have something in mind for me."

"Mountain climbing," Arn answered as he pulled into the back lot of Fat Boy's. "Follow me."

He led Danny through the gate to the back and pointed to the mountain of tires that had been tossed in the heap. "That's your mountain."

Danny looked sideways at Arn. "I bet your explanation about this is going to be a doozy."

"Put your gloves on and I'll tell you."

While Danny donned his gloves, Arn explained what he'd found out at the Ford body shop and what Floyd had told him about buying new tires. "You'll be going through that pile. Whenever you find a

Cooper 235 x 17, set it aside and go get Adam. He's the one who looks like someone pissed in his eye. Have him look at the tire and see if it's one he took off Floyd's truck."

"You have *got* to be kidding me?"

"I wish," Arn answered. "But it needs to be done. Think of it as being in the outdoors. Getting fresh air."

"What will this accomplish?"

"All we have to do is identify *one* tire from Floyd's truck."

"But this might take days," Danny said. "And even if I find the tires that came off the kid's pickup, it doesn't guarantee any of them will have a chunk of sidewall gone. You—or in this case, me—might be barking up the wrong mountain of tires."

"Might," Arn said as he headed for his car.

"But I have other stuff to do—"

Arn stopped and turned back. "Think of this as just one duty a sidekick's gotta perform. And Danny—I wouldn't shake hands with Adam when you meet him."

———

Arn picked Ana Maria up for lunch and they headed across town. "I would have brought Danny along, but he figured he was too dirty to go anywhere in public."

"Ya think?" Ana Maria said. "He's only been rooting around those old filthy tires all morning."

Arn's cell phone rang. He pulled to the side of the road and covered the receiver. "It's Floyd's father."

"I understand there's a problem with the truck my kid bought," Fred Pompolopolis said.

"There's no problem with the sale." Arn explained he was looking at all angles connected to Jillie Reilly's murder.

"Hot damn!" Fred said. "Floyd's got a truck a killer owned. Hot damn! It'll be worth a ton on Craigslist."

"The owner probably killed no one," Arn was quick to point out. He couldn't tell Fred that Dr. Oakert said his special patient was a troller, that he'd travel long distances to meet with his perfect victim, but that this didn't mean everyone driving newer trucks with high mileage were killers. "It's just something I have to rule out."

"Hot damn," Fred said again. "Give me a minute to dig the bill of sale out of my pocket."

There was shuffling on the other end of the line, and Fred cursed when he dropped his wallet. "While I got you on the line, we found some papers under the seat—pay stub, receipt for a tune-up, Social Security statement. You got an address I can send it to?"

"What's the guy's name?"

Shuffling on Fred's end. "Scott Wallace. Some local ranch hand."

Arn sighed. Adding to being a PI and a range detective, he might as well be called a mailman, too. "Scott works at the Circle Trot. Let me know when you're coming back to town and I'll get the papers off you. The ranch is just a few miles from town."

Twenty-Nine

ARN DOWNSHIFTED INTO FIRST gear once he drove off the county gravel onto the ranch road that was little more than a dirt two-track. Hubert and Henrietta Pott had owned the Circle Trot since before he'd worked for the Cheyenne PD. The couple had never had much, except two sections of land that they raised sheep and some milking goats on and an occasional steer they fattened up for butchering every fall. Arn had hunted antelope on their northern range when he was a youngster, and the couple seemed never to age.

At the end of the half-mile drive, a ranch house seemed to rise up out of the ground. Arn recalled Hubert Pott painting the house a bright white every other spring, and painting his shutters a quaint baby-shit brown. To match his eyes, Hub always claimed.

A stooped woman in a baggy dress and baggier apron stopped in the middle of the yard and watched Arn approach. She carried a basket filled with eggs as she walked from the brooder house, and now hobbled over to where Arn climbed out of the car. Squinting, she brought her head up to look through her trifocals. "Arn Anderson."

Arn took off his Stetson. "Mother Pott. Good morning."

"Been a long time, Arn. You here to hunt?" She eyed Arn's Oldsmobile. "'Cause that sure ain't no huntin' outfit."

"More importantly, it's not hunting season."

Her eyes twinkled through her glasses. "Never bothered me before."

Arn smiled. "I'm looking for Scott Wallace."

She chin-pointed to the barn. "Him and Hub are working on our filly what came up lame yesterday."

Arn thanked her and started for the barn when she called to him, "There'll be lemonade and cookies on the porch when you're done."

Some things never change, Arn thought.

He walked into the barn to the smell of fresh horse dung and damp straw that made him homesick, taking him back to when he worked area ranches as a kid. An Australian shepherd greeted him with a stub of a wagging tail and the mandatory sniff of the boot. Arn stroked the dog's head and walked around her when he spotted Scott and Hubert bent over a filly lying on a bed of straw at the far end of the barn. There was a brief moment of recognition and a faint smile before Hubert's grin disappeared as he looked down at the horse with those sad eyes again.

The old man used the side of the stall to stand. He'd developed a noticeable dowager's hump since Arn had last seen him, but he held out a hand deformed by rheumatoid arthritis. "Arn Anderson. Been...fifteen years?"

"More like thirty-five. How are you, Hubert?"

Hubert pointed to the filly. "Better than she's doing."

Scott looked at them over his shoulder. "You're that feller who talked to me at the Archer Complex."

"I am."

"You come here to help?"

"Believe me, I would if I knew what to do. I just want to visit for a moment."

Scott reached around and grabbed a duffle bag. He pulled off a glove and grabbed an ACE bandage. "If you'll hold her head I'll wrap another bandage around her leg before I set her loose."

Arn held the sorrel's head, a beautiful brown horse with contrasting blond mane and tail. She looked wild-eyed at Arn, but remained lying down while Scott wrapped the bandage tightly around her foreleg and over a splint he'd wrapped earlier. When he finished, he stepped back. "I've done what I can for her," Scott said. "Now it's up to the Lord."

They let go of the horse, and she struggled to stand. When she finally stood on wobbly legs, she held the injured one several inches off the floor of the barn. "She stepped in a gopher hole," Hubert said, as if he needed to explain.

Scott shook his head. "Thing I'll never understand is how an animal with as much power as a horse can possess such delicate legs. Prone to twisting and breaking." Tears filled his eyes. "You gotta feel bad for them."

Arn waited until Scott had composed himself before he spoke with Hubert. "Me and Scott needs to jaw for a minute."

Hubert looked at the horse one last time and started for the house. "Cookies and lemonade when you two are finished."

Arn waited until Hubert left before he spoke of the horse. "She's not going to make it."

Scott ran a gloved hand over the filly's twitching withers. "You know your horses. Not much even I can do for a critter who breaks a leg. God or no, this time tomorrow I'm afraid I'll have to put her down."

"Tough thing to shoot a horse you're fond of."

"I won't shoot her," Scott said, slapping dust and straw off his trouser leg. "I got tranquilizer medicine that'll euthanize her. Painless and instant." He stroked the filly's muzzle a last time. "We can talk outside."

He led Arn outside, to where a plank had been nailed to the side of the barn. He sat and grabbed a bandana from his back pocket, wiping sweat from his head that had run down to the neckerchief around his neck. "Somehow I think they always know when it's their time." He hung his hat over a nail jutting out of the side of the barn. "It does look like I won't be able to save her." He forced a smile. "But my track record is actually pretty good. I've saved more critters than not since I've been here."

"How long is that?"

Scott looked up at the clouds as if the answer was floating up there. "I've worked for the Potts for two years now." He peeked around the corner of the barn and withdrew a pack of Marlboros from his shirt pocket. "Got to be careful. Hubert and Henrietta are pretty religious."

"So I recall when I'd come out here hunting as a kid."

"Then you know they'd have a cow if they knew I smoked." Scott lit up and blew smoke away from Arn. "They're good people, but a little set in their ways."

"Wouldn't you be if you were in your eighties?"

The wind blew his sweaty neckerchief into his eyes, and he moved it lower. "Good point."

"But it must be hard on you," Arn said, "working here. If they keep such a tight rein on you they forbid even cigarettes."

"This place has its advantages. I can live with the house rules," Scott said. "Me and Hubert's got an understanding: when I need to leave for a while, he lets me go. In exchange, I make meager ranch wages and he lets me fill up my truck with his ranch gas."

"That's right—you do some freelance shearing," Arn said. He wasn't comfortable with the ease with which Scott told him things. He wasn't used to that.

"I do some doctoring for friends around the area. I got the touch, as they say. But most times as not I'm gone shearing sheep during season. I'm very good." He laughed.

"How good?"

A twinkle formed in Scott's eyes. "Twenty seconds a lamb. Consistently."

Arn whistled. "That's good! "

Scott nodded. "I'm in demand, and I go where the real money is." He waved his hand around. "The money Hubert and Henrietta give me could hardly pay to drive across the state. Even with a tankful of their petrol."

"Which is why I'm here." Arn took out his notebook and flipped pages. "You sold your truck to Floyd Pompolopolis."

"How could I forget." Scott chuckled. "When he told me his name for the bill of sale I thought he was messing with me." He blew smoke, but it hung just above him before the wind took it. "Ford dealership wouldn't give me squat for trade-in, so I figured I'd do better selling it outright. Why do you ask?"

"It had an unusually high number of miles."

"Like I said, I drive a lot."

"Odd to trade a truck in that's only a couple years old."

Scott shrugged and kept peeking around the side of the barn like a little kid watching for his parents to return and catch him smoking. "It was a gasoline truck. Not a diesel. I needed a dependable outfit." He looked at the barn like he could see the horse on the other side.

"The truck started nickel and diming me. I knew it didn't have long before something went to hell and I'd have to euthanize *it*. I was glad Floyd bought it."

Arn stood, thinking of a way to ask Scott more questions about the high mileage. There was just no way to do it cleanly. "I have reason to believe the man who killed Jillie Reilly puts a *lot* of miles on his truck every year."

It took a moment for the accusation to sink in. When it did, Scott's face turned red and he stood. "What the hell. Are you accusing me of killing that woman the newspaper and TV's been covering?"

Arn held up his hands as if to ward Scott off. "All I'm saying is that every time I find someone with mileage as high as your truck had, I get suspicious."

"That's *it?*" Scott flicked his butt onto the ground. "That's what you're basing your accusation on?"

"It's not an accusation. But Floyd did need to buy new tires as soon as he brought your truck."

"Of course he did," Scott said, pacing in front of the barn. "I wasn't about to put new tires on it if I was going to trade it or sell it." He stood and faced Arn. "If you check into it closer, you'll see I just deposited eleven thousand dollars in the bank. That was pay for shearing sheep this past season. As far away as Utah."

"All right," Arn said. "Just consider this interview as going a long ways toward eliminating you as a suspect."

"I thought cops never fully eliminated a suspect." Scott snubbed his cigarette butt out and used the toe of his boot to cover the filter. "But while you're here, what else you want to know about me?"

"All right," Arn said. "For starters: where were you the night Jillie Reilly was killed?"

"What day was that?"

"Two Saturdays ago."

"I was"—Scott looked around the corner of the barn again—"at a bar in town."

"The Boot Hill?"

Scott shook his head.

"Ever been in there?"

"Never."

"So what bar were you drinking in that night?"

Scott lowered his voice. "I was at the Green Door."

"The strip bar?"

"Shush! Not so loud. I was there all night. I brought a wad of one-dollar bills along to stick in the girls' g-strings." He put his finger to his lips. "This isn't going to get out? Like I said, Hubert and his missus are pretty religious. If they found out I was at a titty bar—"

"I won't say a thing to them. But can they at least vouch that you were gone that night, and what time you returned?"

"Do I need someone to corroborate my story?"

"You tell me."

Scott hung his head. "No, they can't. I live in their sheepherder's cabin out on their north range. Half a mile from here. They can't see when I come and go unless they're sitting on their porch."

"Can anyone vouch for you?"

Scott's face lit up. "Sure. A lot of guys will say I was there."

Arn grabbed his pen and flipped to a clean page in his notebook. "Give me names."

Scott rattled off names, none of which Arn recognized, of people who were at the strip club until closing. "They were all by the stage stuffing bills down thongs, same's me. They'll tell you."

"Mind if I take a picture of you?"

"No." Scott took off his hat. "But why?"

"These guys your personal friends?"

"Only time I see them is when I go to the Green Door."

"Then I'll need a picture to show them."

Scott shrugged and grabbed his bandana from his back pocket. He wiped the sweat from his forehead. He smoothed his hair falling over his face. "Profile or frontal?" he asked as he adjusted the bandana around his neck."

"How about both."

Scott stood straight and smiled at Arn's cell phone. "Have at it."

Arn used his phone to snap a frontal and a profile picture of Scott. "That should be all. But if I need to talk further, you'll be here?"

"Unless one of the neighbors has a critter that needs doctorin'. I got no shearing lined up for some time. I'll be here." He nodded to the barn. "Hope I can conjure up a miracle for that filly."

When Arn got back into town, he thought about calling Little Jim Reilly to warn him about following Ana Maria. But it was only another eighteen miles to his ranch, and he felt he could read the man better if he talked with him in person.

When Arn drove into the ranch, he spotted him sitting atop an Allis Chalmers tractor that looked altogether too small for his large frame. Black smoke puffed from the smoke stack every time a cylinder fired, and Little Jim bounced on the hard metal seat as he drove across his pasture. He picked up a round bale of hay and slowly lumbered across the field to a herd of heifers waiting for their dinner, while Jillie's dog seemed content to lope along beside the tractor. Little Jim set the bale down and shut the tractor off when he reached the fence. "You're a ways out of town," he said as he stepped over the fence and walked toward Arn's car. "If you came this far, it must mean you found something out."

"I'm here because you followed me a couple nights ago."

Little Jim shrugged. "I thought we had our little pissing contest that night in the park."

"I warned you not to follow me again."

Little Jim stepped closer to Arn. "What's your point?"

"That went for Ana Maria Villarreal as well."

Little Jim's eyes squinted in the bright sunlight. "I'm not sure I like your tone. What are you implying?"

Arn stepped closer and looked up. He wanted to gauge Little Jim's reaction to his question. Even if meant being within grabbing range of the big man. "Have you been following Ana Maria?"

Veins throbbed on Little Jim's forehead. "I want the son-of-a-bitch who killed Jillie in the worst way. But I'm sure as hell not going to frighten another man's daughter. Of course I never followed that TV lady."

Arn felt his stomach churn. He'd asked Little Jim straight up, and he had answered honestly: Little Jim had not been following Ana Maria.

Someone else had.

Thirty

CHIEF OBLANSKI SHUT HIS office door and sat on the edge of his desk. "You said you had a special favor to ask me."

Arn handed Oblanski a sheet of paper with the names of the witnesses that could vouch for Scott being at the Green Door. "I showed this list to Ana Maria, and I thought I was going to have to cart her to the ER she laughed so hard."

Oblanski's eyes scanned the names and a smile crept across his face. "No wonder. These are names of big shots in town." He tapped the paper. "A banker, two attorneys. A doctor and an elementary school teacher." He handed the sheet back. "What's this got to do with me?"

"That favor I mentioned," Arn began. "I'm an outsider here, and these guys won't tell me squat. And they're damn sure not going to admit to Ana Maria they were sticking dollar bills between breasts and down g-strings at a strip bar. But you're more a ... kindred spirit to them."

"You saying I frequent titty bars?"

"All I'm saying is you've been in the community for a long time. They'll tell you straight up if they were in there and if they saw Scott. They'll know it won't go public if you discreetly ask."

"I'll do it for the entertainment value of watching them squirm. You owe me on this, Anderson," Oblanski said at last as he pocketed the list. "You have any photos of Scott?"

"I'll send you Scott's photos when I get a moment. Just in case these guys don't know him by name."

"I'll hold my breath until they come through." Oblanski nodded to the latte machine. "Want a cup?"

Arn shook his head. "It was too painful to watch last time."

"I got the hang of it now." Oblanski walked to the machine. "I talked with Grimes yesterday," he said from across the office. "Sounds like they set bail for Karen Glass."

"Hopefully it was high enough she won't be back on the street any time soon—"

"She made bail this morning," Oblanski said over his shoulder. "She's out on OR bond."

"Bullshit," Arn said. "She tried to kill me and she got out on her own recognizance?"

"She managed to land a sharp public defender." Oblanski hit the stop button but the machine continued spewing coffee into the cup. He quickly replaced it with an empty cup as coffee sloshed over the sides of the machine. "Watch your backside," he called over his shoulder. "She made some not-so-veiled threats about you."

"I will. And do you need help?"

"No," Oblanski said as he grabbed for a roll of paper towels. "I think I got the hang of this now."

———

Arn walked from the new public safety building to the sheriff's office. Slade was waiting for him in the lobby when he came through the double doors. "Come up to my office. I got something for you."

As Arn followed Slade, he asked him, "So you're finally going to come up with some officers to watch Dr. Oakert's office and his house?"

"Sheriff Grimes put one of the posse members on it—"

"A volunteer?" Arn said. "Even if they're conscientious, they don't even have the powers of arrest."

Slade looked back at Arn. "I pled my case. That's all Grimes would allow me—one civilian. Now when I'm sheriff—"

"By the time you're sheriff, Dr. Oakert's special patient might have racked up more victims. Damn, Slade, posse members don't have much training, let alone experience. They'll be spotted right off."

"I did what I could. I just called the man assigned to watch the office, and there's been no one even approaching the door yet except the mailman."

"So no one is watching his house?"

Slade shook his head. "It was either the doctor's home or his office. I flipped a coin and it was the office. I had little choice."

Arn followed Slade to his upstairs office and shut the door behind them. "This came in this morning," Slade said. He laid a note penned on what appeared to be a Big Chief tablet. It read, *Jillie was swell, and Don went straight to hell.*

Arn held up the note, now encased in a clear plastic evidence envelope. It seemed to glisten under the neon office lights as if taunting him. Then he picked up its envelope, contained within a separate plastic sheet, and turned it over. The Colorado Springs postmark revealed little. "Not much here to go on."

"You got that right," Slade said. "Our questioned documents examiner went over it. She said that by the slant of the writing, it may have been the work of a left-hander."

"Or someone who disguised their writing." Arn laid the envelope on Slade's desk. "Someone's baiting you. And enjoying the hell out of it."

"Obviously." Slade sat in his chair and swiveled around to grab a manila envelope from a drawer. He pulled out a stack of teletypes and laid them on the desk. "I got these hits back. Six agencies had murders with the same MO as Jillie's and Don's in the last four years, as far away as Hays, Kansas."

He slid the teletypes across his desk and Arn read over the list. Police agencies from Rapid City, South Dakota, to Gallup, New Mexico, to Sioux City, Iowa, had reported murder victims killed the exact way: multiple ligature marks on the neck of the victims.

Arn handed the teletypes back to Slade. "Ana Maria pulled up a detailed schedule for Eddie Glass's seminars and dog trials in the last two years." He fished into his briefcase and grabbed Eddie's schedule. "Check the dates against his schedule."

"You're pretty hot on this Eddie Glass character. Anything to do with his old lady damned near killing you?"

"I wish it were that easy." Arn took off his Stetson and sat. "Eddie was the last one to confront Jillie *if* she was still there when he ran out of the bar. And he can't account for his whereabouts the rest of the night. No one at the Outlaw saw him."

"Maybe he was wrong. Maybe he wound up drinking someplace other than the Outlaw."

"He and Karen Glass were both adamant he was there."

Slade leaned back in his chair. "Where were you last Saturday night?"

"I watched a little Forensic Files on the tube before driving out and sitting on a sheep pasture. Why?"

"Anyone vouch for you that's where you were?" Slade asked.

"No," Arn said. "Danny goes to bed early, and Ana Maria was out on a dinner and movie date. Why?"

"My point," Slade said, "is that most people can't bring in *anyone* to testify to where they were."

"Unless they went out of their way to fabricate an alibi."

Slade leaned forward and rested his elbows on his desk. "I think your judgment might be a little clouded. Maybe you'd like Eddie to be the killer—"

"It would make things easy," Arn said. "The bastard's annoying."

"But don't assume he's the killer," Slade said, standing and gathering his teletypes. "Go home and think about it tonight. Maybe you'll wake up a little more clearheaded."

"Sounds like you're convinced Eddie is innocent?"

Slade reached into a metal basket on his desk. "I am now." He handed Arn a copy of a citation. The date was that past Saturday, the day the letter to the police department had been postmarked. "Your boy was in Cheyenne getting himself a speeding ticket when you think he was in Colorado Springs mailing the note."

"When was the last time you were in the Springs?"

Slade shrugged. "Been a while."

"It's only a three-hour drive down. Less if you drive fast. He could have caught his speeding ticket, drove to the Springs to mail the note, and hustled back."

"Kind of convoluted, don'tcha think?"

"Not if you're covering your backside."

"And if he got a ticket at six o'clock in the morning and ran down south to mail this, he would have missed his dog class at eight." Slade held up his hand. "And before you ask, I already checked with Bonnie.

Eddie was at the class the minute the doors opened and remained there the rest of the day."

Arn turned the citation over as if it held some secret before he dropped it on Slade's desk. The postmark on the envelope showed nine o'clock. Unless Eddie had been able to be beamed down to Colorado Springs, Arn knew he had to look elsewhere.

He left the sheriff's office and walked to his car. He didn't need to be lectured by Slade. He'd sounded like his old training officer, Rolf. "Don't discount even the rawest rookie," Rolf had told him one day when they'd arrested a local kid with a baggie of marijuana on a tip from a rookie. "Even the greenest cop can have a good thought now and again."

Perhaps Slade was right. Perhaps he *was* trying too hard to make Eddie the killer. As he fumbled with his car keys, Arn told himself he'd take Slade's advice—he'd go home and think about Eddie. And maybe run it by Danny and Ana Maria.

———————

Danny paraded around the kitchen in his new apron adorned with roses and roosters. He slapped a spatula against the counter in time with Iron Butterfly playing on his boom box. Arn cupped his hand and shouted, "I said when are we going to eat?"

Danny jumped, and took the ear phones off his head. "You scared me half to death. And I can't afford that."

"Sorry. Where's Ana Maria? I'm starved and I need to have a talk with her."

"Not, 'how did it go rooting around on all the dirty tires, Danny?' Or, 'thanks so much for trying to find those phantom tires, Danny.' Give me a break—that's a long time to be crawling around a pile of tires at my age."

"Hell," Arn said. "You can outwork me any day of the week."

"That's because you're too big and you've never had to do manual labor. Now have some tea until she comes home."

Arn poured himself a glass of iced green tea—a step up from Danny's chicory—and was sitting at the table when he heard a scratching at the back door. He cocked his ear toward the sound. The scratching continued, and he slipped his gun from his ankle holster.

"Whoa!" Danny said. "Put that thing away. I don't want you to hurt Sonny." He opened the door and a low-slung dog waddled in. Gray whiskers matted his wrinkled nose, his drooling lips nearly dragged on the floor. He walked with a pronounced limp as he tottered up to Arn. The dog sniffed him once before he sat on his foot.

"What is this?"

"Darwin would say it's a life-form that evolved into what we now call a canine."

"I can tell it's a damned dog."

"Not just any dog," Danny said. "He's a basset hound crossed with something. I'd say a wolfhound."

"I don't want to even think about how that happened," Arn said, rubbing his temple to a rising headache. "What's it doing in here?"

Danny sat on a chair and scratched behind the dog's ears. "If I could read his mind, I'd say he wants something to eat." He reached over and flipped a burger into a dog dish. The hound stumbled to the dish, ate the burger in one chomp, and sat back on Arn's foot. He jerked his foot back and Sonny's testicles plopped onto the floor "See, he likes you," Danny said.

"He's gross," Arn said. "And you still didn't say how he got here."

"He rode," Danny replied, "in the taxi cab with me back from Fat Boy's. He just came up wagging his lonely old tail like he needed a friend. Pretty cool dog, huh?"

Arn shook his head. "He can't stay here."

188

"He'll be good company."

"I got good company."

"I gave him a bath soon's I got him home." Danny motioned to the back door. "And you saw he's housebroke."

"Danny—"

"I know," Danny interrupted. "You want to see how he fits in here before we decide to keep him permanently."

"That's not what I was going to say. I was going to say call Animal Control and have him picked up."

Danny checked his Casio. "Animal Control officers go home at five o'clock. He'll have to stay until the morning."

Arn shook his head. He'd never had a dog all the years he was married to Cailee, and none in the years since she'd died. He just never had found one he cottoned to. Or that had cottoned to him. "Call them in the morning and have him picked up. I mean this, Danny, or you might as well have them pick you up, too."

Danny smiled and went back to the stove.

Sometime during Arn's second glass of tea, he caught himself scratching Sonny's ears, when the dog suddenly lumbered to his feet. He tilted his head back, but all that came out was some type of gravelly cough, like the critter had something caught in its throat.

"Someone's here," Danny said.

"How can you tell?"

"Sonny tries to howl, but I guess his howler is just worn out. Old age and all, I suppose." Danny laughed. "I can relate to that. But that's as good as Sonny barks."

The dog ran as best he could, with his oversized *cajones* dragging on the floor, toward the front door. He sat in front of the door trying to bark, but it still came out as a weak cough. Arn walked past him with his gun in hand.

Ana Maria cracked the door and popped her head in. "What the—"

Sonny remained sitting against the door like some grotesque door stop and Arn moved him aside. The dog looked up at Ana Maria as she stepped around him. "This creature found Danny the Sucker at the tire pile and adopted him," Arn said.

As the dog eyed Ana Maria, Sonny's bloodshot eyes reminded Arn of Adam's at Fat Boy's. Ana Maria squatted and took Sonny's head in her hands. Drool dripped off an oversize lower lip and his tail began to wag. "He's cute. It's about time you got a dog."

"Just until the morning when Animal Control picks him up."

Ana Maria started for the kitchen with Sonny waddling beside her. "We need to set the security alarm," Arn said. "Every time."

Ana Maria stopped and turned to him. "Why the security concerns all of a sudden?"

"When we talked about Little Jim Reilly following you," Arn answered, "looks like I was right. It's not Little Jim."

"Then who—" She stopped mid-sentence and the color drained from her face. "It's ... him, isn't it?"

Arn nodded and reached over to arm the system.

Ana Maria's balance wobbled, and she used the kitchen door jamb to help her sit in a chair. "Someone followed me today after I left the station, too." She held up her hand. "I know it's just a feeling."

"I'm assuming it's *more* than just a feeling," Arn said. He poured her a glass of tea and sat across from her. Sonny sat on his foot again, and he was glad he had boots on. "We better keep the alarm system armed until we catch this guy." He laid his hand on her trembling shoulder. "We'll all be safer. Now did you find out anything?"

Danny dished a pot pie onto Ana Maria's plate. She looked at it for long moments before picking at the crust with her fork. "I went to the Johns' ranch today. When I interviewed Beverly earlier, I made the

190

mistake of telling her I used to turn a wrench for a living. She talked me into working on her sister's truck. The one she hit something with but never reported."

Arn leaned forward. "I saw the damage. Not extensive, but a lot of little dings."

"The fender's caved in and almost rubbing the tire, but it's drivable. Don Whales said he'd do the repair, and he ordered the parts, but of course that's not going to happen now."

"Tell me this truck is a midnight blue."

"If you're clairvoyant, you're a poor one," Ana Maria said. "The truck is beige."

"I was almost hoping she had another pickup," Arn said. "With a broken marker light."

"Nothing that easy," Ana Maria replied.

"When are you going to fix it?"

"I told Beverly I'd take a look at it on Sunday. It's parked in back of the barn with the rest of the equipment needing repair." Ana Maria put her hand on Arn's arm. "You're not going to Slade with this? 'Cause Beverly's mighty worried the law would get involved."

Arn washed his pot pie down with a swallow of tea. "Oblanski's already checked hit-and-run reports for anything substantial. He found nothing that fits Bonnie's damage, so Beverly ought not to worry."

"Good, because she was sure Bonnie was drunk when she hit whatever she hit." Ana Maria grabbed her backpack. "One thing's for certain: if both sisters were as careless and sloppy as Bonnie, the entire ranch would be in shambles." She pushed her supper back half-eaten.

"You find a toenail in your pot pie or something?" Danny asked. "'Cause you didn't eat a whole lot."

A faint smile crossed Ana Maria's face. "No toenail. I guess I'm still a little shaken that someone's been following me. And not Little Jim." She stood and headed for the stairs.

"Re-runs of the Olympics on tonight," Danny called after her. "Might cheer you up."

"I have to turn in early," she said. "I need to study some notes for my segment tomorrow night."

"Anything new?" Arn asked.

"Not much activity on the tip line. But I did find out Bonnie and Eddie are still an item. He even lets her drive his beater truck when hers is down."

"Ain't love blind," Danny said.

Arn called Ana Maria back. "You're certain Bonnie and Eddie are still involved?"

"Beverly thinks so. Why?"

Arn explained about the note sent to the PD from Colorado Springs. Eddie wouldn't have been able to get a speeding ticket, drive to the Springs to mail the envelope, and make it back to class at eight o'clock Saturday morning.

"Unless Eddie *wasn't* at the class bright and early when the arena opened," Ana Maria said.

"And Bonnie lied to Slade," Arn said. "Guess I need to pay Beverly a visit. Make sure Eddie was there."

Thirty-One

I PARK MY TRUCK two blocks away, beside what old locals called the steam plant when it was in operation, and sip the last of my coffee. I cup my hand over my cigarette to mask the glow, but I needn't worry—few people come into this part of town. Bad things often happen here, folks say. People get hurt here, they claim. I chuckle. I'm just about to prove them right.

I wait an hour after the lights go off inside the house.

It's show time.

I snub my cigarette out and sit back in the seat. I didn't want it to be show time, I reason. Maury would be proud of me—self-reflection is how he put it in therapy. Trying to figure out just how to go on with this life. I want this to be a time in my life when I pick the ladies I want to dance with at my leisure, whenever I find one that suits me. No pressure. Take my time selecting. Instead, I've had to silence Jillie Reilly, and also Don Whales, though I admit Don was almost a mistake for me. Almost. Even though he wasn't my type, I still garnered a certain amount of ... pleasure from his predicament. Is that the right word—pleasure? Dr. Oakert insists I never enjoyed what I did, that

I was forced to do it as a result of social upbringing that affected my psyche. That my abusive father made me what I am.

Maury always was wrong about that.

I think I actually enjoy it. At least I'm different from most other patients—I take responsibility for what I do. I don't need some shrink handing me excuses like they were Get Out of the Loony Bin Free cards.

And now I have to take care of Anderson. Even though he angered me the last time I talked with him, I really have nothing against him. But an analytical mind like that—if I believe the Denver news stories—can catch the most careful criminal. And he's shown lately that his mind is working things out. I can't risk him coming to his logical conclusion.

I close the truck door silently and stay in the shadows, avoiding the streetlights as I walk to Anderson's house. How many times have I done this, and how many times have I gone undetected? A veritable Ghost of the Ghetto, one newspaper in Fresno once called me. But it has nothing to do with being a ghost and everything to do with preparation. And I don't mean the "H" variety, either. I've looked at Anderson's run-down house from every conceivable angle. I've figured out from vent pipes and doors where the bathrooms are, where the bedrooms most likely sit in the place. Where the kitchen is located. I know the layout of the house even before I enter. Dr. Oakert would be proud of me.

A car drives north on Snyder Avenue, and I crouch beside a dumpster overflowing with beer cans and pizza boxes and an old broken chair, and I wait. Patiently. I clearly see the house from here: there are no lights except a faint one from a room I know is a bath. Gotta love those night lights. When I walked the neighborhood this afternoon, I saw no dog chained outside, nothing to alert Anderson when I'm at his front door. And ready to dance.

The car fades away and I walk across the street, hands in my pockets, hoodie pulled tight against the chill of the air. Just in case a cop drives by, I'll look natural.

I stop at the corner of the house and run my hand over the phone line that connects to his security system. Unless I'm mistaken—and of course I never am—once I cut the lines, there will be no back-up system to signal I've breached the door.

A quick snip of the line with side cutters, and the system is disabled. And Anderson's lifeline to the police department. If I can get to him before he can use his cell phone.

I swap the dykes for my pick set. A tension wrench, a squiggly pick, and I'll make entry.

I pause.

Anderson has two other people living with him: Ana Maria and some old fart with scraggly gray hair. If I have to silence them, I will. But I firmly believe in myself. Believe that I can get to him without alerting the others. Dr. Oakert taught me that: believe in yourself and your self-esteem will soar. And the doctor was all about raising my self-esteem—something about being all I can be.

I glance around a final time, and I test the porch. It begins to creak under my weight and I stay to one side, away from the center, as I squat in front of the lock. Before I pick the dead bolt, I grab a leather boot string from my pocket, one heavy enough even for someone as powerful as Anderson.

I slide a hook pick into the lock while I put pressure on the tiny tension wrench. One by one, the tumblers click into place. In a moment, I'll dance with the Devil, that being Anderson.

And then I can get on with my life.

Thirty-Two

SOMETIME BETWEEN THE NON-STOP action of synchronized swimming and the semi-final curling game, Arn dozed off to sleep. He woke with a start, disoriented, looking about. What had awakened him? But it was only Sonny, leaving his perch from on top of Arn's slippered feet and wandering from the room. Arn relaxed.

He flicked the television off and leaned back in the recliner. Sonny returned to the room and lay back on the floor, his snoring soon following Danny's, which came from his bedroom down the hall from the living room. Within moments, sleep again crowded Arn's consciousness as he recalled his failures that past week. He'd gone out three nights hoping to catch the Midnight Sheepherder, and three nights he'd failed. Like he always failed in catching the rustler. He fought to keep his eyes open, forced himself to run suspects by the imaginary jury he often thought about.

Slade was right: he *was* putting too much emphasis on Eddie Glass. But wasn't that what good investigators did: compare a set of facts against known suspects to see who fit the profile? Eddie had that raging temper that caused him to beat a married man who objected to Eddie dancing with his wife. And Eddie's temper had landed him court-ordered sessions with Dr. Oakert for anger management. It wasn't a far stretch to imagine Eddie giving Jillie her last ride and ultimately strangling her, and later killing Don for what he might know. If he just knew how to verify or refute Eddie's claim that Jillie had left with the other guy, he could think straighter.

Then there was the Karen Glass factor. She had risked everything protecting her man. She wouldn't have done so without a suspicion that Eddie had killed Jillie. Karen had lied about where Eddie went the rest of the evening. Perhaps even she didn't know where Eddie had been that night.

Where was Karen now? Arn had no idea why the judge had given her an OR bond and let her back on the street. Since he'd found that out, he'd looked over his shoulder more often than usual. The last time he'd been face to face with Karen, she had lethal intentions written all over her. She wouldn't be one to give it up. Except the next time she would be more cautious.

Had she gone into the Boot Hill looking for Jillie, not Eddie? That thought had crossed Arn's mind more than a few times since she'd attacked him. He was certain that if Karen had sought and found Jillie—and took her for that ride at gunpoint—she was more than powerful enough to strangle Jillie with any ligature at hand.

And then there was Slade's theory that Jillie was one of the rustlers. If that were the case, perhaps she got a case of conscience and threatened to expose her partner—the guy in the bar who she'd chased after, threatening to rat him out.

Arn dozed, and sometime after the grandfather clock struck midnight, Sonny's coughing woke him. God, don't make me do CPR on

Sonny, he thought. The dog was looking at the door in an effort to bark or howl or do something besides devolve into a coughing spasm. Sonny must need to go outside to do his thing. Arn stood and grabbed the leash when he heard metal rake across the lock on the front door.

Bolting from the room, Arn clawed for his gun. But he'd taken it off, and he had to run to the kitchen where he'd left it on the counter. Halfway there, he froze in the darkness of the house. Whoever was trying to get inside had unlocked the dead bolt. Now all that remained was the cheap lock on the door knob.

Arn tripped over Sonny and nearly fell before he caught himself and reached his gun.

"What's he raising hell about?" Danny stumbled out of his room rubbing sleepers out of his eyes. He reached for the light switch when Arn stopped him. "Don't!" he whispered.

Ana Maria stumbled down the stairs and Arn jabbed the air. "Lock yourself in your room."

"What's going on—"

"Your room. Go!" Arn said, and she scrambled back up the stairs.

He motioned to Danny. "Hang on to Sonny."

Danny grabbed the dog and dragged him toward the kitchen when the scraping sound stopped, the silence louder than any gunshot. The only sound cutting the darkness was the hacking of a neurotic basset hound mutt, who coughed at the front door like he had emphysema.

Arn duck-walked toward the door, leading with his gun. "Wait," Danny whispered. "The cops will be responding in a moment."

Arn pointed to the keypad on the wall, normally lit with a green light when the system was armed, red when it was disarmed. It showed neither color. "Cops don't know the alarm's been triggered. The system's been disabled."

"Shit," Danny breathed.

"No shit." Arn crawled the last few feet to the door. He gathered his legs under him and crouched to one side of the door. He flung it wide and spied the empty space, looking every place his gun pointed.

Nothing.

The night was cool and crisp with no hint of anyone trying to break in. Except for the boot print smeared in the dirt in front of the door. A print far larger than one from a kid who might have wanted to break in to party or steal.

"Lock it after me," he told Danny, stepping outside. He looked around the street, at the abandoned cars down the block, the dilapidated steam plant kitty-corner from the house, but nothing moved. Arn squatted beside the track and followed it to the next. And the next. They led toward an abandoned car, and Arn slowly walked, hunched over, toward it.

When he reached the car, he paused. Listening.

Sounds of footsteps on the hard pavement bounced off the old steam plant, running east. Arn just made out a form running fast, and he left the cover of the abandoned car after the runner. He tripped on a piece of a trash in the middle of the road and fell. He managed to keep his gun as he regained his footing and ran toward where the intruder had disappeared in the night.

Before he reached the plant that had made steam for the city of Cheyenne fifty years ago, a truck started up and sped off.

Arn bent over, sucking in air, holding a stitch in his side.

When he'd caught his wind sufficiently, he walked to where the truck had been parked. Looking at the ground, he saw nothing to indicate anything other than that it had been a truck containing a chain smoker, given the many butts on the ground. He bent and put the cigarettes—smoked right down to the filters—into his shirt pocket.

Arn looked a final time in the direction the truck had sped off. That it contained the person who'd just tried getting into his house, he was certain. There was only one reason to enter an occupied dwelling at night in this part of town: to do the occupants harm. Much harm. And with the enemies he'd made lately, it could be most anyone.

Thirty-Three

ARN STAYED AT THE house until the city police took the report. They spread copious amounts of fingerprint powder around the door and lock and photographed the indistinct footprint on the porch, scuffed from Arn stepping over it in his pursuit of the intruder. The evidence tech had just left when an alarm company technician pulled to the curb in front to install a new unit. He assured Arn the new wireless system didn't depend on phone lines to alert the police dispatcher.

"Good thing ol' Sonny here was around," Danny said as he passed Arn and Ana Maria cups of coffee, "to tell you someone was breaking into the house."

Arn admitted the dog had woken him when the would-be intruder was on the porch. He had to concede that Sonny was the hero of the night, and by the time he left the house this morning, Danny had guilt-tripped him into allowing the dog to stay. "As long as he doesn't sit on my feet with those ... hairy nuts."

Danny shrugged. "I can't promise that. I'm surely not going to shave him, if that's what you're hinting at. Sonny is his own man. Or in his case, his own dog. Me and Sonny will be holding down the fort." Danny locked the door and armed the system after they left.

Ana Maria slid into the passenger seat of Arn's 4-4-2. "Had to be Jillie and Don's killer last night?"

"That's not the only enemy I've made recently," Arn said. "Don't forget Karen Glass."

"And you can't rule her out? She's a ranch girl. Probably strong as most men."

"I ran that through my mind this past night," Arn said. "And just because her bond conditions say that she's to have no contact with me, I doubt that piece of paper would stop her from coming around. But what I don't know is why risk getting caught coming into our house when we're no closer to catching the killer than we were when this started."

"Maybe he—or she—thinks we're closer than we are," Ana Maria said.

Arn fished into his pocket for his keys when his cell phone rang. "Chief Oblanski asked me to send a patrol deputy to hunt up Eddie and Karen Glass this morning," Slade said. "They were still in bed when my officer banged on their door an hour ago."

"And they couldn't have been acting as if they just woke up?"

"Could have," Slade said. "But my deputy's pretty sharp. He believes them when they told him they were sleeping all night."

"What did your best friend have to say?" Ana Maria asked when Arn disconnected.

"He said Eddie and Karen were sleeping this morning when his deputy rattled their cage."

"And they couldn't have faked it?"

"That was my first thought," Arn said. He stuck the key in the ignition but Ana Maria stopped him. "If you drive this thing like an old man again, I'm walking."

"What would you have me do?"

"Well, blow the doors off some Camaro or Mustang once in a while," Ana Maria answered. "You got a 4-5-5 under the hood, Arn. Drive it like it's hot. And I know it is, 'cause I put that Quick Fuel carb on myself. How else are you going to pick up chicks?"

"The only thing I'll pick up if I drive like you want me to is some tickets and higher insurance premiums."

Ana Maria shook her head and pushed in the 8-track tape. Music blasted from the rear speakers. "What the hell is that?" she asked as she turned down the volume.

"Zamfir," Arn answered. "Playing the pan flute. It's his latest hit album."

Ana Maria groaned. "Get some Three Dog Night tapes. Santana. Something lively."

"I could pop in the Mormon Tabernacle Choir—"

"Don't you dare," she said.

They drove the tree-lined historic streets of Moore Haven Heights on the way to Dr. Oakert's house. Arn turned onto 5th and pulled to the curb in front of the doctor's brick home. "Let me do the talking," Ana Maria said. "If he still thinks there's a dinner date in our future, he might cough up some more info this time."

Arn followed her up the steps. When she got no answer ringing the doorbell, she walked back down and bent to the bay window facing the street. She cupped her hand over her eyes and looked in. "His computer monitor is lit up. He's got to be in there."

Arn banged on the door so hard he thought it would break the hinges, then banged again between ringing the doorbell.

Ana Maria jumped back. "Shit! He scared the hell outta me."

"Who?"

"Maury. He looked out the window as I was peeking in."

Arn slammed his hand into the door with enough force that the sound echoed off nearby trees, and finally the door cracked an inch. "Go away," Dr. Oakert said.

"We need to talk, Doctor."

"Leave me alone."

"A few minutes." Ana Maria beamed her widest smile. "Just give us a couple minutes."

Dr. Oakert shut the door and the chain rattled on the other side. He opened the door and peeked out quickly before slamming it shut after they had entered.

As Arn's eyes adjusted to the dim light, he took in a quick breath. Dr. Oakert's four-day growth of stubble showed scraggly and graying. His droopy lids rimmed his bloodshot and sunken eyes, and he wore his thick glasses askew on his face. In short, it looked as if he'd aged ten years in the past week. Especially without his toupee. He carried a pistol beside his leg and he looked wild-eyed at them. "I'd feel better if you put that away while we talked," Arn said.

"I'll feel better if I have it," Dr. Oakert said. "You want to talk or not?"

The doctor led them through the house, past his computer and over and around trash, into the kitchen. Arn was sure the dishes piled in the sink and spilling onto the counter were the same as the ones he'd seen on his last visit. Dr. Oakert set his gun on the kitchen table next to a clump of dried food and shoved a partially eaten and moldy Swanson's TV dinner aside. "I'd offer coffee, but you're not going to be here long enough." He motioned to chairs around the table.

Ana Maria leaned over and laid her hand on Dr. Oakert's arm, but he jerked away. "What's wrong, Maury?"

Dr. Oakert rubbed his eyes as he focused on her. "Why do you think there's anything wrong?"

"Because you haven't been to your office in two weeks and you look as if you haven't slept in a month. And this—" She pointed to the gun. "Thought you never had use for them."

"So, I had a revelation." Dr. Oakert grew silent as he stared at the floor.

Arn scooted his chair closer to the doctor, and his gun. Given Oakert's state of mind, he wasn't sure what he might do. "We're here to talk about that special patient of yours—"

"Never mind him—"

"—that visited you recently."

"How do you know that?"

"SWAG," Arn answered. "Scientific Wild Assed Guess."

Dr. Oakert rubbed his rummy eyes again. He cupped his mouth with his hand as if he would be heard and whispered, "He came here a couple days after I closed my office. Right after you left. He dared come to my *house*. He threatened me."

"If you exposed him?"

Dr. Oakert nodded. "He said if I told anyone about him, he'd do to me what he did to Jillie and Don Whales. And all the others."

"What others?" Arn pressed. "Who else has he killed besides Jillie and Don?"

The doctor looked at a spot in the corner of the room.

"Maury," Ana Maria said. She laid her hand on his trembling arm, but this time he didn't jerk away. "Let us help you. Tell us about this man, and we'll see that you have protection."

Dr. Oakert paused as if weighing the offer. "I can't. He's still my patient, and I cannot break that trust."

"Don't you think his threats breached that trust?"

Dr. Oakert stared at Ana Maria. "He's sick," he began. "In time, I *know* he will recover. In time, he *will* get his urges under control, like he did before. And he will be a fine person once again. I cannot help you find him."

"This's just stupid," Arn said. "One of your patients threatens you bad enough that you fear for your life and buy a gun, and you still won't lift a finger to help yourself?"

"If I'm wrong about him"—Dr. Oakert tapped his gun—"I've got this."

"When was the last time you shot it?"

"Never have. I just bought it."

"I bet you don't even know how to operate it," Arn said.

"The man at the gun store showed me."

Arn threw up his hands. "This is just stupid. Don't bank on that piss-ant little gun to save your ass. Any man powerful enough to over-power someone as big as Don Whales is certainly powerful enough to take that and shove it—"Arn stood and walked away from the table before he might slap the doctor senseless.

"Give us *something* to go on," Ana Maria said. "Anything that'll help us find this man without breaching your confidentiality."

Dr. Oakert looked up at her.

"Before he kills again."

"He won't."

"If you believed that you wouldn't have bought the gun," Ana Maria pointed out. "Please."

Dr. Oakert rested his elbows on the table into a glob of grape jelly, but he paid it no mind and held his head in his hands. "He's a ghost of patients past."

"What ghost, Maury? What patients?"

"That's all I can say. Now leave. I don't want you two hurt if he returns."

Arn and Ana Maria stood and started out of the kitchen with the doctor following, his gun held loosely beside his leg. *Napa Hospital* was displayed on his computer screen, along with a list of patients, Ana Maria paused to read it but Dr. Oakert hurriedly shut the computer down. "Leave," he said.

They passed through his study and the wall lined with appreciation letters and commendations. "When did you move to Cheyenne?" Arn asked.

"Three years ago."

"When you retired from practice in California?"

Dr. Oakert grimaced. "I called it voluntary retirement. I got tired of dealing with the criminally insane."

"Like your special patient here in Cheyenne? Was he your patient in Napa as well?"

Dr. Oakert's eye twitched. A micro-tic that told Arn he'd touched a nerve.

Unlocking the three locks, the doctor opened the door just far enough to allow Arn and Ana Maria to leave before slamming it shut.

Arn looked over his shoulder. Dr. Oakert had pulled the curtain aside and watched them walk to the car. "Whether his patient killed Jillie and Don is not certain," Arn said. "But my educated guess is that *one* of his patients in Napa Hospital followed the doctor here."

Thirty-Four

WHY ARE ANDERSON AND Ana Maria in the doctor's house so long? Of course, there can be only one answer: the doctor told them about me. Or he gave them enough information to learn who I am. In time, they'll hunt me down. I cannot risk Anderson on my case any longer. Especially after I blew it last night.

I settle back in my truck with a Thermos of coffee. Last night was an exercise in egomania.

I got overconfident.

I went to Anderson's house knowing he and everyone inside would be asleep. Knowing he owned no dog to alert him. Knowing from walking around his house before that his archaic alarm system was tied to the phone lines. And that if I cut them, he would have no way of knowing I entered his house.

Except something went wrong.

How the hell did he hear me at the door? And how did I ever hear him in time to run and hide behind that abandoned car down the street? I only barely managed to leave the safety of that car and run to my truck. I chalk it up to being momentarily taken aback: when Anderson stepped onto the porch, the street light illuminated a gun in his hand. I wasn't counting on that. But I'll remember that gun when I catch him unawares the next time.

As I know I must soon.

They're still inside Dr. Oakert's house. The doctor is a man of integrity and—until just today—I was certain he'd told them nothing.

Now I know he has. He might have told them about the ladies I ... found in California and Utah and Nevada and Arizona, ladies that were all too glad to accept a date from an out-of-town gentleman with disposable money to spoil them with. If only for a night.

I stifle a laugh. The doctor thought he could rehabilitate me, bring me along for eventual release into society. He had me working the hospital laundry and the engine shop and the animal hospital and the carpentry wing until he found I was best suited for something intellectual—the hospital library. Who the hell works a library in the loony bin?

They come out of the doctor's house, and I scoot down in the seat despite being a block away. I check my watch: they've been talking with him thirty minutes, and I know—just know—the doctor has crossed the line; he's finally told them things he ought not to have told them. And it almost makes me sad that I'll have to visit him again and ask him personally. Soon.

Ana Maria is a different matter. Dr. Oakert once told me in session not to feel ashamed that I'm attracted to a woman with a particular look, or a particular air about her. And I've realized Ana Maria is like the others. Yet not like them. Her dark eyes and dark complexion are just like the rest. But her brown hair would take mere moments to snip short.

Then she'd look like the others.

And I suspect that when I talk to Ana Maria like Dr. Oakert taught me to talk to a woman, she'll come around to my way of thinking.

If not, I'll do what I must to convince her.

Thirty-Five

ARN AND ANA MARIA agreed they needed to take a breather and wind down after talking with Dr. Oakert. They grabbed a corner booth at the Village Inn and ordered lunch. "He's close to telling us," Ana Maria said. "He *wanted* to spill his professional guts. He was this close." She held up her hand and the teaspoon in the other, an inch apart.

Arn had thought the doctor wanted to say more, too. Maury Oakert was so frightened that if there'd been a sudden backfire from a car he would have had the big MI right there in his home. "Remember that man I questioned in the death of a neighbor's nine-year-old in Denver that time?" he asked.

"Do I," Ana Maria said. "I still get nightmares now and again."

"Well, after I left him without him confessing, I let him stew. Think things through, and how it would be a relief to get the homicide off his chest. I went back two hours later and I thought he'd crawl right into my lap he was so glad to see me. And glad to get her death off his chest."

"You think if we go back there later Dr. Oakert will tell us about his special patient?"

Arn held up his hand when his cell phone rang. "I got a name of a serial killer in California that fits the MO perfectly," Sergeant Slade told him.

"How close a match?" Arn covered the receiver. "Slade's got a good hit from Sacramento." He tapped the speaker phone.

"A guy by the name of Steve Campbell murdered eight women in four states. At least that's the number they know about. And each died the same way—brought to the point of death before being allowed to live. Then he repeated it until finally killing them."

"With eight victims, the guy must still be in prison." Arn dropped his head with a sinking feeling. "Tell me he didn't get paroled."

"Not paroled," Slade said. "Freed. He was deemed Not Guilty by Reason of Insanity, and they sent him to the loony bin in Napa. After nine years he was pronounced cured—drum roll here—by Napa Hospital shrink Maury Oakert. The good doctor certified Campbell ready to take his place in society four years ago."

"They have photos of Campbell?"

"A detective from San Leandro who handled two of Campbell's victims is faxing them today."

"And you're sure Campbell is our killer?"

"We should know with the pics. Listen." Slade paused, and Arn heard footsteps walking past on the other end of the phone. "Campbell met his victims on internet dating sites. He lived in Sacramento but drove as far away as Utah and Arizona to meet his marks. He fits the troller badge Dr. Oakert gave him."

"As soon as you get the pics, let me know, okay?" Arn said.

"This is one you'll miss out on," Slade replied. "As soon as I get the pics I'll send our guys out beating the bushes for him." He laughed.

"This is one that won't be solved by the famous Arn Anderson but by us local rubes."

Arn disconnected and pushed his lunch aside.

"If Slade wasn't going to let you in one the killer's ID once he sees the photos, why call you in the first place?" Ana Maria asked.

"SOB just wanted to taunt me a little. Let me know he can handle the case," Arn said. "Looks like we better pay Dr. Oakert another visit."

———————

Arn was pulling his car to the curb in front of the doctor's house when he tromped on the foot feed. His tires smoked as he squealed away from the house.

"What are you doing—"

"Something's not right." Arn pulled to the curb a block away and grabbed his Airweight .38 from his ankle rig. "The front door's open the tiniest bit, and the doctor's lights are on. Stay here."

He kept hidden behind trees lining the avenue to mask his approach to the house. An elderly woman across the street rose from pruning her daisies. When she spotted him, she dropped her scissors and ran into her house as he inched up the steps to the front door. He took a deep, calming breath before he flung the door open and button-hooked inside.

"Looks like Maury's been in a fight or something."

Arn spun around in a crouch. When he saw Ana Maria in the doorway, he stood up. "I told you to stay in the car."

"Whatever." She waved the air. "I'm here now."

"At least have the common sense to wait until I clear the rest of the house."

She nodded and remained at the front door while Arn methodically went from room to room, but he found the house empty. "Clear," he said.

Ana Maria stepped around overturned chairs in the living room, and nearly stepped on the doctor's broken ashtray. Old butts littered the floor, and a bottle of Johnny Walker lay smashed against the broken leg of an end table. Arn stuck his gun in his back pocket. "Some fight the doctor was in."

"That's an understatement. Where's Maury?"

"Who knows," Arn said. "His car's gone from the garage. Check his computer while I call Oblanski."

"Looking at his computer is a little illegal," Ana Maria said.

"Whatever." Arn imitated Ana Maria's voice. "The chance he's still alive to press charges is remote."

"You're serious? We just talked with him—"

"Check his 'puter." Arn called Oblanski on his private line. "I think something's happened to Dr. Oakert—"

"I know," Oblanski said. "His neighbor across the street reported some big guy sneaking up to the doctor's house with a gun. I have units responding."

"That was me," Arn said as sirens approached. He quickly filled Oblanski in on what Oakert said, and how pictures of Steve Campbell were being faxed to Slade that afternoon. "And the sooner you put out a BOLO for Dr. Oakert, the sooner we might find him."

"We?" Oblanski said. "The only thing you got to do right now is go outside with your hands above your head. My units just arrived and are positioned around the house. Tell my forensics team where you were in the house. They should be there about the time the patrol officers handcuff you."

"You're not going to tell them I'm one of the good guys?"

Oblanski laughed. "With all the nuts in town, they can't be too careful."

Thirty-Six

ARN DRAGGED IN FROM another failed night of watching for the Midnight Sheepherder. He slipped his boots off and padded barefoot into the kitchen. "Flapjacks," Danny said. "With strawberry syrup." He set a cup of coffee in front of Arn, but Arn waved it away. "I don't want one drop of caffeine coming between me and my bunk."

"Tough night, huh?"

"The toughest," Arn said. "I did the pecking bird all night. Someone could have driven a semi into that pasture I was watching and I'm sure I would have slept through it."

"Wasn't Karen putting the sneak on you, the last time, incentive enough to keep awake?" Danny asked.

"That's the last thing I thought of before I dozed off."

After finding the doctor missing, Arn had remained at Dr. Oakert's house with police detectives and their forensics techs, going through the house, pointing out what he and Ana Maria had touched. The techs needed to eliminate them, along with Dr. Oakert, before they could concentrate on prints that didn't belong. By the time they finished processing the house it had been nearly dark outside—just the time to go out and watch for the rustler.

"By the way, where is Ana Maria?" Arn asked.

"Oblanski called. The police department received a mocking note like the one the sheriff's office got a few days ago. She thinks they'll let her photograph it. She knows a private questioned-documents examiner in Boulder who might help."

"Good," Arn said, using the table to stand. "Then I'll have the upstairs all to myself today. Nighty night." He plodded toward the railing leading upstairs when his cell phone rang. He paused, thinking he might just let it go to voicemail, when he saw it was Slade's number.

"The night deputies may have caught your sheep thief," Slade said. "Just for courtesy sake, I thought you'd want to sit in on the interview."

"Interview of whom?"

"Eddie Glass."

Arn pocketed his phone and walked back to the kitchen. "Better fill my big mug," he said as he downed the first cup of coffee. "I'm going to need it before the morning's over."

By the time Arn got to the sheriff's office, Eddie Glass was already seated in an interview room. Sergeant Slade motioned to a chair in front of the one-way glass and turned the volume up.

Eddie sat half-sideways in the metal chair bolted to the floor, his arms hanging over the chair back as if he had no cares. "I was just out on that county road running my dog. Giving her some exercise. Nothing illegal about that," he told the interrogator who sat across the table from him.

"Running your dog at two in the morning?" the deputy said. "You have enough room on that ranch you work at to exercise her there."

Eddie smiled. "Maybe I didn't want to wake up the boss."

Arn flipped off the speaker. "Your guys brought him in for running his dog?"

"They brought him in because he was running it in Pearly Marshfield's pasture."

Pearly Mansfield was one of the ranchers consistently missing sheep. She'd reported breaches of her fence no less than four times this year, and she'd been one of the forces behind hiring Arn as a stock detective. "I just sat on her pasture three nights ago," he said.

"Then your timing was off." Slade grinned and flipped the speaker back on.

"If you got something on me, charge me," Eddie said.

The deputy interrogating Eddie opened a manila folder. "Night deputies found where you took the gate down to enter Pearly's pasture. And your tire marks show you drove among her sheep."

"I told you what I was doing. About the only thing you can charge me with is trespassing. I'm walking outta here." Without another word, Eddie Glass stood and walked to the door.

"He's right," Slade told Arn. "We got nothing else to hold him on. We'll issue him a trespassing citation and that'll be it." He slapped the wall. "But I *know* he's dirty. I *know* he wasn't just exercising his dog at two in the morning. Damn! He knows just enough law to know we got nothing to make him sweat with."

"I might be able to help," Arn said. "A little sweat will do Eddie a lot of good."

Thirty-Seven

I CAN'T TAKE MY eyes off Ana Maria Villarreal, *striking in the way she looks like the others. I'd love nothing better than to get to know her intimately. Like the others. But like my drunken father said sometime before I killed him: a man doesn't shit in his own nest. That said, I had to silence Jillie before she yelled to everyone in town about my past. And Don Whales had the misfortune of helping with the dog class and demonstrating his dog's ability. I thought he was the Midnight Sheepherder. Sorry, Don, wherever you are now. I was wrong about you, buddy.*

I'm back to driving to find the lady of my dreams one of these nights. I've corresponded with one in Omaha. She's agreed to meet me, but she'll have to wait. I'll string her along while the perfect lady is practically on my doorstep, and speaking into the microphone like she's talking just to me: "Dr. Maury Oakert is forty-six years old," *Ana Maria tells us TV-land viewers,* "with a ruddy complexion and a pronounced widow's peak when he's not wearing his toupee. He was last seen yesterday afternoon at his house," *and she gives the number of a tip line for folks to call if they see him.*

I'm not a betting man, but I would wager no one will find Maury. Not in this life. And not until I want him found.

She continues with her nightly broadcast while a tip number continuously flashes across the bottom of the screen. If anyone has seen the good doctor. Or knows of sheep being stolen or sold belonging to Pearly Marshfield. I have to laugh: they're usually pretty competent, but the deputy last night was inexperienced and botched the trespassing call at Pearly's. It was almost laughable listening to the police scanner. And I know they'll botch their two murder investigations. Three, including Maury now. I'd better send them another brief note just to help them along. And to let them know I'm still thinking about them.

I like Cheyenne, but I know that things are heating up here. So I'm packing my shit, and all I have to figure out is where to move next. I kiss my finger and touch the television screen. I'll have another talk with Ana Maria before I go. And another personal visit with Anderson.

Then it's adios Cheyenne for Steve Campbell.

Thirty-Eight

ARN AND DANNY SAT blacked-out a hundred yards from Eddie Glass's driveway. "This Olds blends in like a colored man at a KKK rally," Danny said. "Eddie's bound to spot you."

Arn refilled his coffee cup from a Thermos and handed it to Danny. "Nonsense. We came in here darked out, and this cottonwood is big enough to hide even this boat. If he comes out tonight, I'm certain he's going to be concentrating on stealing Pearly's sheep that he missed last night when the deputy interrupted him."

"Why would he risk going back there so soon after getting caught?" Danny broke off a piece of donut and nibbled at it.

"That's just what Eddie figures folks would think. No one would think he'd return to Pearly's so soon."

"I hope he's not out too late," Danny said. "I've still got half a pile of tires to sort through tomorrow." He pointed out the side glass. "And right now Eddie's coming out of his house."

220

Arn squinted, but he was unable to see Eddie's shack in the darkness. He'd asked Danny once how he got such good night vision. His "Us Indians are born with good night vision" response answered no questions. But it was the reason he'd dragged Danny along tonight.

Eddie pulled onto the county road, his taillights quickly obscured by the dust kicked up by his truck. Arn let Eddie drop over the first rise before he started around the cottonwood. Danny hung his head out the window, yelling directions to Arn as they followed Eddie in the pitch blackness. "Left," Danny said, and Arn corrected. "Right hand curve coming up ... now," and Arn gently turned the Oldsmobile.

Up ahead, Eddie's taillights merged with headlights of another vehicle, and they both turned into Pearly's pasture. Arn used his emergency brake to stop. "Wonder who he's meeting?"

"Even I can't see that good," Danny said, pulling his head back into the car. He spit dust and took a swig of his coffee to wash it down. "But I'd bet it's his partner in crime."

Eddie and his accomplice slowly drove through a gate and hugged the ridgeline before they doused their lights. "That's our cue." Arn drove in first gear slowly along the gravel road until Danny spotted where the two vehicles had crossed an auto gate leading into the pasture. The gate lay open and on the ground, and Arn inched his car through the field on Danny's direction. "Stop," Danny whispered. He pointed in the dark "They're about forty yards straight down this fence line."

Arn grabbed his flashlight from the center console. "Cover the dome light."

Danny cupped his hand over the light until Arn was out and had closed the door, easing it shut soundlessly. He wiggled his revolver out of his trouser pocket and approached the two trucks, their faint outlines barely visible.

Arn stopped short. Muffled voices rose and fell with the breeze: two people, and one was a woman. Suddenly, a dog barked. Arn flicked on his light and ran the last few yards to the pickups.

Eddie Glass was seated behind the wheel of his truck, blinded by the bright flashlight, eyes as wild-eyed as Bonnie Johns's, who was sitting on his lap. Eddie's dog sat on his haunches in the pickup bed and snarled. "Call your dog off, or . . ." Arn waved his gun so Eddie could see it.

Eddie gave the dog a command, and the Border collie lay down quietly in the bed of the truck.

"Let me see your hands, Eddie."

"What the f—"

Arn shoved the gun into the open window inches from Eddie's head. "Show them."

Eddie held his hands high so Arn could see.

"Now turn on your headlights and get out. You too, Bonnie."

They climbed out of Eddie's truck and Arn motioned them to stand by the hood. The headlights illuminated them, and Bonnie looked scared.

"Now what the hell's going on?" Eddie asked.

Arn backed away. "You tell me. This is the second night in a row you're on someone else's property. And with your dog, too. Just exercising him tonight as well?"

Eddie's fists balled up. "Next time I see you, it'll be without that gun."

Arn smiled. "Next time you see me it might be from the other side of jail bars." He turned to Bonnie. "You've been unusually quiet. You in this little venture with Eddie?"

"What venture?"

"Rustling sheep."

"No way we're partners in that!" Bonnie answered. "I just meet Eddie out here—"

"Shut up," Eddie snapped.

"But he'll call the law," Bonnie pled. "Might as well tell him."

"Mind?" Eddie motioned to his pocket.

"Go ahead."

Eddie fished a pack of Pall Malls out of his pocket and thumbed a match. "Me and Bonnie started to meet out in the country to patch things up."

"As in, romantically?"

"Is there any other kind?".

"Did you forget Eddie's a married man?"

Bonnie put her arm around Eddie's neck. "He's going to leave his wife."

"That right, Eddie? You going to leave your wife and your new baby?"

"When the chance is right."

Arn rubbed his forehead. A headache was fast approaching. "You tell that to all the women you mess around with?"

"Bonnie's my girl—"

"I've talked with three more women who you promised to leave your wife for," Arn lied.

When Bonnie slapped Eddie, Arn thought it was a thing of beauty. His smirk left him and his cigarette flew out of his mouth. "You son-of-a-bitch."

Arn stepped between them. "You visit with me for a moment." He took Bonnie by the arm and led her away from the front of Eddie's truck, far enough away that he couldn't hear. "What are you doing out here? Don't you know he makes it his vocation to bed as many women—other than his own wife—as he can?"

Bonnie looked over her shoulder and glared at Eddie. "And to think I damned near got caught trespassing with him here last night."

"You were here?"

"Almost. I was just coming up the road when I spotted the deputy turn into Pearly's field, so I just drove on by."

Arn remained quiet, letting Bonnie tell her tale at her own pace. "Me and Eddie had a thing last summer, but broke it off when his wife got wind of it." She spit tobacco juice on the ground. "I've been going with Eddie on his out-of-town trips to dog shows, or when he teaches his seminars. With his domineering old lady, it's the only way we could have some quality time."

"You call this quality time?" Arn asked.

Bonnie shrugged. "It's better than not being with him. But now I learn he's messing with more women." She spit again. "I'd lop his nuts off if I didn't owe him."

Bonnie told Arn that Eddie had arranged for her and Beverly to give the dog classes. The fee they charged helped with ranch expenses, which had been getting out of control lately. And he'd loaned her his beater truck to use after she had to park hers in back of the barn with the rest of the crapped-out machinery so the cops wouldn't find it. "Up until tonight, I thought he treated me pretty good."

"And you can stand there and tell me you have nothing to do with sheep rustling?"

"No way!" Bonnie fiercely met Arn's stare.

"And Eddie?" Arn said. "That dog of his is trained really well. He ever into sheep stealing?"

"Mr. Anderson," Bonnie said, glancing over her shoulder, "that SOB's a scoundrel and a bastard, apparently, but he's no thief. I'll swear on that."

"Has he always made it to the dog classes on time?"

"What you mean?"

"You vouched for Eddie being at class that Saturday."

"So?"

224

"Was it the truth, or was that what he told you to say?"

When Bonnie didn't answer, Arn nodded to Eddie leaning on the hood of his truck. "That's what I thought—he wasn't there right at eight. You can join Eddie now."

Arn followed Bonnie to the truck. The thought that Bonnie and Eddie were the Midnight Sheepherder was fading fast.

"You have a schedule of your classes you've given around the country?" Arn asked him. "Something with dates on them?"

"Look it up," Eddie blurted out. "It's all on my website." He took a step closer to Arn. "Now either shoot me with that silly gun or put it away so's I don't have to shove it where you won't like it."

Arn grinned and pocketed his gun. He'd finally had a butt-full of this smart-ass. "See?" He held up his hands. "No gun."

Eddie came away from the hood of the truck without warning, and swung a looping left roundhouse at Arn's head. Arn stepped to Eddie's right and threw his own punch. It wasn't particularly hard. It wasn't particularly fast. But it was a blow that he'd used many times working the street when faced with an assaultive drunk. The blow landed flush on Eddie's liver. He dropped to his knees, moaned in pain, and toppled over clutching his back. Bonnie forgot her anger with him and dropped to the ground beside him. She shielded him with her body as if Arn intended on hitting him again. "My God, don't kill him!"

"He'll live," Arn said. "When he recovers in about twenty minutes, you two clear out of this pasture, or the deputies will have to arrest both of you for trespassing tonight."

Thirty-Nine

"IT MAKES SENSE." ANA Maria waved a spatula around like she was fending off an attacker. "If Bonnie goes with Eddie on his trips, that explains why her place is so run down."

Danny sat on the edge of his chair. He'd argued with Arn that it might not be the best decision to let Ana Maria cook breakfast. "Relax," Arn had told him. "She's got to learn sometime. After all, she'll be little Miss Homemaker one day when she's married and has to cook."

Danny kept a wary eye on Ana Maria's kitchen antics. "Bonnie must not be doing too badly if she paid for Eddie's new truck," he said. "How can she afford that?"

Ana Maria flipped a pancake in the air. It landed on the floor and she looked at it for a long moment. "Five second rule?"

"I'd toss it," Danny said. "We're not so ghetto that we need to eat from the floor."

Before Danny could pick it up, Sonny crawled out from under the table and scooped it up in one bite. He trudged back under the table and sat on Arn's foot while he waited for Ana Maria's next flop.

She shrugged and poured batter onto the griddle. "Beverly said she's about fed up with Bonnie giving ranch money that should go to maintaining the place to Eddie Glass. Sure, she owes Eddie for setting the dog class up, but appreciation only goes so far."

"I just don't get it." Danny eyed Ana Maria's pancake technique. "Why would Bonnie hang around a married man, let alone spring for a new truck?"

"Love is blind." Ana Maria flipped a flapjack onto Arn's plate. This one stayed put, and she handed Danny the spatula. "I think I'm all cooked-out. Better leave it to the pro." She poured herself a cup of joe and sat across from Arn.

"What's the latest on Eddie's schedule?" Arn asked.

Ana Maria pulled a wadded-up piece of paper from her pajama pocket and spread it on the table. "He travels for his shows and seminars. *A lot.* I compared the dates with the teletypes Slate got from the other agencies. Of the six murders, Eddie was out of town—and within driving distance—of four of them."

"I'd think he'd be too tired to drive after a day of giving classes," Danny said, expertly flipping a pancake onto Ana Maria's plate.

"Unless someone else did the driving for him," she said.

"Like Bonnie?" Arn dribbled syrup onto his pancake. "If she bought him a truck, and puts up with his messing with other women, it wouldn't be a stretch to think she might drive Eddie to his … dates. She did admit to me she goes with him on out-of-town trips when she can."

"That's pretty sexist."

Arn looked to Ana Maria for an explanation.

"You're overlooking the other possibility: Bonnie could be the one meeting victims while Eddie is conducting his training seminars."

"Now *that's* a stretch. But it would make for sensational news." Arn winked at Ana Maria. "Bonnie might be a borderline drunk, but there's nothing to indicate she could be the killer. Remember, I'm waiting for photos of Steve Campbell. Slade said there was a problem faxing them through, so the California investigator shipped them overnight UPS."

"Still," Ana Maria pressed, "Eddie *could* take a love-struck woman under his wing. Wouldn't be the first time a man and women teamed up to murder young women."

Arn knew Ana Maria was right. In the history of the country, there had been numerous male-female killing partners. Often the woman lured the victim somewhere, breaking down their natural fear of strangers. Most women would willingly go somewhere with another woman when they might not go with a man.

"And Bonnie is a ranch girl. Used to tossing eighty-pound bales of hay around," Ana Maria continued. "She'd be strong enough to strangle another woman." She finished her breakfast and checked her watch. "We'll know soon enough. I'm scheduled to interview Eddie for a feature."

Arn had a bad feeling about Ana Maria meeting with Eddie all by her lonesome. "What's the feature?"

"What else." She smiled. "His dog class. And in the process of asking my stock questions, I just may throw him a curve ball and ask him directly if he's the Saturday Night Strangler."

"I wish you'd wait until Slade gets the photos of Campbell. If Eddie's the strangler, he might not take that question so well."

"Relax," Ana Maria said. "You can rest assured that whenever I interview Eddie, there'll be witnesses around. Along with that little gun you ... gave me."

———————

Danny tossed the paper plates into the garbage. He was starting out the door with the Hefty sack when he stopped and set the bag down. "You're going to step on your lip again." He motioned to Sonny lying on Arn's foot. "You look like him."

"How's that?" Arn asked.

"You've been moping around here chewing your fingernails like you're starved. Something's bothering you."

Arn swirled a spoon around in his cold coffee. "I worry about Ana Maria. She's taking this thing way too lightly. Even knowing someone's been following her."

Danny sat across from Arn. "I've got to agree. After that night someone tried getting in, you'd think her guard would be up. But the next day it was like nothing happened with her."

Arn flicked a piece of flapjack dangling amongst some drool from Sonny's muzzle. "Ana Maria thinks I'm too paranoid. She's convinced herself it was just some kids trying to get in the house. And she's putting too much store in that gun I gave her."

"Kids usually don't break into houses with the homeowners still there. There are enough abandoned places they could get into for their partying."

"That's what I told her. She insists I blew it out of proportion, while at the same time admitting someone is following her."

"She can take care of herself." Danny offered Arn a piece of cake, but he turned it down. Danny let Sonny lick frosting off his fork before taking a bite himself.

Arn looked at Danny and shook his head. "Sonny just licked his butt and you have him licking your silverware?"

"Protein," Danny said and cut into the cake again. "Didn't you say she went into some pretty gnarly places when she worked in Denver?"

"The worst," Arn said. "But this is different. If she is being followed, the stalker's got a big enough obsession with her to risk getting caught. I sure wish she'd wait until Slade gets Campbell's photos."

Forty

ARN WIPED HIS TIRE-GRIMY hands on his jeans. He sat on a tire at the bottom of Fat Boy's heap and answered his phone. "Dr. Oakert's been located," Oblanski said.

Arn crawled off the mound of tires and turned his back to the wind. "Where'd you find him?"

"We didn't," Oblanski said. "The deputies found him. All I know is he'd dead."

"Where?"

"County road up north. Slade and his forensics people are headed there now with the state crime van. Not a hundred yards from where deputies caught Eddie Glass trespassing a couple nights ago."

"You going to help here?" Danny said, still sorting tires.

Arn ignored him and cupped his hand over the phone. "What did Eddie say about it?"

"Can't say that either," Oblanski answered. "He's disappeared. I'd disappear too. Slade put out a BOLO for him a few minutes ago."

Arn disconnected and checked his calls. Ana Maria had left him a voicemail telling him Eddie had failed to show for his interview with her and she was going to the Johns' ranch to look for him. "I just hope I catch him and Bonnie doing the wild thing," her message concluded.

Arn dialed her phone but it went to voicemail. He left a message. "Dr. Oakert's been found dead where deputies stopped Eddie a few nights ago. Don't go to the Johns' place looking for Eddie. Repeat, don't go."

Danny stood and stretched his back atop the mountain of tires. "Problems?"

"I can't get hold of Ana Maria." He gave Danny the headline version of Dr. Oakert being found and Eddie disappearing. "I'm afraid if she looks for Eddie she'll find him."

Danny rubbed his forehead and a black streak smeared across his head. "I can't blame you. But there is a *little* good news." He lobbed a tire onto the ground. It rolled a few feet before falling over. "That's a Cooper with a good size chunk of tread and sidewall missing."

Arn bent to the tire and ran his hand over it. He didn't have a cast of the tire print he'd spotted in Wooly Hank's pasture—Slade and the sheriff's office had that—but the tire appeared to be a match to the impression the killer's truck had made. "I'll call into the sheriff's office and have one of Slade's guys pick this tire up. Give it to them when they arrive. In the meantime, go inside and grab Adam and see if that's one of Floyd's old tires."

Danny put his hands on his bony hips. "And just what are you going to do while I'm doing the heavy work?"

"I'm going to Bonnie and Beverly's ranch. Ana Maria might have been unlucky enough to catch Eddie there."

Oblanski called Arn as he was turning onto the county road five miles from the Johns' turnoff. "Turns out Sacramento has no photos of Steve Campbell after all. They were just switching to digital booking photos about the time he was released, and they had problems back then. But I sent them photos of Eddie Glass when the sheriff's office nabbed him the other night."

"Any luck with that BOLO?"

"Troopers thought they had Glass's truck on I-25 north of town, but they lost it once they turned around. And before I forget it—Dr. Oakert's car was found parked at the curb a block from his home."

"It just gets better and better." Arn stopped to let a Black White-Face heifer cross the road."

"I'll let you know if I hear anything. And by the way, would photos of the victims help? The task force formed to investigate the murders catalogued them."

"I don't see how," Arn said, "but send them to my phone anyhow."

He disconnected and tried Slade's number again. "I got no time to talk, Anderson."

"Just a quick question," Arn blurted out before Slade could hang up.

"Better be real quick. We're fixing to work Dr. Oakert's crime scene."

"Okay," Arn said. "Was the doctor killed the same way as Jillie Reilly and Don Whales?"

"How'd you guess?"

"Any stock detective could figure it out," Arn said. "And I understand Eddie's on the run."

"He hasn't been located yet if that's what you mean," Slade said. "Right now all I want him for is to interview him. There's nothing to indicate he killed Dr. Oakert."

"Hardly coincidental the doctor's body was found close to where Eddie was stopped a couple nights ago."

"What do you want from me, because I'm up to my ass in alligators here."

"Have you tried the Johns' ranch? Eddie and Bonnie are still having an affair, and he might go there."

"Anderson, we don't have unlimited manpower like you big city dicks did. There's been more sightings of Eddie Glass than there have been UFOs, and we're running them all down. When I get a free unit, we'll send someone out there."

Arn pocketed his cell phone and turned onto the Johns' drive. When he drove into the yard, Beverly had just crawled off an old Allis Chalmers with very little red paint left on it. A cigarette hung out of her mouth and a pair of work gloves hung out of her back pocket. There were days when Beverly was attractive. And days when she wasn't. Today—after hours of hard work—she was less than her best self.

Arn shut off his car and met her as she brushed dirt off her dungarees. "I need to talk with Bonnie right away."

"Whoa," Beverly said as she backed away. "You need to calm down a little. My sister hasn't done anything. She told me what happened when you caught her and Eddie necking in Pearly's pasture."

"I have reason to believe Eddie may be the Saturday Night Strangler."

Beverly tilted her head back and laughed. "He's a flaming jerk, and I hate him for stringing Bonnie along, but he's no killer."

"Are you willing to take that chance with Bonnie?"

Beverly's smile faded.

"Ana Maria was supposed to meet Eddie someplace for an interview, and I think she'll be in danger if she finds him."

"She never mentioned Eddie when she was here."

"She was here? When?"

"She stopped by to start work on Bonnie's pickup. She said she was supposed to talk with someone but they never showed up. That must have been Eddie."

Arn looked around. "I don't see Bonnie's truck."

"The tan outfit?" Beverly said. "That was Eddie's old beater he let Bonnie use until hers could be repaired." She started for the barn. "Bonnie's is here." She motioned to the tarp that covered the vehicle beside the broken-down tractor. "Don was going to fix the old McCormick, but…"

Trailing off, she led Arn to the tarp. She unhooked bungee cords securing it and threw the tarp back. Dust and chaff had settled on the dented navy blue truck, and he didn't have to compare his paint chip to know that Bonnie's truck was the same color as the rustler's truck that hit Wooly Hank's gate.

Arn bent to the truck and ran his hand over a broken marker light dangling from the damaged fender. It had crinkled when Bonnie hit the gate. He straightened and faced Beverly. "Bonnie didn't go out drinking after she was kicked out of the Boot Hill that night, did she?"

Beverly nudged a corn cob with the toe of her boot.

"And no one drove her truck home that night for her, did they?"

"What are you saying?" Beverly asked, her voice breaking up.

"I think you know just what I'm saying. Bonnie was witness that night to Jillie's murder. I think she was at Wooly Hank's to rustle sheep. Probably took your Buckwheat with her." He showed her the paint chip and shards of marker light. "She left this when she fled."

The color drained from Beverly's face. "Are you suggesting Eddie is the strangler?"

"He could be."

"But Bonnie would report him—"

"Think again," Arn said. "She loves Eddie so much, she might not. But if Eddie *is* the strangler—and if he realizes *Bonnie* is the witness—he won't hesitate to kill her, too."

"Oh, God," Beverly said, running her fingers through hair matted with alfalfa chaff. "I'll start checking her usual haunts."

"And I'll call Slade and have him add Bonnie to that BOLO."

Beverly ran to the house for her truck keys, while Arn grabbed his phone to call the sheriff's office. The photos of Steve Campbell's victims had downloaded, and Arn opened them. Each corpse showed where a ligature had choked the life out of them—repeatedly. The killer—like the killer of Jillie and Don—had enjoyed choking them to the point of death before letting up, only to enjoy it again. Until he grew tired of the game.

Arn maximized the photos. Each of Campbell's victims had dark eyes. And dark complexion. And dark hair.

And each was about Ana Maria's age.

Arn shuddered as he looked at the photos of the dead victims. Any one of them—if their hair were long—could have been Ana Maria.

Forty-One

"**HOW AM I SUPPOSED** to drive all the way to the Johns' ranch?" Danny asked. He'd located all four tires from Floyd's truck and caught a cab home. The manager had assured him that Adam would verify the tires were the ones he was looking for as soon as he returned from a doctor's appointment.

"Excuse me," Arn said to Chief Oblanski as he stepped into the hallway to continue his conversation. "I'm at the station, Danny. I can't go back out to the ranch right now—I'm downloading a picture of Eddie and the rest I took since going to Wooly Hank's that morning. Oblanski's sending photos to Sacramento. Maybe someone from the serial killer task force they formed some years ago will recognize him."

"Nice try," Danny said. "You calling me tells me you got your phone."

"I'm using the chief's phone while his tech guy has mine downloading the images. You have to go. To the Johns' ranch."

"Hello!" Danny said. "I don't even have a driver's license—"

"I know you can drive."

"Of course I can," Danny said. "I just chose to have you cart me around. It wouldn't be legal for me to drive."

"Like you've never done anything illegal before."

There was a long pause at the other end of the phone. "So maybe I have. I still don't have anything to drive."

"DeAngelo's beater truck is parked on the front lawn. Ana Maria finished the head job, and it runs just fine. Drive that out there."

"You owe me for this," Danny said and disconnected.

Arn walked back into Oblanski's office as the police IT man returned and handed Arn his phone. "All the pics are downloaded. Even those ones with you parading around the house in just your underwear."

"What?" Arn couldn't recall a photo like that. But Danny wasn't above pulling some prank like snapping a photo in him in his Fruit of the Looms.

"Just kidding," the man said. Then, "I'll send them off to Sacramento right away." He shut the door after him.

"Still nothing on Ana Maria?" Arn asked. Since putting a BOLO out on her, he'd thought of every place she might be, but come up blank at those he'd checked. He hoped Beverly or Bonnie would have news for Danny, or at least a lead by now on where Ana Maria might be.

"Nothing on Ana Maria," Oblanski said, "or on Eddie Glass, either. Sounds like the sheriff's deputies stopped by their place and Karen wasn't there either."

Arn grabbed his briefcase and headed out the door. "Let me know if you locate her."

"I will," Oblanski said. "And I'll let you know if someone can put Eddie's face with Steve Campbell from when he was a patient at Napa Hospital. Where you headed?"

"Floyd's father's train is going to roll into the depot soon. He wants to give me some paperwork he found when he cleaned out the truck after Floyd bought it. Bunch of old maintenance receipts and crap to give back to Scott."

"You work for UPS now?" Oblanski asked.

"At this point," Arn answered, feeling wearier than he had for years, "I'd gladly take that job.'

He left the building and checked his watch: he had another forty-five minutes until Fred Pompolopolis was due at the depot.

By the time he'd fired up his Olds, all sorts of scenarios of what had happened to Ana Maria had run through his head. And the only one that stood out was that she'd gotten too close—like she often got too close to bad people—and Eddie had killed her. Or worse, he took her somewhere to draw out her misery. Arn found himself driving by the church his mother had attended. She hadn't been Greek Ortho-dox, nor had she gone there all her life; she'd been about as conscious of her mortality as Arn's drunken father hadn't been while Arn was growing up. But one day she'd stopped in as she was walking by. The chanting, the songs—as she later told Arn—had beckoned her inside somehow. She walked in that Sunday and she never left.

Just like Arn found himself doing now. He'd parked and started up the long flight of steps leading to the front door before he realized it. He'd only been inside the church once before: at his mother's funeral. An arthritically stooped old priest had performed the services, some in English, some in Greek; nothing that Arn could decipher.

The heavy front door opened, heavy like his heart since realizing he might never see Ana Maria again. He blamed himself for letting her get in over her head, like he blamed himself for not visiting his mother often enough when he'd lived in Denver. After all, it had only been an hour and a half drive, yet he came home to see her only two or three times a year. He hadn't told her enough times how he loved her. And neither had he told Ana Maria.

He let go of the door handle and turned back to the steps, but something tugged at him and he went in. He recalled that icons of the saints lined the front of the church, and they still hung there. Now, perhaps, there were more, as if Arn needed the help of every saint that ever existed. Candles flickered, jammed in a bed of sand off to one side of the entrance, while an icon of the Virgin Mary occupied the space at the opposite side of the entryway.

He cautiously peeked in to where pews eight deep waited for parishioners, as if he were fearful someone might see him. But he was alone in the church. Again, he turned toward the door. He had Ana Maria to worry about, to find before something happened to her. But he had another half hour before Fred's Union Pacific train arrived at the depot. Arn berated himself for wasting time here in church when—

The thought left his mind as quickly as it had entered, and somehow his guilt was taken from him. He had no other place to be right now, no place that was more important, nowhere to be looking for Ana Maria other than right here.

Among the saints.

He walked to the front of the church and sat in a pew directly under an enormous concave dome twenty feet overhead. Icons and images were painted within the dome, and Arn looked away as a man emerged from a swinging door to one side of the pulpit. He was tall and fit, sporting a well-trimmed beard and piercing eyes that belonged to a warrior. And he was, Arn concluded as the man adjusted his clerical collar and approached him. A warrior for God.

He introduced himself as Father Jason, and, without another word, sat next to Arn and quietly waited for him to begin speaking. Much like how Arn had often waited for criminals to begin spilling their guts. So Arn mentioned he was looking for Ana Maria; mentioned the intense danger she might be in. After he'd said these things, he suddenly thought it only natural to burden this man with his fears. "Will I find her in time?" he asked.

Father Jason shrugged. "I'm not a soothsayer. I cannot tell you if you'll be successful. I cannot tell you if your friend is even alive as we speak."

"Then what—" Arn broke it off.

"You were going to ask, 'What good am I then?'" Father Jason smiled. "I can guide you if you wish to know your heart, and if you give your heart to God. Have you heard the parable of the mustard seed?"

"More times than I like to remember," Arn said. "Whenever I doubted myself, my mother would bring that up. She'd say if I had enough faith, I could move mountains."

"As did Jesus," Father Jason said. "And the wisdom of that parable will always be with us." He stood and smoothed his black shirt. "Feel free to remain however long you wish. And Mr. Anderson, remember that what happens is God's will." He made the sign of the cross to bless Arn and left through the door he'd come out of.

Arn sat alone, then, praying . . . to whom? He'd never been religious in the slightest, even with his mother's prodding. But like the old saying that "there are no atheists in a foxhole," there were no atheists when your friend's life hung in the balance. Did the tears he shed sitting on that pew count as a contract between him and God?

———

Arn parked his car in the lot to one side of the Union Pacific building. He walked past the ten-foot painted cowboy boot and stood in awe— as he often did—looking at the red and tan sandstone structure. The stone blocks had been quarried in Colorado and laid by craftsmen so that the whole building had been proclaimed a palace when it was completed in 1887. The railroad had commissioned additions a couple times, all of which balanced out the magnificent edifice. Arn looked up at the clock tower three stories above him and wished he could turn the huge dial back. He would have shackled Ana Maria rather than let her go to meet Eddie Glass.

He walked into the bistro inside the depot, which also housed a craft brewery, and ordered coffee. He was sipping it slowly when he spotted a small, wiry man walking toward him in engineer bibs. The man—an older version of Floyd—shook his hand. "Damn, that Edgemont is a ways off," he said, pulling a manila envelope from his lunch box. He handed it to Arn.

"I'll see that Scott gets this," Arn said. He stuffed the envelope inside his coat pocket just as his cell phone rang.

"Adam from Fat Boy's," the runny-eyed boy said. "I looked at those tires Danny left for me. I remember them like it was yesterday. They belonged to a rancher that needed new skins."

"They weren't from the truck Floyd bought?"

"No," Adam said, and papers rustled on the other end of the line. "It was some real a-hole, pushy bastard. A guy named Glass."

Forty-Two

ARN DISCONNECTED, AND HIS phone rang again. "Forget something, Adam?"

"It's me," Danny whispered into the phone, his voice wavering, his breaths coming in short grasps. "I'm at the Johns' ranch."

"Why are you whispering?"

"I had to break into Beverly's house to use the phone. No one's home."

"What did you find?"

"I didn't find Ana Maria or Eddie, if that's what you mean."

"Then why are you whispering if there's no one there?" Arn asked.

"Because there's a new truck parked by the barn," Danny said.

"Anyone inside?"

"Can't say." Danny's voice broke. "I haven't approached it. But fresh blood is dripping down the side of one window and door. That's why I broke in here."

"Stay tight. Call 911 if you need to. I'm leaving the depot now."

Arn dialed Slade as he hustled to his car. When Slade's phone went to voicemail, he hung up and punched in Oblanski's number. "I just called your number but got voicemail," Oblanski said.

"I was on the phone with Danny. He's at Beverly and Bonnie Johns' ranch, and it looks like someone's leaked all over some truck parked there. I called Slade but no one answered. And those tires I told you about—they were traded in by Eddie Glass. Can you send one of your guys to the Johns' place?"

"It's way out of our jurisdiction," Oblanski said.

"I know you got a mutual aid agreement with the sheriff's office—"

"If they call and request it."

"Well, *I'm* requesting it. Ned, I need you."

Oblanski paused. "I won't send any of my guys. There'd be hell to pay once the council hears a policeman went out that far without a mutual aid request. But I'll meet you at the end of their driveway and we'll go in together. If anyone gets their ass handed to him over it, it'll be me."

Arn started his Olds and shoved the mixer stick into first. He chirped his tires, and by the time he hit Interstate 25, the needle was pegged. He arrived at the end of the Johns' driveway and slid to a stop. He saw the truck Danny had told him about parked by the barn, but it was too far away to tell anything about it. He grabbed his binos: it was Eddie's truck, and blood was caked down the driver's door.

Oblanski drove up behind him and got out. "Did you fly here? I didn't think you'd beat me."

Arn handed him the binoculars. "That's Eddie Glass's truck."

"Where's Danny?"

"I told him to stay inside the house and call 911 if necessary." Arn took the binos from Oblanski. "'Cause after this, you and me might not be in any shape to call."

"Understood," Oblanski said. He stripped off his suit jacket and tie, revealing a Glock in a shoulder rig with two extra magazines. Arn was hoping he wouldn't need all those.

"How you want to do this?" Arn asked as he drew his .38.

Oblanski looked over the terrain. "I'm thinking our approach ought to be from the passenger's side of the truck." He pointed to a shelter belt on one side of the ranch house. "We can make it to that swather without being seen. If you cover me … can you hit something that far with that little gun?"

"Thirty yards? Pushing it, but I can dust someone's head if I have to."

Oblanski drew his pistol. "Okay then, let's make for that piece of machinery."

They jogged up the ranch drive until they came to the shelter belt of Dutch Elm, and cut through until they were parallel with the swather. They ran the last few yards and hunkered down. "Just be ready when I open the truck door," Oblanski said.

Arn held a stitch in his side, but he gave Oblanski the thumbs-up. He rested his hand on a row of sickles and took up a firing position.

Oblanski duck-walked to the truck. When he reached the bed, he looked over his shoulder. Again, Arn gave him a thumbs-up, and Oblanski stayed low under the window as he approached the last few feet. He flung the door open and leaned at an angle, covering the inside of the truck with his gun. He stood and holstered before turning to Arn and motioning him over.

Arn pocketed his gun and joined Oblanski at the truck. A Border collie lay bled out on the seat. Arn looked away and holstered.

Oblanski felt the animal. "Been dead an hour. Maybe two." He pulled the dog's lips back. "At least she got a bite in before she was"— he turned the dog over—"stabbed. Let's find out what your man saw."

Arn waved at the ranch house and Danny walked out. He stopped at the cab of the truck and his mouth downturned in sadness when he saw the Border collie.

"What did you see when you pulled up?" Oblanski asked.

Danny motioned to the truck. "Just that. I ran to the house, but no one answered. Odd to find a ranch house locked, but I broke in to call." He backed away from Oblanski. "You're not going to arrest me for B&E or anything, are you?"

"I think you're safe," Oblanski said. He faced Arn. "I tried calling you—" His words were interrupted by noise coming from the barn, faint but persistent. "Stay behind the truck," he ordered Danny.

Arn stripped off his coat. The manila envelope Fred had given him fell to the ground, but Arn ignored it. "Go and stay by the phone," he told Danny.

"Here we go again, Anderson," Oblanski said. "I'll buttonhook right, you left. You good with that?"

Arn nodded and drew his revolver again. Oblanski positioned himself on the opposite side of the barn door. When he flashed a fist, they entered the barn together. They both crouched immediately, waiting for their eyes to adjust to the dim light. The noises they'd heard before seemed to come from a row of stalls Beverly used for her milk cows. Movement from under a pile of straw, and Oblanski motioned to Arn to stay and cover as he approached it.

He used a pitchfork to move straw from the pile, until Bonnie's head poked out. The straw fell further away, and Beverly lay motionless. Bandanas had been stuffed in their mouths, held tight by a rope encircling their heads. Blood had dried on Beverly's chin where she'd fought the rope, and one of her eyes had swollen shut.

Arn holstered and bent to Bonnie while Oblanski began cutting away Beverly's ropes with his pocket knife. Bonnie spit straw from her mouth as she rolled over to allow Arn to cut the zip tie securing her hands. When the plastic tie dropped free, she turned to Beverly and cradled her head. "Oh God, tell me she's all right?"

"She's breathing and she's got a pulse," Oblanski said. "I'll call paramedics." He stepped out of the barn.

Bonnie stroked her sister's head. "How the hell did we get into this mess?" she asked Arn. Tears cut through the dirt on her face. "How's Eddie?"

"What about Eddie? Isn't he the one that tied you two up?"

"God, no," Bonnie said. "He tried to help us." She pointed to a canvas tarp in the adjacent stall. "He dragged Eddie over there."

"Who's 'he'?"

"Guy from the class. Eddie knew him better than me. He told us his name was Steve Campbell, but I didn't recognize the name from our roster."

Arn walked to the far side of the barn. The tarp that had covered Bonnie's navy blue Ford truck had been pulled off. It covered a body, and Arn peeled it back. Eddie Glass lay face up, eyes protruding, already turning color where a ligature had tightened around his throat.

Oblanski came back into the barn, and Arn called to him. "Better get the DCI and SO evidence techs here for Eddie. And notify the coroner."

The chief went back outside and Arn followed him. "Stay with Beverly," Oblanski said over his shoulder, then yelled for Danny. Danny poked his head out Beverly's door and Arn motioned him over. "Go back in the house and grab some blankets for Beverly. She's in the barn."

Arn returned to the stall where Bonnie still held her sister's head. "What happened here?"

"Me and Eddie drove out here," she began. "I knew Bev didn't approve of him, but we wanted to be alone. You know what I'm talking about."

"I vaguely remember," Arn answered.

"When we pulled into the yard, there was another truck here, but we didn't see no one"—she pulled a piece of straw from her mouth—"until that guy walked up to Eddie's side of the truck, all smiles. Then, quick as that"—she snapped her fingers—"the guy put a knife into Eddie's heart. His dog latched onto the guy's hand, but he knifed the dog, too. 'Don't yell,' the guy told me, and there wasn't a thing I could do. Eddie was barely alive at that point, but the guy finished him off with some leather strap around his throat." Bonnie felt Beverly's neck. "Just checking."

"Understood," Arn said. "Then what happened?"

"That Villarreal woman—"

Arn laid a hand on her shoulders. "Ana Maria was here then?"

Bonnie nodded. "To work on my pickup. After the guy killed Eddie, he led me into the barn. Ana Maria was with my truck"—she kissed Beverly's hand—"along with Bev."

"Where's Ana Maria now?" Arn looked frantically around for other tarps, other piles of straw big enough to hide a body.

"After he trussed me and Bev up real good, he left with the Villarreal woman."

"Did he say where he was heading?"

Bonnie gingerly touched Beverly's swollen eye. "It can't be far. He said for us to relax, that he'd be back soon for us. To dance, whatever that meant." She began crying. "And all this is because of me."

"Because you witnessed Jillie Reilly's murder?"

Bonnie swiped her eyes with the back of her hand. "You know?"

He chin-pointed to the truck. "I figured it out earlier. And it was Jillie's killer who murdered Eddie?"

Bonnie rubbed circulation back into her wrists. "That night, I was at Wooly Hank's—"

"To rustle sheep?"

She nodded. "Except I heard a truck, and a couple fighting. I figured me and Buckwheat could just wait until their little spat was over before we relieved Hank of some ewes."

"Except it wasn't just some family fight?"

"Not even." Bonnie cradled her sister's head in her arms and rocked back and forth, stroking her temple. "When he started strangling Jillie, Buckwheat nipped. Just enough that the guy heard us, and I took off."

"Why the hell didn't you come forward?"

"I was scared," Bonnie answered, her voice faltering. "I knew the law would put me in jail for rustling. Besides, I didn't get a good enough look at the guy to give any description. Even today, I wouldn't be able to identify him from Wooly Hank's." She dropped her head.

"Did he indicate where he was taking Ana Maria?"

Bonnie shook her head and began sobbing again.

Oblanski came back into the barn ahead of Danny. Danny bent to Beverly and wrapped her with blankets while Oblanski motioned for Arn to step outside. "DCI and the SO evidence van are in route. Slade says his guys haven't come across Ana Maria or Scott Wallace."

"Wallace?"

"That's what I wanted to tell you earlier. Sacramento detectives went through your photos. They had no idea who Eddie Glass was. But they recognized Scott Wallace's photo as their Steve Campbell."

"So Eddie taking all those trips with Bonnie—"

"Was legitimate," Oblanski answered. "As legitimate as you can get without your wife knowing it."

"That's the name on these papers." Danny stood up and came over to them. He handed Arn the manila envelope he'd dropped. "The papers fell out. It looks like they're old receipts, but they all have the name Steve Campbell on them."

Approaching ambulance sirens grew louder as paramedics pulled onto the drive. Arn paced. "We've got to find them."

"I phoned Slade. He called all his guys in off-duty and they're looking for them now."

"Tell him to have some units check the Pott Ranch. Scott—or Campbell—works for Hubert and Henrietta."

"Sheriff's deputies have already been there. No sign of anyone at the place." Oblanski motioned to the ambulance crew to drive into the barn.

Arn thought the worst. If the Potts were missing, could Ana Maria be far behind, in some shallow grave somewhere?

Forty-Three

ANA MARIA SQUIRMS AGAINST her ropes, but there's nothing she can do lying on the floorboard of my truck. "We'll dance together soon enough," I tell her as she struggles anew. As I look at her, I'm saddened: we won't have as much time together, her and me, as I would like—I need to tidy up that mess at the Johns' ranch. I would have done both sisters while I was there, but I wanted a little extra time with Bonnie. I laugh. Finally, the Midnight Sheepherder will stop her rustling spree. What irony that I would be the one to finally catch the thief. Wonder if they'll give me a reward.

As I pull up to the boss's house, Hubert and Henrietta sit close together on the porch swing, holding hands like they're eighteen-year-old lovers once again. The evening air is cool, and they often sit like this, the swing swaying gently in the breeze, their hands intertwined like I bet they've done all of their sixty married years. I get nostalgic when I think they've come this far together. Almost like they're right out of a Currier and Ives calendar. They're lucky to be able to be in this world together. And to leave this world together. I envy them, but then that's just me—the hopeless romantic.

251

They wave, and I park the truck by the porch. Ana Maria struggles as she kicks the back of the seat, and I tap her on the head with the tire billy. She stops moving and I slip it into my back pocket. I'll need the billy in a moment.

I climb out of my truck and walk toward the porch.

It's a true shame to do what I must. If it were up to me, I'd stay on this place and work for those old folks for many more years, venturing out whenever I got to scratch that itch I've always had. Coming back when I got it out of my system. But thanks to Ana Maria and that nosy Anderson, I can't stay here. So I'll move on. Like I always have. Except now there's no Dr. Oakert to come back to who'll get me straight. "Cookies and lemonade on the kitchen table," Henrietta *says so me as I step up on the porch. I'll have some—in a moment—as soon as I tell them goodbye.*

Then it's off to the sheepherder cabin in the north pasture, well away from the ranch house, well away where Ana Maria and I will be alone. And if anyone is unlucky enough to drive to the shack, I can see them coming. The cabin is nearly invisible from the ranch house unless you know just where to look.

I will deal with them as well. As soon as I have some cookies and lemonade.

Forty-Four

BY THE TIME ARN and Danny left the Johns' ranch, it was well past dark. Beverly and Bonnie had both been taken to the hospital: Bonnie to get checked out, and Beverly for treatment for a skull fracture and broken orbital socket. Paramedics are no doctors, but they speculated Beverly would be fine after surgery to repair the damage.

Oblanski had remained at the ranch until Slade and his investigation team arrived. He'd had no word on Ana Maria's location, and his deputies had not found Scott Wallace either. Or Steve Campbell, as their BOLO now read. By the time Arn and Danny pulled to the curb in front of their house, Arn was as mentally drained as ever just thinking of places to check.

He unlocked the door and noticed Danny had not armed the security system. "I ran out in a hurry," Danny said.

"Stay put." Arn entered the darkened house and reached for the light, then stopped. If anyone was inside, they wouldn't know the layout as he did, so he kept the house dark as he searched from room to room. When he'd looked everywhere and found no one, he came back to the front door and flicked the lights on.

"A little jumpy?" Danny asked.

"Wouldn't you be after what we've seen today?"

Danny said as much and went into the kitchen to start coffee. "Arn!" he called.

Arn went into the room and Danny handed him a slip of paper. "It was hanging on the fridge."

> *Mr. Anderson: It has been a pleasure meeting you.*
> *Or rather, I should say it has been a pleasure*
> *meeting your roommate. She'll dance quite well.*
> *—Steve*

"The son-of-a-bitch is gloating," Danny said.

"Or a parting shot." Arn rubbed his forehead against a rising headache. "I'm missing something. My first thought was that Campbell and Ana Maria are way out of state by now. But what if they're not? He promised to return and take care of Beverly and Bonnie."

Danny nuked two cups of coffee in the microwave and handed one to Arn. "Surely if he goes back, he'll realize Oblanski and Slade were there."

Arn thought so, too. "Slade left two of his tactical guys there in case Campbell returns, but I doubt he will. I'm *just* missing something. But what the hell is it?"

"Maybe if you go in the living room and think about it. I'll leave you all alone so I won't disturb you—"

Arn slapped the table. "I think you're on to something."

Danny looked surprised. "Me?"

Arn downed his coffee. "Make a fresh pot. I'm going to be gone for a little bit. The one place I bet no one's looked for Campbell is at that sheepherder's cabin on the Pott place. I'd wager no one even knows about it except the Potts, and the sheriff's deputies didn't see them when they stopped there. What better place to be alone with Ana Maria?"

"Want me to call the sheriff's office and tell Slade where you're headed?"

"No," Arn said. "I don't want them pulled off other places they're searching. I'm just going to check that cabin and I'll be right back."

———————

Arn pulled to the front of the Potts' house, the yard light casting odd shadows on the porch swing that was swaying in time with the wind. There were no lights inside, but he didn't expect any. Ranch folks often went to bed with the chickens and got up at the crack of dawn. Right now, the chickens had been in bed since the sun had set.

He grabbed his flashlight from the glove box and went to the door. It was locked—the second time that day a rancher had locked his house, and Arn slipped the gun out of his ankle rig. He raised his hand to knock, but stopped. If they were inside sleeping, he would feel bad waking them up just to talk with him. But Ana Maria's safety was too important, even if he was acting on an off-hunch. He knocked lightly at first, then louder. When he got no answer, he shined his light through the window of the door. It was as if they'd left on a vacation. Again, something ranchers rarely did, with livestock to tend to.

Arn turned to go back to his car and froze. His flashlight illuminated a single blood drop on the steps. The tail of the drop showed that whoever put the blood there had walked *away* from the house.

He turned back to the door and put his shoulder into it. The door broke, splintering from its hinges. Arn flicked his flashlight on and played it around the entryway. Nothing.

He flattened himself against the wall and turned his flashlight off while his eyes adjusted to the darkness. The ever-familiar odor of putrid blood reached him, then, like at hundreds of crime scenes he'd been at before.

Arn inched along the wall, careful not to brush it with his clothing, careful not to telegraph to anyone who might be lurking inside the room his exact whereabouts. Busting though the door would alert whoever might be waiting for him, but he didn't have to tell them exactly *when* he was coming.

He squatted low and flicked his light along the floor for a brief second. Nothing. He stepped another few steps and flicked it on again. Nothing.

Except the odor of decaying blood becoming stronger.

He tried to remember where in the house he was. As a youngster, he'd been inside many times for cookies and lemonade, but that was so long ago ... the kitchen. He was just on the other side of the kitchen.

A fan kicked on. The smell intensified. A dead body lay on the other side of the wall. And the killer might be waiting there as well.

Forty-Five

ARN DROPPED ONTO HIS belly and low-crawled the last few feet to the corner of the kitchen wall. He breathed deeply, calming himself, the blood smell stronger than it had been. He turned on the light and quick-peeked around the corner.

And came nose-to-bloodied-face with Henrietta Pott.

Her bulging tongue protruded from her mouth, and her eyes had glazed over in death. Gray matter spilled from one ear from the pressure of the blows, and she had soiled herself.

Hubert lay on the other side of the room. Like his wife, he had been beaten to death. Blood had seeped out onto the floor. Hubert had been alive, then, for some time, leaking over the kitchen floor before death thankfully took him.

Arn stood and turned his light off. When his eyes had adjusted to the darkness, he began going room to room. He didn't expect to find Campbell there, but he was taking no chances. When he'd cleared the house, he returned to the kitchen. Grabbing his cell phone in his trembling hand, he breathed deeply several times before calling Danny. "The Potts are dead," he sputtered. "Looks like Campbell beat them to death."

"Are *you* all right?" Danny asked.

"Just a little shaken. I need you to call Slade and Oblanski directly. Their numbers are in my notebook on top of the fridge. Tell them what I found. Tell them I'm betting Campbell took Ana Maria to that sheepherder's cabin north of here, over the hill."

"The place no one's looking?"

"Unless you know it's there, you can't spot it from the main house."

"Are you going to wait for backup?"

"Negative," Arn answered. "Ana Maria may not have time for me to wait for help."

Arn returned to his car and paused for a moment to orient himself. He had seen the sheepherder's shack once when investigating stolen ewes that spring. It was over the hill about a half mile away.

He kept his lights off as he drove slowly along the dirt road. When he crested the hill overlooking the cabin, he carefully kept on top of the deep mud ruts of the two-track, the trail illuminated only by the flashlight Arn hung out the window. He'd gone several hundred yards before he spotted the light from the shack in the distance. He inched the Olds along, the oil pan scraping against the hard dirt, using the emergency brake to slow the car when needed. He wished he'd taken Ana Maria's advice and replaced the mufflers with a quieter exhaust, and he shut the car off fifty yards from the cabin.

Arn tucked the flashlight into his back pocket and reached up to take the dome light cover off. He pried the bulb out of the socket with his fingers before opening the door.

Outside, he paused to listen. The only sound was wind flattening gamma grass and slicing through sagebrush, the bleating of sheep in the nearby pasture, and an owl calling close by.

His hands started to sweat and he wiped first one, then the other, before taking his gun in a tight grip. He hadn't gone a dozen yards when he froze mid-stride. He turned his head slowly, trying to pick up movement in his peripheral vision, which he knew was more light-sensitive than frontal vision. His cop instinct had kicked into overdrive: someone was following him. He turned slowly, three-hundred-sixty degrees, looking, testing the wind with his nose, using all his senses.

After a few more tense moments, the feeling subsided. Arn didn't know if he should feel relief or not. All he knew was that Ana Maria might be inside the shack. And in peril.

He walked the rest of the way, stopping now and again, testing the wind, trying to recreate the feeling he'd had that someone was stalking him. When he reached the corner of the shack, he paused and breathed deeply. "Take five breaths, dummy," he heard his training officer Rolf tell him. "Then maybe you won't shit yourself when you come face-to-face with evil." By all accounts, he'd taken Rolf's advice: he'd never shit himself. But he was getting close to it as he duck-walked under the windows and peeked in.

Ana Maria sat tied to a chair to one side of the small one-room cabin, alone. Her head bobbed on her chest as she fought for consciousness. Her hair had been lopped off, her locks littering the dirty floor. A leather thong encircled her neck, and Arn could see where ligature marks had cut into the flesh in several places. How many times had Campbell strangled her to the point of death before letting her live? Arn couldn't tell. He only knew he had to help her soon or she'd die.

But where was Campbell? Arn was certain he'd put the sneak on the place so that no one could have seen his approach. Had Campbell gone back to the Johns' ranch to finish his work there? Or worse, fled Cheyenne only to turn up somewhere else to do his grisly murders?

Arn tried the cabin knob: it turned free and he entered. He dropped beside Ana Maria and gently lifted her head up. She opened her eyes, and for a brief moment there was recognition before she closed them once again. Arn moved behind her to cut her hands free from the zip ties with his pocket knife when movement in his peripheral vision caught his eye a moment too late. Campbell swung a tire billy down hard on his hand. His pistol flew from his grasp and skidded across the floor. Arn leapt for it when he felt a stout ligature—a rope, perhaps a leather thong like Ana Maria's—tighten around his throat.

He shot his hand up, struggling to get it between the leather and his neck as Campbell tightened the noose. His hand became trapped there. Pressure mounted. Consciousness was leaving him.

Arn's high school wrestling kicked into high gear and he dropped to one knee. Campbell flew over him, but he didn't lose his death grip as Arn's hand slipped out.

The leather tightened.

Arn felt his windpipe constrict. The air cut off. He had mere moments before—

He turned into the leather, just enough that—

He cocked his elbow and dug it in tight to Campbell's side, burying the blow under Campbell's ribs. Campbell coughed violently, relaxing his hold on the leather.

Arn slipped out of the thong, sucking in air, as Campbell swung the tire billy at his head. Arn raised his arm, but the short stick glanced off the side of his head and he dropped to his knees. Campbell lashed out and his boot caught Arn in the chest. He fell against the bed frame. Campbell drew a knife stained with Eddie's blood. "Now we talk," he said. He backed up a foot, the knife cocked to deliver the final slash across Arn's throat.

Arn rubbed circulation back into his bruised neck. "Talk about what?" Raspy. Gravelly, as he struggled to speak against the bruising deep inside his throat.

"What do you know about me?"

Arn tried to sit up, and Campbell took the blade off his neck but kept it within slashing distance. "I know you're Steve Campbell."

"Campbell. Wallace. Or the dozen other names I've used. What's in a name? Now unless you want an extra gash right under your chin, tell me what you've found out."

Arn slumped back against the bed. "I know everything. I know you murdered Jillie. And Don. Maury Oakert. And for good measure, that blowhard Eddie Glass. And Sergeant Slade knows it all too."

"Bullshit," Campbell said. "Everything points to Eddie Glass. Once I go back to the Johns' and take care of them, I'll make it look like a murder-suicide. Bonnie knifed her lover Eddie, then killed her sister and herself. Airtight."

"Slade and his investigators have already been there. Bonnie and Beverly are both safe."

"You're lying."

"Am I? We figured out right off that Eddie had nothing to do with any of the killings."

"I got to call bullshit again."

"Is it?" Arn said. "You carry a bandana around in your pocket."

"That's your evidence?"

"It is when you got another one around your neck all the time that you never take off. Did Jillie or Don gouge your neck so badly you have to hide the marks?"

"That's still not enough to send me up the river."

"It's not, but I picked up several cigarette butts from the street that night you followed me from Dr. Oakert's office. As I recall, you're damn near a chain-smoker."

"Eddie smokes. Who's to say he wasn't the one following you?"

Arn tried sitting again, but Campbell pressed the blade against his neck. Blood trickled down the front of his shirt. "Eddie smokes Pall Malls. No filter. You smoke Marlboros. Filtered. Just like I found on the street."

"So go lock up the Marlboro man." Campbell grinned.

"Does the Marlboro man have to find his dates hundreds of miles away?"

Campbell's smile faded.

"And then have to strangle them to get his rocks off?"

"You son-of-a—"

Arn was only vaguely aware of his assailant hurling through the air. Campbell's body smacked against the wall and a window pane broke. Glass cascaded down on him and he shook shards of glass from his hair. Blood seeped from a gash on the back of his head, and he picked a splinter of glass from his neck as he struggled to regain his footing.

The gun cocking was louder than any Arn remembered as a policeman. Little Jim Reilly stood framed in the doorway, a large caliber revolver leveled at Campbell. "Untie the TV lady," he told Arn. Campbell's eyes widened.

Arn turned to Ana Maria and cut the plastic ties around her ankles with his pocketknife. She collapsed in his arms and—once again—opened her eyes for a moment's recognition and a faint smile before closing them. Her breathing was shallow, her pulse thready when Arn felt her wrist. But she'd live through this.

Which was more than he could say for Campbell. Little Jim had his single action Colt aimed at the killer's head. "Mr. Anderson, I knew if I tagged along you'd lead me to this monster," he said. He nodded to the door. "You'd better get the little lady to the hospital."

Arn eased Ana Maria onto to the bunk and slipped a pillow under her head. "What are you going to do, Little Jim?" he asked. "Murder Scott—or, I should say, Steve Campbell?"

"You have a better idea?"

"I do," Arn said, making sure he didn't step between Campbell and Little Jim. "This bastard killed at least three other people here besides your Jillie. Probably murdered the Potts, too. And how many more victims in his travels? We have him dead to rights."

"Listen to him," Campbell said. He stood on wobbly legs, holding the back of his head where Little Jim had crashed his pistol down on it. He grabbed a can of Copenhagen from his back pocket and stuffed his lip. "Anderson's right. I need to stand trial." He grinned wide. Besides"—he winked—"not too many people can kill another like I did and sleep well. But I do."

"I just want to know why," Little Jim asked. "Why my Jillie?"

Campbell shrugged, and Little Jim took a long step toward him. He hit Campbell on the temple with the barrel of his gun. Campbell dropped to one knee and his hand shot to the side of his head. "All right, big man, I'll tell you why I killed your little girl." He spit tobacco juice on the cabin floor. "She was drunk at Boot Hill that night when I stopped in. I didn't know she'd be there. I was there for one quick beer to wash the dust down."

"Still doesn't answer why you murdered her."

Campbell wiped tobacco juice with the back of his hand. "Sure it does. She spotted me that night. Recognized me as Dr. Oakert's patient. And she knew why the doctor and I...had to get acquainted some years ago. She taunted me that night. Threatened to tell everyone why I was seeing Dr. Oakert."

Arn closely watched Little Jim's finger whiten as he tightened pressure on his trigger finger. "You were Dr. Oakert's patient in Napa Hospital," he said.

"Oh, you are good," Campbell said. "But not good enough to save the doctor. Sure, I was his patient. Intense one-on-one therapy. I was his test subject, and all I had to do was go along with how he thought I was rehabilitating. And when another patient tried stabbing him in the commons area, I saw my golden opportunity. I saved the good doctor." He laughed. "And that's all it took for him to certify I was cured."

Little Jim's gun hand drooped ever so slightly.

"I tried to go the straight and narrow," Campbell said. He leaned against the wall holding his bloody head. "But the urges ... got the better of me and I back slid, you might say. I *wanted* to stop. I really did. So I found out where the only shrink who'd ever helped me moved to. I found Maury had moved here."

"But Jillie would never have violated your confidentiality," Little Jim seemed to plead. "She never even told me about any of the doctor's patients."

"I couldn't take that chance. See, when I showed up in Cheyenne a few years ago, Dr. Oakert was actually glad to see me, now that I was rehabilitated. But when I told him how many new ... ladies I'd been with, he snapped. Said he didn't want me as a patient anymore. I could live with that, but I convinced him—in my own special way—to keep me as a patient. What I couldn't live with was Jillie spilling the beans on me. She typed up all Dr. Oakert's notes. She knew *all* about me."

"And when you followed her out of the Boot Hill you grabbed her?"

Campbell stared at Little Jim's gun. "That boob Eddie Glass got the blame in some people's eyes. Reinforced when I dumped Dr. Oakert's body right where deputies had stopped him for trespassing the night before."

Little Jim snapped his gun up and Campbell cringed. "Jim!" Arn yelled.

Little Jim glared at Arn.

"Don't do this. You're the one who'll go to Rawlins." Arn held out his hand. "Jillie wouldn't want you to go to prison."

Little Jim seemed to think it through, his trigger finger whitening. Then he decocked the gun and handed it to Arn. Arn held it pointed at Campbell.

"You've got enough to send him away forever?" Little Jim asked. "Or send him to death row?"

"We do," Arn said. "Besides Bonnie and Beverly testifying against him, I'm certain Slade can get a DNA matchup from Dr. Oakert's house, and from the cigarette butts. And after Slade works up the Potts' crime scene, Campbell here will die in prison." He turned to him. "But why the Potts?"

"I was truly sorry I had to kill them," Campbell volunteered. "The Potts were loose strings, though." He motioned for a chair.

"Drag it away from Ana Maria," Arn ordered.

Campbell looked down at her head resting on the pillow before dragging the chair to a corner and sitting while he held the side of his head. "The one thing I wanted to know—who exactly was the witness to Jillie's murder? So I followed you around."

"Why did you think I'd know?" Arn asked.

Campbell smiled. "I studied up on you. The way you went around looking for paint matchups, I know you'd figure it out."

"As did you."

Campbell nodded. "But not until just today when I followed Eddie there. After I ... took care of Eddie, and dragged Bonnie and Beverly to the barn, I noticed Bonnie's truck. Saw her broken marker lens that matched the one I picked up at Wooly Hank's. Am I right?"

Little Jim slumped against the door jamb. He rubbed his head as if fatigue would overtake him at any moment and he'd topple him over. "If there had been a way to save Jillie, I would have."

"There wasn't," Campbell said. "Your Jillie fought hard. You can be proud of her for that. In the end, she begged to live. As they all do." He winked at Little Jim. "She begged the most of any, I think. But it pained me to have to kill her quick once I spotted that dog and Bonnie peeking over the hill—except I didn't know it was Bonnie at the time."

"At least you'll rot in prison," Little Jim said between clenched teeth. "Until that lethal injection—"

Campbell shook his head. "Who but a crazy man would just up and confess like I did to you two? Slade will interrogate me, and I'll spill my guts. Like a crazy man. The county attorney will bring murder charges on me, but the state will send me to the state hospital in Evanston for evaluation. I'll be deemed too nutso to stand trial." Campbell smirked. "And you know what—I'll probably meet some kindly shrink in there who believes he can work miracles. Thinks I can be rehabilitated. Another Maury Oakert. And in a few years, I'll be out." He grinned. "I'll be hunting again. And there's nothing you two can do about it."

"That's not going to happen, is it?" Little Jim asked Arn.

Arn looked away, and the color drained from Little Jim's face as he realized it would happen. He knew it was true. "He's going to walk, isn't he?"

Campbell laughed heartily. "Go ahead and tell him, Anderson. You've dealt with our less-than-perfect criminal justice system long enough. Tell Jimbo there I'll be seeing him again one day."

Arn couldn't lie to Little Jim. Campbell would fool some other institutional psychiatrist and be out in a few years to prey on women again.

He wanted none of that. All throughout his police career, he'd pushed for justice, told himself that what he was doing made people's lives safer. And it had. Except those times he'd run into the Campbells of the world—those who'd skirted the system, using whatever loopholes fell their way to evade justice. If it were up to Arn, Campbell would never be free to hunt again. But it had never been Arn's decision.

Until now.

"I need to get Ana Maria to the hospital," he told Little Jim. "She's in a bad way, and I can't wait for the ambulance to arrive."

"What about him?" Little Jim said. "I don't want him getting away."

"You have a point," Arn said. He handed Little Jim his gun back. "Watch him close," he said as he bent to scoop Ana Maria up in his arms. "Some psychopath like him is likely to try anything."

"You're leaving me alone with him?" Campbell asked. He stood from the chair and stepped toward Arn. Little Jim cocked his gun and aimed it at Campbell's head. "Anderson—you know he'll kill me once you leave."

"Nonsense. Unlike you, we're civilized. Unless"—Arn winked at Campbell—"unless you make a play for the gun and it goes off." He nodded to Little Jim's .45 Colt. "And a gun that size would be likely to put a hole in you big enough to stick my fist in."

"You can't leave me with him!" Campbell shouted. He stepped closer and Little Jim's arm extended. Campbell looked down the barrel at the crude sights and froze.

"Don't do anything foolish like try to get Little Jim's gun," Arn said as he wrapped his arms under Ana Maria and lifted her off the bunk. "'Cause that'd be self-defense, wouldn't it, Little Jim?"

Little Jim only nodded, his trigger finger whitening once again.

"Watch him," Arn said. "With Campbell's history, he's sure to try to wrestle the gun away from you."

"No!" Campbell yelled at Arn's backside as he carried Ana Maria outside toward his car. "I'm not trying to get it—"

The shot—which came as Arn was easing Ana Maria into the front seat—didn't even surprise him. He could only smile in the darkness. "I guess Campbell tried to get Little Jim's gun after all," he said to himself.

Forty-Six

A KNOCK ON THE door hard enough Arn thought it would break the hinges reverberated throughout the house. "I got it," Danny called out.

"Guess that's Little Jim coming from his interview," Arn said.

"I'll put a pot on," Ana Maria said through clenched teeth. It was hard for her to talk with a swollen jaw and the two broken teeth that had to be extracted. Arn laid his hand on her shoulder. "Stay seated. I'll make coffee."

Danny led Little Jim into the kitchen. The man stopped in the doorway and grimaced as he checked out Ana Maria's neck from different angles. "You and Jillie were about the same age. You need anything while you're on the mend?"

Ana Maria smiled and winced. Her split lip was healing slower than it should. "I'm doing just fine, Mr. Reilly."

"Coffee?" Arn asked.

"I shouldn't," he answered. "Darned bladder. But what the hell—I have a reason to celebrate."

"Sergeant Slade called and said the interview proved you acted in your own defense," Arn said.

Little Jim sat on a metal folding chair and the legs bowed. "Thanks."

"For what?" Arn handed him a mug of coffee.

"For telling Slade it was probably self-defense even if you didn't see what happened."

Arn shrugged. "I just told him what I saw until I left with Ana Maria—that Campbell acted like he would try to get your gun if he had the chance."

A smile tugged at the corners of Little Jim's mouth. "I never thought a little feller like that would go for it."

"And with a light trigger like most Colts have." Arn shook his head. "A shame is what it is. Just a damned shame."

"I talked with Wooly Hank and Pearly this morning," Little Jim said. He wolfed down two cookies that Danny had set on the table and eyed the plate for another. "The Wool Growers Association voted to give you a bonus for catching the rustler."

"Give Slade some credit," Arn said. "He's the one who coaxed the full confession from Bonnie."

"Did I miss something while I was in the hospital?" Ana Marie asked out the side of her mouth. "'Cause if you're hiding anything—"

Arn held up his hand and she stopped talking. "I know—I was going to tell you when I got the chance. Slade invited me to listen in on Bonnie's interrogation. She gave a full confession to being the Midnight Sheepherder, and a witness to Jillie's murder that night."

"What did she do with the money she got from the stolen sheep?" Ana Maria asked. "Her place is so run down, I'm sure she didn't spend a nickel on it."

Arn dribbled cream into his coffee and stirred lightly. "Eddie. She was so in love with the guy, she blew her money on him. Remember the new pickup she bought for him? And whenever they went out of town, Bonnie would foot the bill."

"She's being charged with the thefts?"

Arn nodded. "She's in a solitary cell in the county jail as we speak."

Little Jim stood and grabbed the coffee pot for a refill. "Did she say why she fought with Jillie that night in the bar?"

"Bonnie needed an alibi," Arn said. "By making a scene and getting 86'd from the Boot Hill, she could tell everyone that was her first step in bar-hopping that night, when instead she went directly to Wooly Hank's after she picked up her truck and trailer. And Buckwheat."

"So there was no guy who gave her a ride from the bar, or no accident she left unreported?" Ana Maria asked as she sipped her coffee with a straw.

"That was just a ploy to draw anyone away from her truck if they asked about it. The only thing she hit was that gate. She parked her truck back of the barn and tarped it, and Eddie let her use his beater truck."

Little Jim chuckled. "Tight ass. Since she bought it, he should have let her use that new one." He sat back down, and Arn thought the metal chair might collapse under the man's weight. "Did Eddie Glass know about Bonnie's rustling?" Little Jim asked.

Arn shook his head. "She kept it from him. Even in that, she loved him enough she didn't want him to be an accessory."

"And his wife knew nothing of Bonnie's activities?

Arn sipped his coffee. Thank God Danny had gotten off that chicory kick. "She *thought* Eddie might be the Midnight Sheepherder. And she was willing to protect him at all costs."

"But she's still in hot water for trying to kill you?" Little Jim asked.

"I'm not so sure charges won't be reduced." Arn broke down and took another cookie. "As I was leaving the interview, Karen was waiting."

"For her interview?" Ana Maria asked.

"For Slade," Arn said. "Soon as she saw him, you'd have thought she was going on a prom date. All smiles for Slade. Hanging all over him. She mentioned something about going to lunch somewhere— just the two of them—to talk about her late Eddie."

"Apparently she got over his murder," Danny said.

Arn nodded. "A born opportunist."

"Isn't love grand," Danny said. "If Slade doesn't have his nuts handed to him—between that banshee Karen Glass and his own wife—I'll be surprised."

Little Jim smiled. "Guess the sheriff's race doesn't mean as much to the good sergeant as he thought."

"Where's Beverly fit into all this?" Ana Maria asked.

"She always protected her younger sister," Arn explained. "Every time Bonnie got into some pinch, Beverly was there to smooth things over. When Slade and I talked with Beverly at the hospital, she finally admitted that she strongly suspected her sister was the Midnight Sheepherder."

Arn grabbed the pot for another refill, but Little Jim waved it off. "I got work to do. Now that I'm doing it alone ... " He turned his head and swiped a calloused hand across his eyes. He started out of the kitchen when he stopped in the doorway and turned to Ana Maria. "Anytime you got a hankering to sit a saddle, Jillie's horse would just fit you."

"I can't ride," Ana Maria said.

"Sure you can. Let me and Jillie's mare teach you. Once you're mended up," Little Jim said, and he left before they saw him cry.

"What do you think he means by that?" she asked after he'd left the house.

"I think with his daughter gone, the man is lonely," Danny said.

Arn recalled Danny telling him how he'd lost his own son one night when the kid got drunk and fell to his death off Mt. Rushmore.

"I think it would be good for you to spend some time with Little Jim," he offered. He patted Ana Maria's arm. "Looks like between Little Jim's riding lessons and Beverly's implement repairs—and the television reporting—you're going to be mighty busy."

"On top of replacing the dented transmission pan in your Oldsmobile from bottoming out in those damned ranch ruts." Ana Maria forced a smile. "What the hell am I ever going to do with you?"

Epilogue

ARN SHUT OFF THE car. He sat at the curb looking up at the stone structure while he checked his watch. Services began at 9:30, the website had said, and he climbed out of his car. He was early; maybe that would hedge his bet the next time he needed the Man to step in and help save a friend.

He walked the flight of concrete steps and hesitated when he reached the doors. Did he really want to be here? "Of course I don't," he found himself saying. Church had never been his thing. He thought it good for weddings and funerals, to stop by for a bake sale now and again or bingo if one felt lucky. Not for weekly attendance. Not for services. But he'd made an agreement, and he stepped inside.

The candles burned to one side of the entrance, the icon of the Virgin Mary on the other side, just like the day he'd wandered in here. The day he'd made a pact with Him.

Father Jason was the only person there early. He stood at the pulpit looking down at notes. He glanced up and nodded at Arn before returning to his reading. Arn eyed the rows of pews and sat in the farthest one back, closest to the door. Just in case he needed to make an abrupt escape.

He looked all around the church, at the icons that he knew must represent something, as his mother had hung so many in the house when she was alive. The dome overhead told a story, though Arn didn't know what that was either. All he knew was that he'd come in here last week and sat. He had prayed—he thought—and asked Him to save Ana Maria. "If you do that, I promise to come back," he'd said in the tearful prayer.

So here he was: Ana Maria was safe. The Saturday Night Strangler would never kill and terrify again. And Bonnie, he was certain, would somehow straighten out her life after she paid her dues. If all it took for things to come out right was dropping by, Arn told himself, perhaps he'd come back and sit in this pew more often.

The End

About the Author

C. M. Wendelboe is the author of the Spirit Road Mysteries (Berkley/Penguin). During his thirty-eight-year career in law enforcement, he served successful stints as a sheriff's deputy, police chief, policy adviser, and supervisor for several agencies. He was a patrol supervisor when he retired to pursue his true vocation as a fiction writer. Find out more about his work at www.SpiritRoadMysteries.com.

WWW.MIDNIGHTINKBOOKS.COM

From the gritty streets of New York City to sacred tombs in the Middle East, it's always midnight somewhere. Join us online at any hour for fresh new voices in mystery fiction.

At midnightinkbooks.com you'll also find our author blog, new and upcoming books, events, book club questions, excerpts, mystery resources, and more.

MIDNIGHT INK ORDERING INFORMATION

 ### Order Online:
- Visit our website www.midnightinkbooks.com, select your books, and order them on our secure server.

 ### Order by Phone:
- Call toll-free within the U.S. and Canada at 1-888-NITE-INK (1-888-648-3465)
- We accept VISA, MasterCard, American Express and Discover.
- Canadian customers must use credit cards.

 ### Order by Mail:
Send the full price of your order (MN residents add 6.875% sales tax) in U.S. funds, plus postage & handling to:

> Midnight Ink
> 2143 Wooddale Drive
> Woodbury, MN 55125-2989

Postage & Handling:

Standard (U.S.). If your order is:
> $30.00 and under, add $6.00
> $30.01 and over, FREE STANDARD SHIPPING

International Orders (Including Canada):
> $16.00 for one book plus $3.00 for each additional book

Orders are processed within 12 business days. Please allow for normal shipping time.
Postage and handling rates subject to change.